The
Proper Order
Of
Things

Tara Benwell

A NOVEL

The characters, events, places, and incidents in this novel are a product of the writer's imagination or are used fictitiously.

Visit the author's website at www.tarabenwell.com for contact information.

Cover art and design by Karen Thompson.

www.karenbenwellphotography.com

For Mama Bird
You were always there.

TARA BENWELL

CHAPTER 1—MOTHER

Mother always said there was nothing special about being called a sweetie pie. *All pies are sweet,* she would say, and not one of us would disagree. It wasn't that we didn't know about the chicken pot or mincemeat kinds. We had seen them in the grocery store flyers that lined the ditch along Whirl Creek. It's just that we weren't allowed to talk about things like trash in our family, so we didn't.

Mother didn't like names like honey or pumpkin either. She said those were for people who didn't put enough thought into their own babies' names—either that or men who didn't have babies of their own. The worst thing a man could do around Mother was to call her child a *babycake.* Mother didn't sit around for hours sorting through Neil Diamond lyrics to find the perfect names for us just so some stranger could call us whatever he damn well pleased.

Dad said my name came from the song about the good times. *Sweet Caroline.* I knew when he said it that the good times came before I was born.

"Just tell me one thing, Mother. Why do I get to pick and the others get to do as they're told?" I asked.

"It's just that you're special, Caroline," Mother told me from the floor inside her bedroom closet. We looked like freaks, Mother and I, sprawled among the shoeboxes eating strawberries and fake cream. *Whipped Dream.* The kind that squirts out in waves and never goes bad for seven more years.

Mother had called me to her bedroom, hissing my name from the wedge in her half opened door, jiggling the coiled stopper until I looked up. All I could see through the crack of light were the red treats and her index finger motioning me away from my favourite episode of Family Feud. *September Baby*. The one where the host asked, "During what month of pregnancy does a woman begin to look pregnant?" and the contestant answered, "September." I don't think any of us kids got why it was funny back then, seeing as those were the days when Mother looked pregnant almost every month of the year. Just watching the game show host crack up that much got us every time, though, and besides, there was nothing better than seeing a grown-up laugh harder than a kid.

You're gonna miss it! Desiree had said as I got up off the floor and walked towards Mother and Dad's room. We all knew the baby question was coming up right after the commercial. I told her it wasn't even funny anymore, but Neil shushed us and waved me away, meaning that everyone better laugh as hard as usual even without me in the room. When I got closer to the bedroom I knew I had to wash my hands because Mother was doing that thing where she wiggled her fingers in front of her chin as if there was something hot in her mouth.

"How do you mean special?" I asked. I knew the others would never let me forget about this day. This wasn't about getting to pick what flavour of frosting Mother used for some movie star's birthday cake. This was about *how* I wanted to grow up, or more importantly, *who* I wanted to grow up with.

I licked the red fuzz from my front teeth, careful to collect any evidence of seeds while I waited for her to answer, *Why me?* I wished she'd use the word small instead of special, or even *petite* like Chester's mom had called me the time she braided my hair right from the top of my head, pulling small bits from each side as she worked her way down. Mother had ripped out the braid the moment I got home, saying it hurt her eyes the way it went all crooked like a broken bone. It was true that the braid went off to the left almost right from the start. Chester's mom had shown me how to look at the back of my head using two mirrors. She said if I kept the braid in all night I would have waves in the morning, like her. I never got the chance to tell her that your hair goes crinkly like French fries if you only leave it in for a few minutes.

Mother showed me her teeth, and I nodded to say there were no strawberry seeds showing.

"You know, like the special that means a good kind of different," Mother said. She picked out one of the larger berries and filled her mouth with it. As she chewed, she took all the green strawberry tops and arranged them in perfect rows in the lid of a shoebox. Her tongue licked her whole mouth clean before she spoke. Then she told me I had a few hours to decide where I wanted to do the rest of my growing up. I could stay in my own home with her and the little ones, or move with Dad and the others to a flat in *stinkin' Waterloo.*

"Kitchener," I said. "Waterloo is where Chester moved, Mother. You keep mixing them up. Maybe you need to say it over a bunch of times or something. Kitch-en-er. Just remember the kitchen. Not the loo."

"Same difference. They're both the city, Caroline."

I knew it was a divorce even though Mother and Dad never gave it a name. Divorce was one of those invisible words that didn't exist until it suddenly mattered. It popped up everywhere the summer before it happened. You had to turn the page or hum a loud tune to get rid of it. Sometimes even the clouds looked like a divorce.

The others had been assigned a home the night before. In the morning, Desiree had pulled me up into the kids' room and asked me which envelope had been on my pillow.

"What do you mean which envelope?"

"Mother's or Dad's?" she wrote on her palm with her finger. She always whispered her secrets in finger writing. Even though it looked like it was only us in the room, you could feel at least one other kid hiding nearby, and you could never tell for sure who was siding with Neil.

"I didn't get any envelope," I told her, but she didn't believe me.

I sat on the floor by the book tower Rosie had made before breakfast and watched Desiree hunting through all seven beds, pulling off the pillows and sheets and then putting them back, smoothing the creases and wrinkles as best she could.

"I told you, I didn't get an envelope," I said again after Desiree wrote *NEIL* in capital letters on the ticklish part of my back. We both knew the book tower would come toppling down if she called Neil in. If the sound woke up Melinda, we'd have to scrub walls in wide circles to help put her back to sleep.

"Come on, Caroline. Even the baby got one," Desiree said out loud.

Desiree took me into Mother and Dad's room to show me the mini envelope that was still inside Melinda's crib. Inside was a tiny slip of paper that said in Dad's handwriting: *You'll live with Mother.* Desiree had already told me that her note was written by Mother and that it said she'd be moving with Dad.

"I'm sure Neil is playing a stupid joke. What'd you do to him this time?" she asked, shaking her finger up and down as if she were older than me. Desiree was a year and a half younger than me, but people thought she was the older one. She was only an inch or so taller for most of grade school, but Neil always made us compare our hand sizes. The top joints on Desiree's finger curled right over mine even when our palms were lined up perfectly. Mother said there would come a day when I would be thankful that I looked younger than my age. *The queen still hasn't lost her baby face,* Mother always said. If you took me out of the family, the others all lined up properly, tallest to shortest, oldest to youngest, according to their birth month. When the midwife had trouble remembering who came first, Mother reminded her how to use her knuckles and count out the months, like teachers taught us to do to find out which months had thirty-one days. *Start with the knuckle on your left pinkie and work your way across.*

"Don't use the thumbs," Neil liked to remind Marie. "And don't include Carolswine. She screwed everything up by coming in July."

Whenever she introduced us to someone, Mother would nod for us all to hold out our knuckles before she went through our names, showing how we came out like a magazine subscription. *January. February. March.* Neil. The twins. Desiree. *Simon is my April baby. Rosie, Magdelene, and Melinda are May, June, July.* I never saw her do it that way after Melinda was born, even though Shilo came along in August, just as Mother would have planned for her youngest. I was the only one who didn't fit into Mother's birthday plan. Whenever Neil commented about how I messed things up, Mother jumped in and blamed the twins. She said Les and Lee were more work than one baby, and she needed extra time between them and Desiree. *Especially for a special baby like Caroline,* she liked to say. During the introductions, she always skipped me and then came back to my hands at the end. She'd say my whole birthday while holding her own fists close to her heart. *Let's not forget our Sweet Caroline. July sixth.* Whenever she said my birthday, Neil would automatically whisper *Sith* to one of the twins. *She's from the dark side.*

"I hate when you say that, Mother."

"What, special?"

"Yes."

"Well you are, Caroline."

"Well it sounds like Special Ed." I switched hands before dipping another berry into the cream. It felt awkward eating with my left, but I was sure Mother had noticed me lick one of the fingers on my right by accident. The berry dissolved under my tongue while I played with the pen that hung from a plastic spring on the knob of the closet door. It wasn't a normal pen for a house. It was the kind you see in banks, only the words were scratched off from old age. Mother once said that the pen was one of those things that came with the house, like the fireplace Dad had wallpapered over, or the fence that once had pigs in it. It was one of those pens that never ran out of ink no matter how many letters you wrote. I wondered if other people's closets had pens inside.

"I told you, it's a good special. Not that kind you kids think of. I want to tell you why," she said, taking the pen away from me and watching it snap back, trapped with us on the inside.

"Then why?"

"Just promise you won't tell your dad."

The *your* dad and *your* mother were new since the d-word.

"Pinky swear."

I held my pinky out for her to lock onto, but she was too busy fiddling with the fruit. It was left at that until the berries were gone and there was nothing left to occupy our mouths. Mother hugged her knees and rocked against the indoor shoes for a minute before the story came spewing out.

"You were baptized, Caroline. The day you were born. The very hour. You are the lucky one."

"Lucky? Why? What's baptized?"

Mother bit her lip with one of her pointy teeth. She despised it when people asked more than one question at once. She felt that if the first question wasn't important then there wasn't a point in asking it. Mother hated pointless things. I waited for her other teeth to show.

"Blessed by God," she said. Her eyes crossed as she stared too hard at the pen.

"What's blessed?"

I wished she'd say that I was so small I could sneak into heaven without anyone seeing me, but I knew that wasn't it. Simon said God probably had some kind of equalizer, anyway. Some machine he dropped dead people into so we'd all be the same size when we passed through the gates.

"I mean to tell you everything, just not all at once. You're too young to know *everything*, Caroline."

"I'm nearly thirteen."

Mother winced when I said that number. She told me to shut up. She'd wash my mouth out. She spoke quickly, in a whisper that was vicious like a scream. She said life wasn't going to suddenly get easier by moving to the city, if that's what I thought. Then her voice got different again. It was like a fairy godmum. She said it would make God happy if I picked her. She called me Sweet Caroline, like when I got perfect on windows or mirrors, like she did when she looked into my eyes and sang her favourite Neil Diamond song between sips of fizz from the neck of Dad's too-warm beer.

I sucked hard on my empty mouth a few times and then whispered that I didn't know God had feelings.

Mother took my right hand and forced me to rub her head. Front to back, back to front. Her naked scalp was sweating, and my fingers, stained with strawberry juice, left faint pink trails as they walked. I counted up to two minutes until she pushed my hand away and began to part my hair instead, tucking it behind my ears again and again. The way it was supposed to be. The mother-daughter way. I counted in my head another minute before Mother stood up and put the empty fruit bowl in my hands. Mother had once caught Chester and I putting peanut shells in the fruit bowl and she had made us wash and dry it seven times. *Which one of you is allergic?* Chester had asked while he waited to dry the fruit bowl the final time. I told him Mother was allergic to peanuts and Dad was allergic to popcorn, which was why we weren't allowed things like Cracker Jacks in the house. *Allergic* was the only way I knew how to say it, and I hoped he never saw Mother dip chocolate chips in the peanut butter jar.

Mother balanced the shoebox lid with the green stems under her palms like a serving tray, and wiggled the closet door open with her feet.

"Do the right thing, Caroline Quartz," Mother said. She took one hand away from the shoebox and pinched the skin on her left knuckles with her teeth as she finished her instructions. "Feel what's in your bones. That's when you know you're following God's plan."

"Yes Mother."

"And remember, you can't have a swing at an apartment. There are other rules than just no pets, you know. You can't take your thinking chair to the city, Caroline. I don't know where you'll do your thinking with no trees around. You'll disappear in the crowd, you know. The damn city'll stunt your growth even more. Besides, your dad's never even baked a stinkin' birthday cake."

The last thing she told me was to leave an envelope with my decision under one of their pillows by five o' clock that day.

"You know which pillow is which," she reminded me, pointing to herself as she said it.

I did. We all did. Mother's was the only pillow in the house without any brown circle stains underneath the case.

CHAPTER 2—DAD

"Psst, Caroline."

Dad's nose was poking out of the chicken coop. It was always the first thing you saw of him—either that or his ponytail if you saw him from behind. He had found me hanging from my swing by my calves, my fingers draped along the ground. I was counting the blades of grass in the patch of dirt beneath the swing. Every time I got to twenty-one, I went back to the piece with the brown sun-dried tip to make sure I hadn't miscounted. It was raining, but the rain never took long to finish up in Mitchell, Ontario.

"Come here a sec, sweetie," he said.

"You come here."

I switched to standard swinging position, thinking he wouldn't come, but then he was at my feet, clutching my shoes hard enough so that one popped off and landed in the dandy flowers. We weren't allowed to call them dandelions, and Dad was not allowed to go near them with his mower. Mother held a ceremony in the front yard every time the dandy flowers went to seed. She'd make each of us lie down on the grass and take a deep breath. We had to blow the closest flower to us as hard as we could, and when we finished blowing, we had to stand by our flower so she could come by and check how many seeds were left on the stem. She got Simon to write down the numbers every year to see if God had changed his mind about how many babies each one of us would have. Mother said that when it came to babies it wasn't unlike God to change his plan.

Dad hated the day of the dandy flowers. He wished Mother would just let him *do away with the pests* with his mower. Apart from cutting down trees for our thinking chairs, mowing the lawn was Dad's favourite thing to do.

"Wanna go for a walk, just you and me?" he asked.

"What for?"

"Fresh air," Dad said, slowing me down by my stirrups, forgetting we were already outside.

All that was left of the rain was what came off the tree in the odd poof of wind. Dad pulled me by the elbow, which is what he did with any of us who were too old for holding hands. He led me towards the back trail even though we always went the front way with parents.

"Where are we going?" I asked. I still had only one shoe on. Wearing one of anything that was supposed to be two was bad luck according to Simon. It was also bad luck to place shoes on a table or let a beetle crawl in your shoe. Simon said the left shoe should never go on first, unless it was by mistake on a Friday morning. Then, and only then, God might forgive you.

"Whirl Creek. Where else?" Dad said.

"How come? Through the back?" I didn't think Dad even knew the way us kids went.

"Who do you think made the path to the creek? Neil?"

None of us ever questioned Neil to his face. He was the *eldest*. Not the *oldest*. Neil would make us pay if we said it the wrong way. Neil said he had carved the path out of the bushes before any of us were even born, and that he had dreamed about how it would look even before he moved to Canada with Mother and Dad. The rest of us had to call it Neil's Passageway and ask him for permission to use it.

I stopped at the twins' thinking chair to put on my shoe. Neil loved to tell the story about the day the twins were born, and how Dad had started to chop the new thinking chair in half, and how Mother had run outside and grabbed the axe yelling that the stump was plenty big enough for two boys to share. Dad had already carved the name *Leslie* across the back of the chair months before. Whenever the twins called Neil a liar, he would laugh and point to the place on their tree chair where Dad had shaved off the last three letters of their original *girl* name. Dad had used the L from Les and carved out Lee going down like a crossword puzzle. No matter how hard the twins tried to sand it down, you could still see the trace of the word l-i-e. *Mother wanted one of each,* Neil always reminded them. *Which one of you screwed it all up for the rest of us?*

Dad tossed my shoe towards the house and told me there wasn't time to fiddle around. I was surprised that Dad knew where all of the low poking branches were, and how to avoid the spitball bushes. It was obvious by his breathing style that the walk had something to do with not telling *my mother.* When we reached the banks of Whirl Creek, Dad pulled me down beside him. He sat right in the goose poop while I took off my shoe and socks in a squat.

"Your mother and I have made a decision."

"No you haven't," I said into my shoe. I pretended to look for a tiny stone at the bottom of it.

"What did she tell you?"

"Can't you just put me somewhere? Like the others." I was worried he would tell me the real reason for the divorce, even though I was sure I already knew. Neil and the twins knew too, but not because they had heard what went on in the bedroom like I had; they were just older and better at assuming than the younger kids.

"We could put you in Kitchener," Dad said, more to the geese swimming by than to me. He got up and took his shoes off, then his socks. As he got closer to the water's edge, he rolled his jeans up to his knees and pulled his T-shirt over his head. Then he waded into the creek. We didn't talk for a few minutes while he got used to the cold water. His fingers played with the surface of the water until he was ready to talk. While he spoke, he drew semicircles around his body with both hands, making a swooshing sound that forced me to listen louder. I shook my shoe again.

"Do you know anything about the day you were born?" He pulled the elastic out of his hair and floated to his back, letting his arms spread out to his sides like water wings. I cringed at the thought of the wet jeans sticking to his hairy skin.

"Nope."

"Nothing?"

"I know it was on my birthday."

"We were here. Your mother and I. You were still inside her, with no signs of being ready to come out."

I wanted to say that I wished he wouldn't talk about me like I was a lasagna, but I also wanted him to tell me more, so I said nothing and waited until he was ready to speak again. He floated for a while, tapping his stomach like a drum until his watch beeped four times and I knew that Family Feud was over and the others would be looking for me. For us.

Dad's chest was the last thing still dry, besides his nose and eyes, and when he looked like he was going to tell me the rest of his story, a siren in the distance flipped him over to his feet. In our family, you had to pray for sirens even though you didn't know who was in trouble. Dad never looked like he was praying, though, not even during grace when he stood over the food with his eyes closed and his knuckles in a knot. When the sirens were gone, Whirl Creek got silent again, and Dad suddenly looked ready to tell me everything.

"We had left Miles with Neil and the twins that day. Miles begged us to go out and leave him alone with them, just for half an hour so he could get his badge for Scouts. Imagine a forty-year-old man wanting to babysit. I didn't want to do it, but your mother insisted. She had this thing, *this feeling*, she called it. She felt it would be okay. *Just this once.*"

"Sure. Why wouldn't it?" I said. Us kids weren't allowed to make fun of Miles, or his lisp, or the dent that cut sideways through one of his eyebrows. When Mother talked about Miles she called him Dad's friend, but Dad always corrected her. *He's our friend,* Dad would say and Mother would roll her eyes and nod and say *yes, Peter, just like Marie is our midwife.* Neil once asked Miles whose friend he was, Mother or Dad's, and Miles answered the question backwards. *I'm their best friend*, he said, and you could tell he really thought it was true.

"Your mother and I thought we were alone that evening at the creek," Dad said.

"You weren't?"

"We didn't notice until the stars came out. There was a man bathing in the water. Right about here." Dad pointed straight ahead of us and then looked up into the sun.

"What kind of a man?"

"A tall one. He was—nude."

"Dad!"

I sat staring at a different part of the water while I waited for him to continue with his story. The water didn't move; even when he dunked his head under and came back up, the water ring stayed still around him. I was sure we were both picturing his story differently. His face was calm and dreamy, like at the start of a fairytale, and mine was scrunched up like a Muppet. I finally got the nerve to look straight at him and signal that I was ready to hear the rest. I swallowed hard and blew air out my nose.

Dad walked slowly out of the creek and sat beside me, shivering like dads aren't supposed to do. He put his dry socks on his wet feet, and tried to force his right foot into his left shoe. He looked confused for a minute, and I was sure he had changed his mind about telling me anything. Then he looked right into the sun again and smiled as if the brightest idea had come to him.

"That man. He just popped out of the water while we were lying on our backs on this bank, looking for the dippers." Dad pulled the elastic off his wrist and tied his hair in a bun. He always did that when he got out of the shower. He'd let it out when it was still damp so Mother could smell the *Head and Shoulders* instead of the hair. Mother thought he looked like Charles Ingalls when it was down. She even called him Pa sometimes. Dad loved tucking his elastic in Mother's pocket and pulling it out whenever he needed it. He hadn't done it in a while, though. Not since Melinda had been born, or at least not since Chester had left.

"You're not going to tell me something sick, are you?" I handed Dad his right shoe and undid the laces on the left one. It was something a mother should do. My hands looked like they belonged in kindergarten.

"Your mother screamed. She couldn't catch her breath. It was like she was hyperventilating. I remember that part clearly."

TARA BENWELL

"Maybe it was me. Maybe I was having a bad dream," I said. "Babies dream, don't they? Even on the inside?"

Dad continued struggling with the shoe and wouldn't take the other one when I offered it to him.

"The man took a few steps towards us and then reached for a robe behind that tree. He checked on his picnic basket and then came right to us. He wasn't a ghost, Caroline. Your mother would kill you if she heard you say it that way. She liked the word angel. Don't say he was a ghost."

"I didn't say he was," I said, but I started to think it by how fast Dad got talking, and the way he smiled and shook his head at the same time. I continued to listen to him tell the story of my birth, though it turned out he wasn't even there for the coming out part. I had always assumed I was born at home like the others, with Marie waiting quietly at Mother's side to catch me and find out my name. I figured Dad would have been managing the record player, in case I turned out to be a boy and Mother needed to think of a different name.

"The man took off his robe again so that your mother could lay on it, something to catch the mess until the birthing sheets arrived, he said. She begged me to fetch Marie. I didn't want to leave her with that man, but he had this way with her. He calmed her down. It was almost like she knew him. She begged him to stay and for *me* to go." Dad pointed towards our house, even though the midwife lived the other way.

"You left Mother alone with the—naked man so you could get Marie? You left Mother *and* me?"

"He said he was a priest or something. No. An earth angel. That's right. An angel of God. Or was it a guardian angel?"

The rest of Dad's story was really Mother's because he wasn't even there. He had run off to find Marie, but Mother couldn't wait for the midwife. It was like I had to get out right then and there, and I did, without even a push.

"And there was no mess," Dad said. "It was as if her thingy was a throat and you were some kind of noodle." He took his hair out and fluffed it for a minute before he wound it back up.

I covered my eyes as if something x-rated had just popped on the TV. I knew childbirth was supposed to be an untidy painful thing. I had heard and watched parts of it, and it was always loud. It was always pretty quick with Mother, but not like that. Not like a squirt of ketchup or something. Dad said Mother felt giddy with me. The way he pictured the scene while he spoke it was like he was looking at her right then and there, only she was a younger, more alive version of Mother, the Mother who used to sit cross-legged on the circle stool for hours listening to Neil Diamond songs just so she could find the perfect name for her next baby.

"But we almost lost you," he said. He looked up again and bit down on his lip.

"When?"

"On that night."

"When? July sixth, my birthday?"

"July sixth, right. You bounced and rolled in, head first." He made a rolling motion with his hands.

"In where?"

"The creek," he said pointing in front of him. "That's what they said when we got back here. Your mother was wrapped in the man's robe, and when Marie tried to make sure everything was okay, your mother refused to let either of us near her or *the baby.*"

"What do you mean *the baby*? You mean me."

"She said she was fine. She said you both were doing fine."

"And were we?" I asked, but Dad ignored my question.

"As soon as I saw your mother, I knew you were the lucky one she talked about. All she kept saying was *Sweet Caroline.* You were at least two months early, but you were perfectly normal. The priest guy said you shouldn't have even survived. Then he walked away with that damn picnic basket and we never saw him again."

I couldn't speak. Dad looked at the creek as if the ghost man were back. He didn't say whether or not the guy took his robe back from Mother. I figured he did since there was no mess, but I didn't ask. Maybe she swaddled me in it. I hated how he called me *the baby*, but I figured that's what happened when you were the fourth born.

"Promise you won't tell your mother what I told you," he said. "She wants to be the one to tell you this, to tell you everything. She says you need to be a woman first, whatever that means. Maybe when you're thirteen you'll be big enough, old enough. You'll have to act surprised if she ever tells you any of this. Pinky swear you'll act surprised?"

"Pinky swear," I said, holding out my crooked finger.

"Don't tell the others, either. Not even Chester, if he ever shows up again," he said. "Your brothers and sisters aren't as good at holding on to secrets, Caroline. You have to be careful what you tell Desiree if you don't want the world to make fun."

Dad held out his pinky and locked it with mine. I was sure it was his way of saying he knew that I knew about everything, not just why he and Mother were breaking up, but what had brought them together in the first place, way back in their life in America.

"Pinky swear," I said, a second time, but hardly any voice came out.

Dad's eyes were like hoops of fire while he locked his finger with mine. For a second I thought he might jump back in the creek and swim into the deepest part for fear that I might tell somebody what he had told me. Instead, he got up and started for home. I followed without being told. At the turn, he disappeared and went back the parent way. From the back he could have been a teenage girl.

"I'll beat ya," I said and began to run. I wanted to get back to my swing before the others could ask where I'd been. As I ran, I thanked God for September babies. I knew none of the others could have followed us out to the creek with everyone's favourite episode on. Even if they looked for us after the show was over, they wouldn't have got to the creek on time to hide behind a bush or bench. I vowed to never tell any of them my birth story, not even Chester, if I ever found him again. I had pinky sworn and it was the easiest promise I had ever made, and I would die before I'd let Mother tell me her *everything* version. *Maybe when you're thirteen.* It would be just like Mother to tell me about the unluckiest day of her life on the unluckiest day of mine.

As I ran, I tried not to count how long it was until my thirteenth birthday, but every time I tried to block it out, the counting came back to me. Every thirteen steps, my voice whispered into my ear. *She's going to tell you everything.* I knew right then what my moving decision would be. The special feeling was so strong it practically swallowed me up.

Dad was standing with one foot on my thinking chair when I reached the yard. Mine was the furthest tree chair from the house, the closest to the pathway, and the one with the most rings. *Why did the runt get the biggest chair?* I once heard Neil asking the twins. *He coulda used a sunflower stalk for Carolswine.* Dad was cleaning out the last few letters of my name with his fingers. That was what he always did when he needed to get out of the house after he had already cut the lawn. He would sweep leaves and dirt off our chairs and then clean out the grooves of the letters until you could read the names on them from as far back as the house. It wasn't something he ever did just after it rained, though. Mother insisted rain was the purest form of water in the world. She would call it pointless if Dad went out to clean the chairs after a storm.

"Beat ya," he said. He pointed at my other shoe, which had been tied to a boot and thrown up high into the maple tree, either by Neil or by someone Neil had threatened.

"I stopped to pee."

"Better go wipe. Your Mother'll kill ya." He made a pretend gun with his fingers.

He was right. She'd smell me in an instant. Mother was almost always pregnant, so she could smell practically anything—dust, crumbs, boogers, stolen cupcakes, even mail. I made my final decision at that moment; I just hoped she didn't ask why. By my next birthday she'd be ready to tell me everything. Everything I already knew and maybe even more.

There was an envelope waiting at the top of the stairs when I got in. It had my name on it in Mother's handwriting, but there was no piece of paper inside. As I reached for the pad of construction paper in the zipper compartment of my knapsack, I heard her slippers sliding by the open door. She almost never came upstairs except to use the attic or to do a bedroom check, and it wasn't time for either of those things. It was 3:29 P.M. We all kept digital watches because Mother didn't trust clocks with faces. She especially hated the kinds that had a few straight lines with wide gaps in between instead of numbers. I flipped through the paper and counted as the plastic bottoms of Mother's slippers went down each stair. Her bathroom door clicked shut.

Mother always used the toilet at 3:30 in both the P.M. and the A.M. I had plenty of time to write down my decision. Thirty-one minutes exactly. There were ten colours of construction paper to choose from. Someone was coming for me. Surely Simon. He'd have something to tell me, something that didn't matter unless you were going on Jeopardy, like the fact that there are more chickens than people in the world, or that rubber bands last longer in a refrigerator. I picked a piece of blue paper, blue for a man. At first I thought pink, but then that felt cruel, like dangling a rubber duck too high above a baby's head. At the last minute, I decided something neutral would be better than blue. I tore out a piece of yellow, slowly so as not to rip it at the edge. *Yellow is for friendship,* Mother always said about the frosting or balloons she chose. Simon was calling my name. With a purple crayon sharpened at both ends, I quickly wrote *Dad* smack in the centre of the paper. I folded the sheet into four to make sure there was a D on both sides of the crease, and then stuffed the paper into the envelope and took the stairs down two at a time into Mother and Dad's room where the bathroom light was on. I placed the envelope under and between the two pillows, making sure there was a little more of the edge on Dad's side.

"Caroline. Sweet Caroline. Is that you?"

I knew Mother would hear me if I walked past the bathroom door. I still had twenty-one minutes to get out. When she flushed, I ran for the exit. She wouldn't hear me with the faucet on. The kind of water Mother used was always loud. But then the bathroom door opened. Her elbows were on the knob. Her wrists awkwardly up in the air, soapy wet. She kept her eyes inside. I turned back and disappeared under her bed. It was the only bed in the house that had nothing under it. My heart was in my neck, doing circles. I heard her slippers on the door kicking it open further. She had a full view of her bedroom. I watched her from the small hole in the wood of the bed frame that Chester and I called the lookout. Soap up, rinse, soap up, rinse, dry, repeat. Six times. One more to go.

Simon was shouting that he couldn't find me, and Desiree was saying that if I wasn't on my thinking chair I was probably on my stupid swing. Desiree told him to check there first as if he hadn't already. Mother sat on the bed and found the envelope.

"Well? What's the verdict?" It was Dad at the door. His voice squeaked like Neil's had started to do. He saw me under the bed. Upstairs Rosie's book tower came crashing down.

"I won't have it," she said to him in a weak whimper. "Not my Caroline. Not my birthday girl. The envelope was on my side. It was supposed to say *Mother*."

Dad looked right into my eyes before he walked out of the room. He turned back and winked so quickly it could have been a twitch to anyone who didn't know I was under the bed. As soon as he was gone, I felt the mattress spring up, and then the closet door closed, and I knew she was inside.

I waited for the sound of the paper. When it came it wasn't just a rustling or flipping sound like usual. This time it was a slamming and scraping and tearing as if Mother was wrapping a present she didn't want to give away. The sound of Rosie and Simon whimpering through the heat register didn't make the paper sound go away. I could tell by Desiree's singing that Dad had told them my decision to move to Kitchener. I tried to concentrate on Desiree's cheerful song, but the paper kept getting in the way. *Sweet Caroline...ba, ba, ba.* What was Mother ripping?

I was sure if I slid out from under the bed and opened the closet I'd find her shredding pages with her teeth. My baby pictures, maybe? My report cards? Letters to a dead relative she never sent because she didn't know the address? No. It was the sound of newspapers. I wanted to shout for her stop, but I couldn't. I knew it wasn't plain old obituaries from the *Mitchell Advocate*. Mother was tearing up the stories from her childhood. Hers and Dad's childhood.

I wished Chester had been there to confirm the smell. He always sneezed when those old newspapers were around.

CHAPTER 3—DESIREE

Desiree didn't ask why Mother and Dad had given me a choice where I wanted to live. She just wanted to know how I came up with my decision. I told her it came to me in a dream, a dream where God was lying under my bed with a sign that said *Waterloo*.

"What'd he look like again?" Desiree said into her pillow the third night in a row. I knew she wanted to know in case God ever appeared in one of her dreams. Desiree was afraid of dreams, unless they were ones that came back again and again, and you could tell yourself to wake up because you knew they weren't real.

"Like Santa Claus, only he was all in white instead of red," I said.

"So God is fat?"

I told Desiree there was so much light around God it was hard to see his body shape. I wasn't sure if he even had a body.

"So God is just a head?"

"It doesn't matter what he looked like. He'd probably look different to you if you saw him anyway," I said. *He might be some naked guy in a bathrobe that looked like a ghost,* I thought to myself. "The part that matters is the sign."

"And you're sure it said Waterloo, right? Maybe God can't spell Kitchener."

After my third time explaining the dream, a strange thing happened. I wasn't sure if it started in my head or in my heart, but I started to believe I had really had the dream about moving. Each time I described the Santa God dream to Desiree, I became more convinced that moving away from Mother was part of God's plan for me. Instead of thinking of myself as a liar, or a person who was afraid of the truth, I focused on Mother's golden rule.

"Don't let me ever hear you kids doubting God," Mother always said.

"John Henry did," Desiree said one time when the sun hadn't come out for over a week.

"John Henry's from a book," Mother said.

"God's from a book," Simon said.

"The book," Mother said, before forcing us all to sing Orphan Annie's theme song in a round.

Desiree told me she doubted God would come into a dream about a divorce. A love dream maybe, but not one about a family breaking up forever.

"Well, he did," I told her.

"If he did, it must have been a silent dream," Desiree said. "A God dream should have woken me up."

"I said it was a sign. There wasn't any sound."

I didn't believe for a second that Desiree doubted my dream. She had a thing about not being the last person to fall asleep, and she would have said anything to keep me awake that night. We all knew her biggest fear was that the whole house would fall asleep and then everyone would start talking in their dreams.

"Want me to read you a book?" I whispered to Desiree. Though we were the only two still awake in the kids' room, we could hear the baby crying downstairs. We knew that if Mother heard us up she'd make both of us take a turn shutting up Melinda.

"Okay, but I don't know which book I want," Desiree said, tiptoeing to the shelf.

"How about the wedding book?" I whispered, and then wished I could take it back.

"No!" Desiree said. "It will make it harder to sleep. Maybe you could *tell* me a story instead. Like a story about how it was before Chester left. Before the stupid agent man came and broke us all up. Neil says the agent screwed us. That's what this moving is all about."

"I said a *book*, Desiree. I don't feel like making up a story."

"You don't have to make up a true story, Caroline. You can just tell it."

"I don't feel like telling."

"Fine then, read. Just not the wedding one. Weddings are stupid, anyway. Neil said weddings jinx you."

Our books were from a thrift shop in Mitchell called *The Second Chance*. Miles said they were books that were going to get thrown away, either doubles or ones with *mithing pages*. Miles spoke like a kindergartener and got excited about things like free crayons. He came by the house at least once a day for a piece of cake, which Mother wrapped up for him to take home because he licked his hands while he ate. Mother read to us every night, except for Fridays, and we had to take turns picking the book we wanted. Dad said we should give every book a chance, even if it was just a brown one with black lettering. He said if Mother judged him by his cover most of us would have never been born. It was true what he said; the book with the big whale and the bad word on the front that Neil had chosen for Mother to read on his thirteenth birthday wasn't worth reading at all. We learned not to always pick the books by the covers; sometimes we picked them by the size or the smell.

"Let's read this one tonight," I had begged Mother one evening when Chester was at our house for a sleepover. I must have been in grade five at the time because Chester and I had started keeping each other's secrets. I held up the skinny novel from the new pile of books called *The Member of the Wedding*. "It smells like the basement," I said to Mother by accident.

"How would you know what a basement smells like?" Mother asked. I looked away because I knew my face was going to turn pink. I was just about to lie and say I had been dared to put my nose to the crack of the basement door when Neil saved me.

"Who cares about weddings," he said, giving me the shut up or else eyes. Mother and Dad had only just gotten married by then, but it wasn't a real wedding. "You like that book 'cause it's scrawny like you."

There was one part in the wedding book we all liked, except Mother. It was where John Henry and Frankie Adams talked about what God did wrong in the very beginning. Each night that week after Mother kissed us each the proper amount of times and told us to say sorry and thank you prayers, we took turns pretending to be Frankie or John. There was always enough time for each of us to take a turn discussing God's mistakes while Mother was washing up. We called the game *The Eighth Day*. Every night that week Desiree said the world should have been created with chocolate dirt and lemonade rain.

"Let me guess, and candy flowers," Neil had said, the second time Desiree said it. Even though Desiree swore she made it up in her own head that was exactly what John Henry said to Frankie Adams in the wedding book. The rest of us made up different things every time we played.

"On the eighth day, God gave pregnant women buttons to press to say if they wanted a boy or a girl," Neil said, the second night.

"Like belly buttons?" I asked.

"Only on their butts," Neil said.

"On the eighth day, God gave babies fireproof skin," I said.

"Babies don't smoke." Simon said.

"No, but they can still burn," I said, looking at Chester and thinking of the American newspaper clippings we had read in Mother's closet. I could still see the headlines with Mother and Dad's names in block letters beneath the newspaper titles. I tried not to picture them too closely. I didn't want the dreams to come back that night.

Chester was the only non-family member who was allowed into Mother and Dad's room. When I said the word *burn* I opened my eyes wide and looked straight at him. Chester nodded his head and swished spit around in his cheeks. I had never told him I thanked God every night that I hadn't discovered the shoebox on my own or with someone who couldn't keep secrets like Desiree. The thought of being the only one knowing Mother and Dad's secret scared me even more than the stories of the fire.

"It was the eighth day and God decided to make babies out of rubber," Chester said, "so they could bounce and not be so breakable."

"What would you know about babies," Neil said. "You're an accident."

"He is not," I said.

"Families with only one kid are always accidents—either that or mistakes. Even God makes mistakes."

"Your mother tells me things," Chester said, trying not to cry. Chester wouldn't dare call her just plain Mother in front of Neil, even though he swore to me that Mother said he could call her Mom, or even Maman if he wanted. Desiree once called Mother, Mummy, and right after she said it Mother put Desiree in a corner and made her spin around and around while the rest of us covered her in toilet paper. Desiree had to unravel herself, and Mother made her put the pulled paper in a margarine container to use every time she went to the bathroom as a reminder of what she had done wrong.

"On the eighth day God made babies out of glass," Neil said, getting back to the game. "So they'd smash into pieces when they hit Mother Earth."

The twins went next. They both agreed that all babies should be born as boys who looked the same.

"Two more boys and then Mother would be happy for the rest of her life," Simon whispered.

"She only needs one more boy," I said, counting the boy knuckles in my head and looking at Chester. We all knew which boy she wanted, but we couldn't say it around Neil.

When Rosie finally spoke that night, she changed the theme. She said a stupid thing, which she almost never did even though she was the youngest one playing. She said she wished God had made vegetables nicer colours, like fruits.

"Tomatoes are red. Carrots are orange. What else do you want?" Neil asked.

"Maybe purple vegetables," Rosie said. "They would taste better than green ones."

Rosie was the only one who had noticed that Mother was done in the washroom and that she was standing at the door listening to our game. We had lost track of time because Neil had taken two turns. Neil said it was Rosie's fault Mother made us eat beets and brown sugar for breakfast the next day, mustard and beets for lunch, and beets with salt and pepper and BBQ sauce for dinner. And it would happen again if Mother ever heard us questioning God. Not only that, but if she ever caught us questioning babies.

We learned a lot of things about life and how it was supposed to be from books. It was from old-fashioned books set in England where we learned that it was normal for people to name their houses.

"How come our house doesn't have a name?" Simon asked one day at the dinner table, long before the separation.

"I guess because we never gave it a name the day it was born," Mother said.

"When was it born?" he asked, but nobody knew the answer to that either. Dad said it was already born the day he and Mother arrived from America.

"Morehead, North Carolina is in America." Simon said. "It's where they have the bald conventions. I hope I'm bald when I grow up. I want to be beautiful like Mother. I bet all the relatives had no hair."

I filled the silence as quickly as I could. Simon knew better than to bring up relatives, but sometimes he needed to know things and his brain did the talking instead of his mouth. I suggested we name our house Circle Square. I knew it was a bad name as soon as I said it, but anything was safer than mentioning uncles or grandparents.

Mother had said that if we insisted on naming the house it ought to be something significant. "It won't stick otherwise."

"Something like Mouse House," Neil said, and then walked away from his dinner. Mother asked what was significant about that.

"It ought to have something with Manor in it," Mother said.

"Circle Manor," Desiree said. "Or Square Manor. We can use crazy glue to stick the name on right at the front by the number."

Mother didn't snort or sigh like Dad did when Desiree said something stupid. She had convinced the school board to let Desiree start kindergarten the year after me, and she never once admitted it was a mistake. I remember standing beside Desiree in the K-2 schoolroom when Mother sealed the deal. *We usually only do this with the January babies, Mrs. Quartz,* the teacher who was in charge of the elementary class said, as if Mother had mixed up her own children. *She'll be just fine.* Mother said. *She'll have Caroline and Chester. Besides, she shares a birthday with Albert Einstein.*

"Think of the smell, the feel, the taste, the sounds. The everything," Mother said, about the house naming. I looked away when she said the word *everything.* Her eyes waited for me to look back, but when they didn't, she walked away and left our house nameless.

Bleach. Bare walls. Purple frosting. Papers turning. Nothing seemed to sum up our house in one or two words. It was a week later when Dad suggested that Maple Manor had a nice ring to it and was highly appropriate considering the only tree left standing in the backyard was the giant maple.

"And both words start with M and have five letters," Mother said, double checking with her fingers. "It's perfect, Peter."

"Like you, Sherry."

"And we always have maple syrup," I said, opening the fridge and pointing at the sparkling glass bottle, which had come special delivery from Connecticut one July. Mother had soaked the bottle in vinegar for a day and then rinsed it seven times before pulling the half used container of Aunt Jemima out of the paper bag at the back of the fridge. She poured the syrup into its new bottle without spilling a drop, and then spent the next hour peeling the paper sticker off the empty syrup container. When she finally got it off in one piece, she handed it to Dad who ripped the nice lady into shreds. Miles had told us later that Mother did that 'cause she *din't want no more kids askin where's their aunties.*

"And ever since the eighteen hundreds the maple leaf has been the emblem for Canada," Simon said.

TARA BENWELL

"Our home and native land," Neil sang in the sarcastic girly voice he used when he thought something was dumb.

*

Desiree thumbed through the books on the shelf, but still couldn't decide on one for me to read. The baby had stopped crying, which meant Mother and Dad were probably asleep too. Dad was still sleeping in the same room as Mother, but he slept in a kid-sized sleeping bag on a pillow bed by the door. Every time Desiree noticed me nodding off, she whispered something to keep me up. *I wonder if the little ones will even remember us when we're gone. I bet our teachers will wear blue jeans. I wonder if you'll grow faster in the city. Dad said we can't get a cat. Do you think we'll go for walks after supper at our new house? Maybe Dad doesn't even care about walking like Mother does. Maybe Dad just goes down to the creek every day for Mother's sake. He probably wishes every day was Friday. He likes folding laundry better than walking. He says it all the time. He's a Friday man. Mother says people are fatter in the city. They forget they have feet.*

Even though we didn't have a car, walking wasn't something we did to just to get somewhere in Mitchell. Every evening, except for Fridays, we formed a family ring around the maple tree, said a prayer for nature, and went looking for dippers, big or small, along the Whirl Creek trail. Dad felt we should count our lucky stars every day for just being alive, but Mother was more interested in stuff that was closer to the ground. She said the trail was the only place in the universe where humans had not disturbed the perfect balance of God's creation.

Mother always walked in front on the way to the creek, and at the back on the way home. We followed behind or ahead of her two by two, just like Noah's animals, smallest to largest, by height, not hand or foot size. If there was an extra person, Neil stayed at the back or the front, and we pretended he didn't belong to us.

With Mother's shaved head she looked different than most women, though we only knew two or three others. The dark roots that bloomed from her scalp took seven days to really be noticeable. On the eighth day, she washed it with shampoo more expensive than our dinner before she slid a pink plastic razor over her head. She shined it up with peppermint cream, and by the end you could almost see yourself in it. It took her three hours to complete the procedure. Afterward, she would sit on the floor in the living room and hang her head upside down, and we would all stand around her and fight to be the first to touch the smooth skin. Mother was at her most womanly when she was clean-shaven with a belly as big as our globe. We knew so by Dad's eyes. He would sit on the floor in the opposite corner with his legs outstretched and crossed at the ankles, pretending not to want to touch her all over, as he watched us from the side or the top of his newspaper.

We didn't use chairs inside Maple Manor. We had a table that stretched across half of the main floor where Mother set out the meals every morning and night, at a quarter to seven. Dad told Chester that chairs were too dangerous with so many of us piddling around. There were lots of other things we could sit on—pillows, book boxes, or laundry baskets. The circle stool with the stuffing falling out. Other than the tree stump chairs that were scattered throughout the backyard and rooted to the ground, the circle stool was as close to a chair as Dad permitted. When Mother wasn't using it, Neil took charge of it. He would turn it on its side and roll it out to the centre of the living room, kicking it over, and snapping the belt from his housecoat to call a meeting.

"Why doesn't he just sit on it?" Simon asked in my ear every time. No one called Simon by his Neil Diamond name back then. *Soolaimon.* No one except Mother and that was only on his birthday in the birthday song. *Happy Birthday to Soolaimon, Wayne Newton, and Doris Daaay. Happy Birthday to you.*

Neil liked to stand on the stool and make us sit on our knees around him. He got his idea from Mother. She made us hop on one leg in formation around the circle stool when she wanted a confession. She didn't stand in the middle like Neil did. We had to face the outside as she paced around us looking for blinkers or shakers. Mother said it was impossible to balance when you weren't telling the truth.

"This is the last time I am going to ask," she would say. "Who put the peanut butter in the fridge?"

Mother was different when we went on our evening walks, and she almost never got mad after seven. Dad once said that after seven was kind of like Mother's Sabbath because she never did any cleaning or sorting after that. Mother was religious, but in a different way than church people; besides bedtime prayers and grace, she didn't believe in bringing God indoors.

As soon as we got to the part in the path where the gravel turned to smooth gray stone, Mother would stop and do her thing. The breath she took was so long and deep she got more than her fair share of the world. She closed her eyes just enough so her eyelashes twitched like butterflies. Then she crossed her arms in an X. She did it all backwards when she was ready to let the air back out. And she did it all with her nose. It wasn't until the very end when she used her mouth, and that was to whisper one word: *equilibrium.* She said it slowly and then opened her eyes. The last thing she did was suck her lips together, tilt her chin back as far as it could go, and kiss the air.

"It's so perfect. How'd he do it? It's the first thing I'll ask him when I get there," Mother said.

"Get where?" Simon asked because it was his tradition. We all knew she meant heaven, but none of us agreed what it would look like, or what you would do when you got there. Mother said heaven wouldn't feel like something fancy. "It's going to feel normal, like doing the dishes or brushing your teeth. It'll be something perfect and natural, like love for a newborn baby. You won't know it till you get there, but you'll see."

"I'll know it by the sugar mountains," I said one time after Mother's usual explanation. "You can jump off them and not worry about falling down 'cause you can't die twice."

"I'll know it by the maple mountains," Desiree said. "You can swim up them and you won't drowned 'cause you can't—"

"Heaven doesn't have mountains," Neil said. "Heaven doesn't even exist."

"Then where are all the dead people?" Simon asked. Mother was too far ahead on our walk to hear what Neil had said, but Dad heard, and Dad always made us touch the first tree or wooden bench we saw after anyone said the word *dead* or *die*. One time Neil suggested we surprise Mother for her birthday by trying to find all of the famous people who had died on *our* birthdays. None of us thought it was a good idea, but Neil had insisted it was exactly the kind of thing Mother liked, so Simon got out his notebook and divided up a page with all of our birthdays, ready to record any deaths we found. We had already figured out that a queen had been beheaded on Rosie's birthday, and the founder of Mack Trucks died on Desiree's when Mother walked into the living room and realized what we were doing. She grabbed the circle stool and asked us if we all wanted to go to hell. Other times when she wanted to talk about the opposite of heaven she would say h-e-double hockey sticks, but not that time. "Your birthdays are sacred," she said, after the hell word. "What have you all got to say to God?"

It wasn't until after we were double checking that all of the encyclopedias were away in the proper order that I realized none of us even knew when Mother's birthday was. Even if we wanted to surprise her with a gift, we couldn't. We celebrated Dad's birthday every year, but not once had we celebrated Mother's. Chester didn't understand why we didn't just ask her when it was.

"I'll ask," Chester said one day when we were all making guesses.

"You will not," Neil told him. "You ask and you die."

For a few years I was sure Mother's birthday was on Labour Day. At Maple Manor, Labour Day was the most important day of the year. Mother said it was like having all of our birthdays on the same day. She'd spend the weekend before it counting candles to make sure there were enough to put all of our ages on the big cake. We used the same candles for every birthday because Dad didn't allow them to be lit. It was the year I caught Mother singing Happy Birthday in her closet when she was supposed to be looking for vanilla that I started to suspect that Labour Day was her birthday. *Happy Birthday to me. Happy Birthday to me. You have all these children. Now be filled with glee.*

When I asked Dad if I was right, he looked up at the ceiling and laughed, as if he had some sort of inside joke with the walls. "Labour Day is on a different day every year, Caroline."

*

Desiree fell asleep after the first few pages of *The Velveteen Rabbit* while I sat awake thinking about the story she had begged me to tell her, the story about how it was before the agent came along and took Chester away. How we used to do whatever we wanted on Friday nights and Saturday mornings because Mother and Dad were busy having adults only time. I figured that if I thought hard enough about it I might have a good dream about the good times.

The agency had no real reason to give us Chester. The fact that Chester was born on the same day as Michael Landon from *Little House on the Prairie*, and that Mother sobbed like a baby whenever she saw Charles Ingalls wasn't enough of a reason, according to the agent. Mother even went as far as to tell the agent that she had named me Caroline after Charles' wife, hoping it might convince him we were *meant to* have Chester. That only made things worse because the agent didn't like being lied to and didn't believe in *meant to* things like Mother did. Everyone, even British people, knew *Little House on the Prairie* was a new show. Besides, the agent had heard Mother singing my Neil Diamond song on my birthday. He had been the one to pull her out of the closet and dry her eyes that day while everyone else couldn't get the words '*good times never seemed so good'* out of their heads. Desiree and I had watched him do it from the hole underneath Mother and Dad's bed. Dad had been out in the backyard tying balloons to a sprout that had grown from my thinking chair. The agent dried Mother's eyes differently than Dad did. He did one at a time and looked at each one separately to make sure neither was going to start up again. Then when both eyes did, he sat on the floor by her feet and rubbed them until she seemed almost finished. His feet stuck out so far from the closet we couldn't help but see them. The agent was a giant compared to Dad. I could fit both of my feet, and a hand, in one of his shoes.

"What's brought all this on, cupcake?" the agent had asked. "I thought this was a celebration?"

"Mother always cries on Caroline's birthday," Desiree whispered. "It's part of the tradition. She probably wants her to grow."

Mother spat out something about happy tears and her first-born daughter, but she didn't look at him once when she said it. She never looked straight at anyone on my birthday, though I had caught her more than a few times staring in her bathroom mirror, patting her own head, and bugging her eyes out like a monster, while everyone else was demolishing my birthday cake.

I was standing beside Mother at the table the day she told the agent her plan to take all of the shoeboxes out of her bedroom closet and turn it into a room for Chester. The way she looked at me when she said *shoeboxes* I was sure she knew Chester and I had found and read the newspaper clippings she thought were hidden safely behind her red clothes. When I looked away and tried not to blink nervously, Mother told the agent Chester would be more comfortable in the closet than any of us were upstairs. *There are just so many beds and snores and nightmares in the kids' room.* Mother said it was important for Chester to be close to her in case of an emergency.

"I'll take the doors off the hinges if it will make a difference to your decision. He'll be like one of the babies. Nice and close at all times," she told him. "He hasn't got anybody else."

When Desiree asked Neil why Mother and Dad were breaking up, Neil blamed it on Chester. He said Mother and Dad wanted to keep Chester more than they wanted to keep each other. He was their little orphan Annie. That was what Neil said he heard the agent say. *Orphan baby. Why do you need an orphan baby when you got so many of your own goddamned kids?* Neil's accent wasn't very good, but we all laughed anyway. Even I laughed, because I knew that if I didn't Neil would threaten to cut my tongue off with the letter opener.

Orphan Anne, not Annie, I thought to myself. I didn't think the others knew Mother's theory. Mother was certain Chester was named after Lucy Maud Montgomery's first son. *Why else would you call a kid*

Chester? Mother had said to me that first day we met his family. Mother was like Marilla and Daddy Warbucks. She wanted a boy. "Chester is an ideal name for a boy in a single child family. Lucy Maud's son was born on July seventh. The luckiest day of the year."

The agent agreed that Maple Manor was big enough for one more member, but said that since Mother and Dad didn't balance their books there was no proof that the Quartz household could provide for him financially. It was Simon's idea to show him that the Quartz's could balance their books just fine.

"I think Simon needs a lighter book. He can't seem to keep this one on his head," I told Neil.

"He's hopeless, that's why. He's going to ruin everything."

"Am not!" Simon said as the book came crashing down again.

"No wonder this won't stay on," I said looking at the nursery rhyme book Neil had chosen for Simon. "It's missing its cover."

"So?"

"So, it's flimsy. You need hard covers for balancing."

"You're flimsy," Neil said. "This is a dumb idea. Let's just forget it."

We all knew that just because it was Simon's idea it wasn't a dumb one like Neil said. One time we found an IQ test at the back of the newspaper and Mother made us all take it and Simon got almost triple Neil's score.

"Caroline, did you tape that thing to your head?" one of the twins asked. They had the history of World War II balanced between them, and despite them being exactly the same height it kept slipping off and landing between them.

"She chose the Bible for good luck," Neil said.

"Did not!"

"Then your head is as flat as Mother Earth," he said.

I felt the top of my head to make sure it was round; the Bible fell to the floor. Some of the red pages folded into the spine, and as I was smoothing the creases out, we heard the sound of shoes near the front door.

"Wait!" Simon yelled down the stairs. "We have a presentation!"

The book on Neil's head fell down front side up. We all gasped. It was the pig book.

"Not that book," I said.

"I'll use whichever book I please." Neil held up his middle finger.

"Let's just forget it," I said.

"No. Let's go," Neil said. "After me."

"At least go in the middle and *hold* the pig book on your head," I begged him. "Like spread your fingers out over the picture. She might not notice which book it is." He ignored me, but it didn't matter. We all knew she'd still notice.

"I'm first," Neil said. "I always am. Carry your books till you reach the bottom."

We followed behind him down the stairs, balancing our books on our heads and putting our hands out at our sides as we walked towards the agent. Neil held the pig book on his head with one finger. He looked like the ballerina from a jewelry box.

"See. We can all balance our books," Simon said. "And so can our Dad and Mother. We're all their kids. So we're born with their gift."

"Yeah, it's like in our jeans," Desiree said. She held out her pant leg and her book fell to the ground.

At first the agent looked annoyed, but then he started rolling back and forth on the stool, watching Mother instead of us. Every few moments he licked the corner of his mouth and closed one eye for a better look at some part of her. When Neil passed Mother, his book crashed down to the blond man's feet. Mother jumped up from her spot on the kitchen floor and grabbed the pig book. She held it close enough to suffocate herself before she pulled Neil out of the lineup and positioned me in front of Desiree at the front, then she marched the side-by-side twins behind Desiree, followed by Simon. Last was Rosie, balancing two copies of *The Mitchell Advocate,* holding one hand over her outie belly button. We always had extra copies of the local newspaper because one got delivered, and Dad always brought at least one home from work. Even though he worked at the paper, he complained he never got to read it there because people kept dying and needing obituaries.

"Okay. Now one circle of the kitchen, darlings," Mother said. She couldn't help making her voice sound like the agent's when he was over. We snaked around the kitchen, and without Neil in the lineup nothing fell down. He stood in the corner and huffed and puffed, trying to blow down our books from afar. Mother clasped the pig book between her knees and stared up at the books on our heads, circling her hips around as if there were music playing.

Another day, in a lullaby voice, I heard the agent telling Mother they couldn't let Chester fall through the system like so many other orphan kids.

"I would do anything for you, sugar," he said. "Anything but this." He whispered it over and over from inside the closed-door room where Mother was supposed to be feeding the baby.

"But God has a plan for this family," Mother said. "We need another boy."

"It's the man's job to make the boys, dumpling," he said. "That's what my mom always used to tell my dad. She had three girls before me. Maybe Sweet Peter hasn't got any boys left in him, doll."

"You're messing with God," Mother said.

I stood still, making sure not to push down on the creaky part of the carpet by Mother and Dad's bedroom door. It took a few moments before the agent's next words came rolling out.

"There might be a way, babycake," he said. "Let's just say we may not need to take this closet door off the hinges just yet."

Dad came home early from work that day. I tried to keep him out of the house by telling him my thinking chair had a chip in it. He was on his way to his toolbox when he heard a curious whimper on the same side of the house as their bedroom.

"Is it me, or do you hear a cat?" Dad asked, pressing his ear up to the house where their bedroom was.

"Uh, it's pretty windy outside. Maybe that's what caused the chip in my tree chair. You need to fix up my C; it's starting to look like a Z or something." The Z was the first letter to come to me, but I wished I'd said O, which might have been more convincing than a letter that sounded like C, but had no resemblance in shape.

"That's no wind," Dad said, heading inside with his shoes still on. "I am sure I heard a cat."

The agent came out of Mother and Dad's room a few minutes later with pen scribbled all over his face. Dad followed behind, waiting until the agent's van was out of sight before he grabbed his toolbox from the front porch and headed out to the thinking chairs.

When Mother finally came out, her hands were black and she had fingerprints all over her scalp. It wasn't like Mother to come into the kitchen without washing up first, but Chester and I had seen her come out of her closet looking that way many times before. Chester could smell the newspaper on her even from under the bed. He had to plug his nose until she washed up so he could let out his sneeze while the water was running in Mother's ear.

"Where's your dad?" Mother asked after the agent left, and I pointed out the window past the maple tree, and pulled myself up on the counter to reach a washcloth for her. I didn't want the other kids to see her that way; I didn't want them asking questions. If they did, I knew what I would tell them. I'd say Mother got caught reading the obituaries again. I'd say she gets sad even when strangers die.

Mother put the cloth up to her face and neck, but refused to wash the newsprint off her hands.

"We'll get Chester," she wrote on the window in the cloud from her breath. She traced 07 07 on top of Chester's name as she stared at Dad out the window. He looked up at her and then went back to polishing the chairs in the rain.

*

"Caroline, wake up," Desiree whimpered. I had fallen asleep thinking about Chester and the agent and how it once was. Saliva was spilling out of my mouth onto *The Velveteen Rabbit* cover. "You're having it again. I'll stay awake with you if you want. I'll read *you* a story. Just don't have that dream anymore, please. I'm begging you."

I didn't have to ask which dream, even though I didn't remember having it just then. I knew she meant the one about the burning cupcakes. Desiree said it gave her nightmares when I had that dream.

"It's like *I* can smell them too. I feel like I'm in your dream, Caroline."

CHAPTER 4—APARTMENT

Desiree sang and skipped rope right up into the moving van.

"First comes love, then comes marriage, then comes baby in a baby carriage."

As she disappeared up the ramp, Magdelene asked Mother where babies came from. I heard Mother say that almost all babies came from angels, except for ones like Melinda that came too soon by accident and you couldn't do a thing to stop it.

"Even God makes mistakes," Mother whispered, looking at me. When she caught me listening, she pretended she was talking about Dad and how men make mistakes about whom they want to be married to. She told Magdelene about the television that Dad was loading into the truck, how it came by a special delivery the day after Mother and Dad's pretend wedding when he promised to live with her forever. Mother said the TV was the wedding ring she never had, and she was sorry to see it go. Even that was a lie because the only time Mother ever watched TV was for *Little House on the Prairie*.

"I'm telling you, Peter, I don't want any part of it. Till death do us part, my foot," Mother said. She was following behind with the original box, even after the TV was wedged between the two bunk beds. Dad smiled and took the box as if it were fragile. What he really wanted was the waterbed, and Mother knew it. What he didn't know was that Mother had already arranged to put an ad in the paper to sell the waterbed, and that Miles was on the lookout for a single canopy bed with dresser drawers.

*

We were skipping school the day the TV arrived at Maple Manor. I was in grade five and Dad had written a note for the bus driver to give to Ms. Ticks that said we were all taking a day off for a family honeymoon. It was the first Monday after Mother and Dad's fake wedding, but it felt like a Saturday, until the delivery. Desiree and I had decided to get out the jump rope, and we were about to start skipping when a black van with a white bunny rabbit head painted on the side of it pulled up our driveway. Two men wearing navy blue jumpsuits got out, and the first thing I noticed was that their names were stitched on their pockets. *Chip and Dale.*

Even though it was cold outside, they had their white T-shirt sleeves rolled up to their armpits with cigarette packs tucked inside. I watched their blue veins bulging as they carried a cardboard box up to the door past Desiree and me. Chip knocked two times and then followed Dale back to the bunny van. Desiree ran up to check on the box. I heard Dale asking Chip why we weren't in school, and Chip saying he didn't fucking know fuck. I was glad Desiree didn't hear, or she probably would have yelled back that we were on our honeymoon and that if they wanted to go to heaven they better not use the f-word. They drove off and left us with a new TV.

The only thing we knew for sure was that the box was mailed from Connecticut, and that Connecticut was somewhere in America. Dad said we had better shut up our questions if we wanted to keep the dang thing. It was always like that when a gift arrived from America. Something big and expensive came at least once a year in early July, though the TV was one of the only things useful to us kids. Other years it had been a long wool coat or a snow blower. When Dad finally got the TV working, we only got two English channels and both of them had a wavy line running through the middle of the screen that made people's heads look like aliens. The only way to make it go away was if someone stood to the left of the TV and stuck a thumb in the silver wire that came out of the back. Neil said Simon gave the best reception, especially if he faced the wall.

"Oh, so I get to keep all the junk!" Mother shouted after Rosie walked back down the moving truck ramp with Desiree's Easy-Bake Oven.

"Mine don't need much in the way of toys anymore," Dad said from inside the truck.

"Yours?"

"I mean the ones coming with me."

Mother watched as the trail of things got dragged and bumped down the front stairs of the house, up the rubber ramp, and then back down again after Dad shook his head. I was watching closely, too. I wanted to see if Dad tried to take any shoeboxes with him. The newspaper clippings were as much his as they were hers, and I was sure he didn't know she had torn them to pieces the day I handed in my decision.

Mother stood beside the closed door, not bothering to help prop it open when Dad came out with something heavy. She never did much in the way of helping when she was expecting.

Dad had said weeks before that they should wait until the last baby was born before they decided who was going with who.

"With whom," Mother said. As she walked away, she tucked her chin into her shirt and said that if he thought he was taking any of us he was dreaming.

"I don't know about the rest of you, but I'm staying," Neil had said, later that day.

"Me too," the twins said.

"You're dreaming," Desiree said.

"I think I'll try the kitchen place. It's near the water," Simon said.

"Waterloo," I said. "Where Chester lives now. Dad says it's really close to Kitchener."

Mother walked back in with her feather duster when she heard the word Chester, and we all lined up in the proper order to get dusted.

"Where's that one going?" Simon asked poking Mother in the belly while she checked if he was spotless. His notebook was open to a page of rows and names, and he stared up at her for an answer.

"What is this chart?" Mother asked trading the notebook for her duster. "Quartzmart?"

"It's for just in case. I can tell you whose kid is Dad's and whose is yours," Simon said, dusting off her belly and asking the baby if it tickled.

"This isn't an auction, Simon!" Mother said.

"I didn't write prices. We're all free."

"This baby will not be going anywhere," Mother said. "None of you will." She tore Simon's notebook in half and handed it back to him.

"But Dad said—"

"Your dad and I have talked it over. Children belong with their mother."

We knew that was a lie because Mother and Dad hadn't talked nicely except to get the butter passed across the table since the day the agent left covered in ink.

It took more than an hour for the moving truck to get to Kitchener from the Whirl Creek Flats. Desiree was riding in the front with Dad, and in the back the twins were each lying on a top bunk pretending they were sick people in an ambulance. I was the nurse. It was the first time the three of us had played anything in our whole life, and it felt almost like having new friends. We were supposed to bang on the front wall of the truck if something went wrong during the drive. Dad had given us a map to look at and said he would honk his horn once when we passed the first sign that said Waterloo, and two times when we got to our own street in Kitchener. At first, Dad had protested when I asked for a Waterloo honk, but when I promised to brush his hair before bed for a whole week, he agreed to do it. The twins almost rolled out of the beds when the first honk came. The next horn was a minute or two later.

"Oh my God! Chester's going to be like our next *store* neighbour again!" I shouted. Dad had promised there would be payphones all over the city, and I couldn't wait to call Chester and tell him Mother had ripped the evidence of her past to pieces. I knew Chester would say that paper could be put back together if it was all in one place, and I probably would have agreed Mother might have regrets, but even if she saved the shreds, I knew it would take her years to piece them back together. By then, I figured I'd be old enough to change my name or live somewhere far away where no one would care that my family was freaky.

Dad unlocked the back door of the van and we all jumped out before he could pull out the ramp. We were parked in front of a tall building made of mostly windows. The sign on the front lawn said King's Tower; we didn't have to give it a name.

"This is our house?" Desiree said.

"Our new home," Dad said. "I'll give you a tour before we bring anything in."

"And Chester's new home is like only a few minutes away," I said.

"You're so excited about him being close and he's not even part of our real family," Les said.

"Yeah. Why don't you feel sad about Rosie or Simon or Neil being far away? How do you think that makes them feel that you care more about somebody else's kid?" Lee said agreeing with Les.

"Mother says he'll be a Quartz one day, even if it's over her dead body," I said reminding them.

"Yeah," Desiree said, taking my side. "The agent said there might be another way."

I ran towards the building before the twins had a chance to laugh or say that the agent's *way* didn't work.

"Wait up!" Desiree shouted as I did a cartwheel by the sign before noticing the *Please Keep Off Grass* part. I couldn't help thinking that maybe Mother was right. Maybe you couldn't do much in the city. Maybe I'd look even smaller in a place like Kitchener where you weren't even allowed to play on the grass. Desiree said she was telling, but then realized there was no one to tell.

There was a fountain near the front door with water shooting out of an angel's butt. I was purposely wearing the shoes where you put a penny in and you're lucky all day. I pulled out the left coin and threw it in the turquoise water.

"I wish for all sunny days like today," I said.

"Why'd you go and wish for that?" Desiree asked. "Now it's going to rain for the rest of the year."

"God's not like that."

"Not God, dummy. The devil is in charge of wishes."

"It doesn't matter what Neil says," I said. "Not anymore." I handed Desiree the penny from my right shoe and she wished for no more clouds for the rest of her life.

"Fridays are never going to be the same," Les said, as Dad pulled down the door of the moving truck.

"Yeah," Lee agreed.

"We'll probably never go for walks again," Desiree whispered, siding with the twins.

"Yes, we will," I said.

"But not with everyone. The Creek Kids will be with Dad. Remember what Dad said about the switch?"

Neil was the one who had come up with the term Creek Kids. He had tried to coax the twins into coming up with a name for our group too, but every time they suggested something he snorted and called it gay. He wanted us to pick the name Sewer Rats, but none of us liked that for a group name, and we knew Neil couldn't make us do everything he wanted anymore. For the first time in our lives we could call him things like Freckleface out loud instead of writing it in the palms of our hands.

"I'm sure Dad won't mind sitting around for a while at the house after he visits with the others on Saturdays. Maybe he'll even walk with us, and then we'll all be together again like old times," I said.

"Fridays will never be the same," Desiree said, looking up to make sure the twins heard her. "Maybe Dad will turn into a Sunday man or something."

It was true about Fridays. Even I agreed that those would be the hardest nights to get used to in our new home. Mother had always told us that the reason we didn't have family walks on Fridays was because there was too much to do. Most of the kids believed her because Friday was the day that Mother and Dad folded the sheets. I was the only one who knew what really had to be done on Fridays. I had seen the thing that the others had only heard from the upstairs bedroom. I never told anyone what I had seen, not even Chester. It wasn't because I didn't trust Chester not to tell the others; it was more because I didn't know how to describe the thing they did without making sound effects.

Once a year, we woke up to piggies in a blanket for breakfast to go along with a newborn baby. Except for Desiree and me, Mother's babies almost always came a year and a month after each other, and on the day they were born Neil would separate the chubby legs from the white cloth to check if it was a new brother or sister. When Neil's finger pointed out to the wall it was for a boy, and when he made a finger circle it was for a girl. Melinda was the ninth baby. The fourth knuckle if you started at January with Neil. It was that morning when Dad discovered we were out of sausages.

"No piggies!" Mother screamed, startling Melinda who began to cry. Then Magdelene began to cry because Melinda's cry had no tears. Then Rosie cried because the babies were crying, and Simon got out his pen and paper to record the scene.

"What's wrong with Melanie?" Simon asked.

"Everything!" Mother said. We waited for her to send Simon to the bathtub for saying the wrong name, but instead she put Melinda in the middle of the table and walked out of the house as though we should divide the new baby up for breakfast as a sausage substitute. The blue blanket came untucked, and Melinda was a little pink wrinkled up creature without a single thing wrong with her. She may have come a few weeks late, but she was still a July baby, and as far as I could tell she was perfectly finished. While I silently counted everyone's birthday over and over on my knuckles, Dad held Melinda to his shirt pocket and fed her milk from a rinsed out ketchup bottle. None of us dared tell Mother how Dad got Melinda to take the milk by warming it under his armpit.

TARA BENWELL

*

Dad searched all of his pockets before he found the new apartment key in his sock. He put it in the door and turned it right, then left, then pushed and turned, then pulled. There was a woman on the other side of the glass. She was smoking and putting on lipstick at the same time, and I noticed her red bra peeking through her white hooded T-shirt dress when she turned her back to us and opened a metal box on the wall. She pulled out some coloured papers, closed the box, tore them in half, and tossed them into the wastebasket on her way out the door. I put my hands to my ears until I was sure she was finished ripping. Even with the glass door separating us, I could hear the paper splitting in all directions.

"Hey mister, you gotta use your hands to pull the door. Don't let the weasel catch you pulling the door with the key. He'll charge you for the locksmith. Happened to me once. You don't want to know what it cost me." She held the door open with her arm and motioned for us kids to duck under. When we were all through, she let dad hold the door for her and then vanished into the back seat of a taxi that looked more like a limousine. As Dad and I stared out after her, Desiree gathered the coloured paper that had been abandoned. She rolled one of the torn sheets up and put her mouth right up to it. "Presenting the family Quartz," she tooted through the cone. "Well, half of it."

"Desiree, you can't do that here. You'll bother the others!" Dad said. He pulled the paper away from her face where there was already a circle indent.

"What do you mean bother the others? The Creek Kids are like a million miles away," Desiree said. "There's no way Mother can hear us from here."

A honk sounded from the blue car and the back window rolled down halfway. The woman with the red bra hung her head out and started to say something as she took the grape gum out of her mouth. She pointed at our moving truck and gave a thumbs up.

"Lacey.1205."

"Peter. 1405," Dad said, and then wiggled his hand in our direction to show that there were too many of us to bother saying all of our names. Too many still, even though we were less than half.

"Buzz me if you need anything," she said and rolled the window back up. As the car drove away, she blew a bubble as big as a balloon. It popped over her nose and she collected it with her tongue as she waved with her fingers.

Dad led us to the elevator and that's when we started to get what was about to happen. We'd be sharing King's Tower with many others, including the bubblegum lady. In fact, there were about fifteen hundred others living in the same house, according to the twins' calculation. We were about halfway up in the elevator when Chester's face came into my mind. *One more person would hardly even be noticed in a place like this.* Mother's way didn't work, but I was sure I could think of my own way to get Chester. Dad said things were going to be easier in the city. Maybe I'd find Chester's mother, too.

The fourteenth floor of our new home turned out to be the thirteenth floor, only without the proper number. Dad said it was probably just a typo and not to go worrying about things for no reason, like our mother.

"You can keep your shoes on, kids," Dad said as we entered our new home where everything was either white or black. We unpinched our noses once we were out of the hallway, and Dad told us to go on in and explore. Desiree followed me from room to room as if she were afraid of getting lost. We bumped into the twins around every corner, and when they stepped out of the shower that was shaped like a telephone booth saying, *Nanoo Nanoo* I knew exactly what they meant. *This place is so weird it doesn't even have a bathtub.* There was no scale in the corner by the tub, either, and no Neil forcing Desiree and me to compare our sizes or search each other's armpits or scalps for freckles or moles.

Dad said the main room was kind of like two. He drew an imaginary strip with his finger and said we could decide which one was the living room and which one was the dining room slash kitchen. The rooms stunk of fresh paint, which was worse than the bleach we were used to, but not as bad as the smell coming from the halls of the building. Dad tried to open the windows, but none of them would budge. There was a sticker on the front one that read: *DO NOT OPEN.*

"So, if there's a fire you have to smash the glass," Les said.

"Yeah, and tie some sheets together and wait for help," Lee agreed.

Dad glared at the sticker while we all looked down at the ground. Miles was standing by the curb waving at the cars going by. He looked like Fisher Price.

It only took a few minutes for us to inspect our entire home, including the cupboards and closets. When we all met back in the front hall, Dad said he better get down to the truck before Miles forgot what he was doing in Kitchener and hitched·a ride to America. He said we could keep looking around if we wanted, but there were no more doors to open, so we followed him out.

"Wait, Dad. Where's the basement?" Desiree asked.

"Good question. I'll show you on the way back down. You kids'll be in charge of your own laundry now, so you'll need to get used to going down there."

Desiree looked at me funny, and I knew she was confused. She didn't mean the basement to King's Tower; she meant our own personal apartment basement.

*

Mother and Dad hadn't know we had been using the basement at Maple Manor as our playroom every Saturday, ever since Magdelene was born. According to Mother, basements were places where families kept lots of junk they had either outgrown or never loved. She felt that if something belonged under the ground it wasn't something a family needed all year round. Mother didn't believe in seasonal things like Christmas decorations—we had to make our own decorations each year if we wanted the house to look festive. The basement door was always locked, but one winter Neil heard Miles bragging to Dad about how he had picked the lock to his trailer with a paper clip after losing his keys. That gave Neil the idea to break into our basement, and he succeeded on the first try.

From that day on we spent Saturday mornings underground. Once we were in, and Neil had closed the door behind us, we couldn't leave until we were sure Mother and Dad were awake and showering. When the pipes began to sing their song it meant the coast was clear to go back up and lock the door behind ourselves. Neil was always the first to go down and the first to go back up. At Maple Manor Neil called the basement Nelly's Dungeon. He convinced Simon and Desiree that Nelly was his dead identical twin. He said Nelly lived in the walls, and that the pink cushy stuff behind the stapled plastic was her pillow. When Simon learned that identical twins had to be the same sex, Neil convinced Simon he had a hearing problem. "I said *un*identical. I've always said it that way. Nelly and I looked nothing alike. The only way you would have known we were twins was cause Nelly looked like Mother and I looked liked Dad. Don't tell me you haven't heard Dad call Mother *Nelly* by accident." That part was true. Though Dad never mixed up any of us kids, I had heard him call Mother the wrong name many mornings before he drank his breakfast coffee. I sometimes wondered if Mother was his second wife after some lady named Nelly or Nel.

Saturday was the only day of the week we went down to the basement because Mother and Dad never woke up until noon after doing the Friday night laundry. When we first started going down, Neil drew up a list and convinced Miles to help us furnish the space with stuff from *The Second Chance*. Miles brought us one item at a time, hiding whatever it was under some leaves in the back corner of the pigpen. He managed to get a chalkboard, a stand-up lamp, a timer, a tea set, a kettle, a rug, a small fridge, and one gold pillow. Miles was told to rub the dent in his eyebrow to show that he had hidden something in the bushes. Folding chairs were on the list, but Miles kept saying he forgot to look for them. Even with most of the list checked off, the basement was still just a big open space with a few cold beams that we swung around on when we pretended to be firemen. Neil would make a siren sound when we were all sitting on the rug in the middle of a game, and we had to climb up and slide down the poles and put out imaginary fires.

I always made the tea on Saturdays, and Neil was in charge of the milk and sugar. He used the sugar from the paper bag instead of the bowl so Mother wouldn't notice any missing. After the tea was made, we had to wait at the top of the stairs until Neil called our names from his pillow on the basement floor. He made each of us march up to him, so he could measure us from side to side to see if we had fattened. Then he handed us a tea and made us drink half of it right away while it was still too hot. Each week I prayed that I would be bigger than Desiree or even the same size, but each Saturday I seemed to be shrinking as the others grew. Neil said even Rosie was catching up to me. He'd flatten Rosie's fingers out and pin them against mine whenever she tried to scrunch them up to look smaller. "Yep, still a freak," he'd say to the others every time he finished with me. "Tell us the way of the Sith," Carolswine.

The first game we would play in the basement was called Insults. We sat in a circle and began with the letter A. Neil always started. He would turn to any one of us and call us an asshole no matter if we were a girl or boy. Usually, he said it to one of the twins who would turn to one of us girls and call us a bitch. It was important who got called a bitch because that person got to choose whether to call a boy a cock, or a girl something even worse. Even though we didn't know what all the words meant, we knew it was bad to say them, especially the girl C word. Neil held the timer from the Spill and Spell box and counted us out if we took too long. When anyone got out they had to sit with their backs up against the stairs underneath Mr. Green's framed obituary. Mr. Green was Dad's first Canadian boss. Before Dad started working for the newspaper, he did part-time meat packing at the local grocery. When the head grocer died, Dad wrote an obituary for him and sent it to *The Mitchell Advocate*. They liked it so much they offered him a full-time job writing nice things about dead people. Neil said Mr. Green's ghost slept behind the glass and had a thing for the dead twin Nelly.

After the insult game was over, we always sang the Neil's the Champion song and then played the sausage game, where one person had to ask another person a question, and no matter what the question was, the answer had to be sausage. Neil would ask Desiree,

Hey what's that you just shoved up you nose with a chopstick? Then she would have to say, *a sausage.* After that, she would turn around to Simon and ask something like, *What's that you just put up your nose with your finger?* The difficult part was you were not allowed to laugh. Whoever laughed had to swing from a pole and practice laughing as hard as they could. If you didn't laugh hard enough Neil would get mad and make us all do fire drills.

Another basement game was called I saw you. If Neil said to Desiree, *I saw you picking your ears and putting something yellow in your mouth when you were out feeding the chickens yesterday,* the rest of us would all call Desiree a sicko and her cheeks would fill up with red air as Neil asked for a show of believers. An accusation like that would be easily voted as a lie because Desiree never went into the coop alone. Rosie hated this game because she was the whitest of all of us, and her blushing showed through when she lied. She'd bribe Neil with stolen cigarettes from Miles to get out of participating. Sometimes, if she didn't have a cigarette to give him, Neil would make her take a turn, or worse, he'd make her swear. She didn't have to say *shit* or *piss off;* he made her say the full version of f-you. Usually, when she finally said the words, they came out so softly it was almost like poetry. After she swore, Neil sometimes made her take a turn anyway. While we waited for her to think of something she saw someone doing, we'd pretend to drink from our empty teacups. Either that or we'd try to make each other yawn by opening our mouths as wide as they could go. Rosie's turn was like our basement game intermission— except for one time. It was a few weeks after Chester had been taken away.

"I saw you, Caroline, checking the circumference of your nipples to see if they had grown in the night," she said. She looked straight at me when she said it, then she turned to the others. "She used the tape measure first thing yesterday morning. Check by the lucky bed if you don't believe me. She always sits there to measure herself. Take her fingerprints and compare if you want to. You'll know they're hers anyway because they're so small they look almost like tiny dots."

The lucky bed had a mirror on the headboard and it was the oldest bed in the house. Every time Miles came upstairs to drop off a box he told us the story of how the lucky bed had come all the way with him from America, and how Peter promised it would be his again one day when he could afford an unfurnished place of his own. There was silence in the room after Rosie said *nipple*. She never used private part words without being forced to. It didn't matter that nobody knew the word circumference, because she had used her hands and fingers to demonstrate. Neil asked for a show of believers.

I knew what Rosie was doing—she was getting me back for what I had just said about her. I had told everyone that I saw Rosie writing in a diary and stuffing it in the upstairs bookcase next to the Scrabble dictionary. As soon as the pipes started banging in Mother and Dad's room, we all knew the boys would race up and raid the shelf to find the book that sounded like a butt barf. After they read it out loud, they would rip out the best parts, crumple them into inky balls, and then toss them at each other with high-pitched girly voices.

The vote was unanimous. Everyone believed what Rosie said she saw me doing. When she did lie, it was more like a fib. Like she would say, *I saw Neil saying his prayers last night for a second time*, and we would call her liar liar, check if her pants were on fire, and move on to juicier questions.

The day the nipple story came out was the day I realized Chester and I weren't the only ones who knew Mother and Dad's secret. What Rosie had said about me was true, except for the part about the lucky bed. The measuring tape I always used was in Mother's closet under the shoebox that glowed in the dark. The only way Rosie could have seen me measuring myself was if she had been lying under the waterbed and peering through the lookout hole when I stashed it away. Rosie wasn't trying to get me back for tattling about the diary; she was sending me a signal. We needed to prevent the others from finding her diary and reading about what she had found in the shoebox. Just by looking at each other it was clear what we both had to do. She would go with the others to the lucky bed while I took her diary and moved it to a safe location.

"Did you read it?" Rosie asked, holding up the Scrabble dictionary later that night. I knew what she meant, and I shook my head no. I had opened her diary briefly, but had closed it as soon as I saw the flames and the tiger and the little girl with the pigtails being hauled out of a tepee. When the others finally gave up looking for the measuring tape, I had put the notebook under her pillow where I knew she would find it.

I didn't Rosie's diary again until moving day. "You mustn't forget your pillow, Caroline. Mother says it's going to be hard to sleep in the city, so many cars and trucks. The city is like a circus, you know," Rosie said, holding her lips tight. She twisted her arms in front of her body and locked her pinkies together as if she were making a promise with herself. I knew she had put a package of some sort inside the pillowcase because it was heavier than normal, and because she had tied it up with one of her shoelaces, making long bunny ears, as Mother had taught us to do. She must have known her picture diary would be safer with me in the city, or maybe she hoped I would pass some of the pages on to Chester when I found him.

CHAPTER 5—CHESTER

"Guess what today is?" I asked Desiree, as we searched for clean pajamas in the suitcase. Dad said furniture like dressers would have to wait until after we bought a car and a telephone.

"Today is Thursday. I know because we're going to the house for visiting hours tomorrow," Desiree said. "Duh."

"Visitation," I corrected her.

"Same thing," she said, and I thought she was probably right, thought I knew it sounded wrong.

"Which means it's the eighth day," I said.

"Eighth day for what?"

"The eighth day at the apartment."

"So?"

"So, don't you think we should play the game? We haven't played The Eighth Day once since we've been here."

"We're not allowed to play that game anymore. It's against God."

"But Mother can't catch us here, and Dad won't care. Plus, there's no Neil, which means you can go first."

"First?"

"Yes, first."

"But doesn't God come to apartments?" Desiree asked, looking around the room as if God might suddenly appear and shake his big head at us.

"Yes, but don't you think God has more important things to do than listen to our stupid games? People are always praying, you know. There are people starving and running for their lives as we speak," I said.

"Well, shouldn't we invite the twins to play?"

"Let's just take turns going back and forth. You go then I go. That way we can take as many turns as we want."

Desiree had never been first at anything, and when she tried to start she couldn't think of anything to say. She kept repeating the opening line, *On the eighth day God made, um, um…* until I finally looked around the room and pointed to the beds.

"Beds?" she asked. "I thought people made beds."

"It's imaginary, Desiree. Don't you remember how to play the game? I don't mean he made ordinary beds. These are the kind of beds that when you fall asleep you can actually go to the place you dream about."

"No way. I don't want those beds, Caroline. On the eighth day God took away those dreaming beds and made regular wooden beds from trees. Beds that stay put on the floor and don't come alive."

"That's boring. What about glow-in-the dark sheets or something?" I said.

"Uh-uh. Then if you were awake you'd be able to see other people's dreams instead of just hearing them."

"Speaking of beds. Want to try having our own beds for once? No more swapping and fighting about whose night it is like we did at the house. We can pick the bed we want and stick with it."

"For forever?" Desiree asked.

"Sure. You can even pick first. Pick the bottom bunk if you want. I don't have those falling down dreams like you do."

Desiree's smile quickly turned into a pout. "You're afraid I'm going to fall on you. Mother's going to say I'm already getting fat when she sees us tomorrow. Neil says he's going to measure us every time we come. I hate the city. It's probably making you smaller." She threw her pajamas up to the top bunk and started climbing carefully up the ladder, steadying herself after every step.

"Maybe I'm trying to be nice for once. Ever thought of that? Maybe the city is rubbing off on me, and I know that you don't like heights."

"You just want to be in the colder bed. You're going to change your mind in the winter when you want the warmer one."

"Pinky swear I'll keep the top," I said.

TARA BENWELL

Desiree stepped back down the ladder and grabbed on to my crooked pinky before I could put it behind my back like Neil always did with his when he made a bad pact.

"A deal is a deal, Caroline. You said forever."

I climbed up the ladder and threw Desiree's pajamas down to the bottom bunk. Simon had once told us that it was hotter upstairs in Maple Manor because of how heat rises, but Desiree had remembered it backwards, probably because mountains are cold. She went ahead and accepted the bottom bunk just like I knew she would. I wasn't sure, but I figured dreams worked the same as heat, and I hoped that by being in the top bunk mine would escape into the apartment above us where the people were strangers, instead of going down through the wood of the bed into Desiree's ears. The top bunk also had a broken part at the back of the headboard where I could hide Rosie's diary.

There were five quick knocks at our bedroom door. Then two slow ones.

"Caroline, there's a letter here for you," Dad said. "Can I come in?"

Desiree climbed out of her bed and opened the door. At Maple Manor we weren't allowed to close the bedroom door, but Dad believed young girls needed privacy and he told us we could keep the door closed as long as we came quickly when he knocked, in case there was an emergency.

"First, you must take your shoes off, Dad," Desiree said. "Leave them in the hall. Side by side. Toe to toe."

"Mail? Who knows where we live?" I asked. I hoped Chester had somehow figured it out.

Dad threw the envelope up to me instead of coming in. He had insisted that we could keep our shoes on whenever we wanted at the apartment, even though none of us did, except him. The letter was from Mother, and after I read it to myself, I shaped it into an airplane and shot it across the room. It went straight up to the ceiling and did a nosedive, landing with its tip in the heat register. Dad asked who it was from, but he wouldn't look at me when he said it. Of course it was from Mother. Who else taped stamps to envelopes to avoid a lick? I told Dad he could read it for himself if he really cared what it said, but my throat was too hot. Desiree saw me wiping my tears on my pillow, and got back into her own bed and began to sniffle. She didn't even know what the letter was about.

"I'm sad cause I didn't get a letter," Desiree said, when Dad told her to act her age.

"There's one for you in the kitchen. It says, Dear Occupant." When Desiree ran out, Dad closed the bedroom door behind her and pulled the airplane out of the register. He poked himself in the temple with the tip of the plane a few times and then asked me if I wanted to read it to him.

"I already read it," I said. "Why would I want to read it again? How did it even get here this quickly?"

"We don't live that far away," Caroline. "It probably only takes a day to get mail back and forth. Don't tell your mother how quick it got here or she'll say we don't need phones."

Dad sat on Desiree's bed so that I couldn't see his face. He fidgeted with the paper for a while, but I knew he wouldn't read it without my permission. When he finally spoke he made it sound like my reading the letter to him would be good for me. He said that sometimes sharing something with one other human could save you from having sleepless nights. "It's not good to keep your feelings in a bottle, Caroline. I would know."

A haunting feeling came over me right then and I knew I had to stop Dad from telling me something about his past. I spoke as quickly as possible, hoping to stop his confession.

"The letter says Chester isn't living in Waterloo anymore. He was, but now he's not. He moved to some other foster home the same day we moved here. He's probably moving to another next week. Read it yourself." I wrote the f-word on the palm of my hand with my finger and then closed it in a fist, hoping God wouldn't see it.

Dad opened up the airplane and read the letter, which explained that Chester had been transferred from his foster home in Waterloo to a foster home in another town starting with a W. Mother had written down a list of cities and said that Chester could be in any of them: *Woodstock, Whitby, Wallaceberg.* The agency had been trying to track him, but with all the moving, Chester had disappeared into the system. At the bottom of the letter in red ink there was a P.S. *Where do you think he is Caroline? Can you feel it in your bones? Do you still think the city can help you find him?*

The day we moved out of Maple Manor, I had left a note for Mother on her pillow that said the reason I had decided to move to Kitchener with Dad was to find Chester. *It will be easier to find him from the city because of things like phone books and libraries. My goal is to get him back by his birthday. I bet orphans don't even get to dress up for Halloween. This is the right thing to do, Mother. I can feel it in my bones.*

It was true that I hoped to find Chester again, even if it wasn't my main reason for moving away from Mother. I had heard Dad talking to Miles one day before the move, telling him that Waterloo and Kitchener were like second cousins and that they didn't even have separate phone books. I pictured us walking into the grocery store to buy new spices and finding Chester in the bread section pushing a cart for his new mom. I had a special feeling that we would find him by Halloween. It was the first prayer I said in our apartment. I was sitting on the new toilet staring at the white tiles on the wall when the prayer came into my head and started repeating itself over and over: *God, please let us find Chester by Halloween.*

*

The first time we met Chester and his family was on Halloween. We only did the dress-up part of the holiday because Mother didn't trust other people's candy. It was her rule that half of us had to be bad things like ghosts and half of us had to be good things like angels. In the years where there was an uneven amount of us, one person had to be half-good half-bad. It was up to God to decide who got to be good or bad each year. That was what Mother said every time she passed around the hat with the paper slips.

The year we met Chester there were eight of us. I had chosen *good* and Mother dressed me up like a clown. She started the night before Halloween, waking me up when everyone had fallen asleep to make me take a shower. When I got out she twirled my wet hair up in pink sponge rollers and told me to sleep on them. When she took them out in the morning, they bounced around like Slinkys, and Mother kept sliding her fingers in and out of the curls saying how perfect they were. Just before it was time to go for the Halloween walk, she took me into her bathroom and painted my face white. When all of the pink was gone, she drew blue tears on my cheeks and a red frown on my lips.

"Why am I sad?" I asked her. She was already dressed up like Dorothy on her way to Oz. You had to imagine that she had brown pigtails on her naked head, and that she wasn't pregnant.

"Clowns turn other people's smiles upside down," Mother said, "but on the inside they only wish someone would love them." She clicked her sparkly heels together as she showed me how to pout my lips. The shoes had arrived in a package from Connecticut one Christmas and the only way Mother could fit into them was if Dad stretched them first by sticking his own feet in them. Dad and Desiree were waiting at the maple tree for us when Mother finally finished with my clown makeup. They were dressed as Gomez and Wednesday Addams.

"We're Adam and Eve," Desiree said. "Hi Clown."

Dad ran behind the maple tree when he saw me, and yelled something at Mother about my costume. At first I thought he was upset because I was wearing makeup. "I thought Caroline picked *good* this year!"

"I'm a clown," I said running up to him. "Peek-a-boo."

Dad's face turned purple, and he pushed me away harder than a play fight push. "You get that evil makeup off your face and go find a princess hat," he said. "Or grab a sheet and be a fucking ghost."

"But I'm supposed to be good this year," I said. I had never heard my dad swear. The only people I had ever heard swear were kids or Miles.

"Then be Casper. Just get *that shit* off now."

"I tried to talk her out of it," Mother said. "She wanted to be a clown so bad, Peter. She didn't mean anything."

I ran back into the house to change, wishing the whole way that I could tell Dad the truth—that my idea was to be a sunflower, but that Mother had changed the plan in the middle of the night. *I dreamed you were a clown,* she whispered to me in the middle of the night.

"Grab the pink sheet off the line. It'll take a second to make you a princess cape," Mother yelled after me. She also said to bring tape or a stapler, and a piece of pink construction paper.

"Hurry up, Caroline. The fireworks are about to start," Miles yelled as I ran past him. Miles always came for a walk with us on Halloween, and according to Neil he went out to the houses nearby to collect treats on our behalf after we went to sleep.

"We only have fifteen minutes!" Miles yelled. It wasn't that we were afraid of missing the fireworks. It was that we had to be home with the door locked behind us before they started.

As I ran hot water over the soapy washcloth, Mother came in and told me there wasn't any time to change my makeup into a princess. She tied a flowery sheet under my chin and tucked it in my jeans at the back so I wouldn't trip over it. I would have to hold the pink paper cone on my head when it got windy because we didn't have time to find an elastic, she said.

We only got in a ten-minute walk before Dad said it was time to turn around and go home. When I spun around at the front of the group, the cone flew off my head and began to blow towards home. We all started running to try to catch it, but it seemed to have a plan of its own.

"There it is!" I shouted when we turned down the street to our house. The hat was caught under the wheel of a car with a Quebec license plate that was parked in front of our house. I skipped up to the car and pulled the hat out from under the wheel. As I stood up and looked at myself in the window, I noticed a small boy sitting on the hump in the back seat. He was staring up at our house as if it were made of candy, and when I followed his gaze I saw a man walking out of our open front door. A woman stood behind him shaking her head. Dad told us all to stay put just as the first firecracker went off. He covered his head with his arms and ran up to the house to find out what the people had stolen.

"Désolé. We thought this was our new house. We saw the pen. We have pigs too," the woman said to Dad. She was shaking a map as she followed behind the man.

"A pig," the man corrected her.

"We've only seen our house once before, in a newspaper. It's around here somewhere."

"Ours is for flowers," Dad said. "The pig pen. We don't keep pigs."

"Anymore," Mother said.

When the couple reached the car, Mother looked in and smiled at the boy.

"We're off to see the Wizard," she said to Chester who had his head and hands out the window.

"Why is the princess sad?" Chester asked, pointing at my blue tears.

"She ate a rotten apple kid," Neil said.

"Did not!" I said.

"We did," said Desiree. "Daddy and me did. We're from the red pages of the big—"

"This is Caroline," Mother interrupted, pulling me in front of Desiree. "She can't find her true love." She grabbed my hand and held it out as if Chester should kiss it. My pinky finger stuck out to the side and I pulled it back in.

Chester's mom walked up to the car and whispered hello to us. I could tell she was trying not to stare at Mother's baldness.

Mother told Chester's mom "Happy Halloween," and by the look she got I figured people from Quebec didn't celebrate the holidays. Chester's mom took her eyes away from Mother's head and looked down at her pregnant stomach. Mother began to rub the baby from the outside, as if it were cradled in her arms. Up and down, side to side, then round and round in a circle. She looked at Chester and said to his mother that her boy had to be close in age to some of us.

"He's four today," she said. Her voice sounded fancy, like a violin. "He's our only one."

"Happy birthday," Chester said, without singing. "To me."

"Where's your party?" Desiree asked.

"What kid is born on the day of the dead?" Neil said, but Mother was already singing Happy Birthday. When she got to the name part she waited for Chester to say his name, but he didn't seem to know what to do. His mom looked at us funny, probably thinking the song was over too soon.

"What's your name, birthday boy?" Mother asked.

"Chester."

"Say again?" Mother said. Her voiced changed. It wasn't sweet anymore. She looked at him as if he had just lied about stealing an expensive piece of jewelry. Chester said his name one more time, and Mother looked up into the sky and hugged herself nicely. She took Chester's right hand into both of hers, even though he had just rubbed his nose on his sleeve. *You're my birthday boy, aren't you?* she whispered. She wiped a tear from her cheek and then finished the birthday song in the loudest singing voice I had ever heard, adding *dear Chester and Michael Landon* at the end. When she was done, she asked Chester if he wanted to come in for some birthday cake. "You simply must," Mother said, not even looking at Chester's mother.

"It's orange with black icing today," Desiree said. "I picked. Yesterday it was blue. Ocean blue, not sky blue."

Chester nodded his head yes, but his mom shook her head no, and pulled him away.

"You should send your boy over to play some time," Mother said, almost begging. "He's a special kid. I can see it."

"She means she feels it in her bones," Desiree said. "You have to come over by walking. We're old fashioned, like Laura Ingalls."

As the car drove away, I watched Chester turn around in the back seat and point at us. His eyes were the kind you knew still stared even after you could no longer see them.

It was spring before we saw Chester again. We were on our walk, and Mother decided she didn't feel like going to the creek. She wanted to continue straight. The pattern sometimes changed without warning if Mother saw other people heading our way. She didn't like how other people always made such a fuss over babies, and how they'd put their big hats on her babies' heads and laugh and say how cute they were and act like the rest of us were invisible. Mother said lice weren't cute.

"Perhaps we should see if they've settled," Mother said.

"Yes, perhaps," Dad said.

"Who?" Neil asked.

"The little family that thought our house was theirs," Dad said. He always knew what Mother meant without asking. "It's been six months now. That's how long it usually takes people to get used to a new home," Dad said.

The trees were so overgrown you could hardly tell there was a log home at the end of the street. We might have walked past it except we could hear the pig.

"It's the Woodsey house!" Desiree said when we finally saw it. The Woodseys were a toy chipmunk family we had that couldn't sit up without toppling over. You had to squish their tails through the back of their chairs and they still didn't sit still unless you took them out of their house and sat them on a flat surface. Sometimes Mother would struggle with them when none of us were even playing. It was one of the only packages that came from Connecticut that was addressed to *The Children*.

Desiree was right. Chester's house looked like you could pull it open and closed with Velcro, just like the Woodseys'. Dad didn't think anyone was home. There was no car out front and no lights, or any sign of life, he said.

"Yes there is. The boy's there. In the pig pen," Mother said, but Dad was already walking towards the house. Chester was lying on the ground on his stomach, making a mud pie. He stood up and waved as soon as he saw us, and it was almost as if he was expecting us all along.

Dad went up to the front door while the rest of us walked up to Chester. I had just taught myself to cartwheel, and I made it all the way to the pigpen that way, and ended in a handstand. Chester bent over and put his head between his legs to get a better look at me. I took a hand away from the ground and waved.

"Show off," Desiree said to me, then she got down and tried to do a somersault, but ended up plopping over to one side and scaring the pig.

"There's nobody home!" Dad yelled down to us.

"Of course somebody is home," Mother said too softly for Dad to hear. "He's just a baby." I could see that Mother was making double o sevens with her foot in the dirt.

Dad kept knocking and ringing while Chester told us his Ma had a pain and his Papa got mad and his Ma cried so hard she got blood and his Papa told him to go play in the pen 'cause they were going for a bike ride without him.

Dad found an open window and went inside to write a note for Chester's parents to say that we were taking him to Maple Manor. He told Mother it was no crime because Chester's dad had gone into our house uninvited, and hadn't even apologized. It was easy to convince Chester to come with us. We just said "come on" and he did.

That night Mother made a pillow bed for Chester beside hers, in case no one came to pick him up. I caught her praying before she did it. She was out by the chicken coop, sweating and swaying on her knees. Her hands were put together in a point, so I knew she meant whatever she was asking for.

"Can't he sleep with us?" I asked, when she came back in.

"No, Caroline. It isn't a good idea," Mother said.

"What isn't good about it?" I asked.

"When it comes to beds, you only sleep beside your family."

Chester's dad arrived to pick him up the next day, and Mother sent Dad to answer the door. The rest of us listened and watched from the kitchen table. At first Chester's dad said, "Thanks a lot," and we waited for Dad to say "You're welcome." When he didn't, Neil said it was a different kind of thanks—the kind you say when you really want to swear but can't, either because you'll get in trouble or you don't know someone well enough. Chester's dad said it was our family's fault that their pig ran away. He didn't say pig right at first, but Chester translated for us and then ran up to the dads to help them understand each other.

When they were finished arguing, Chester's dad raised his right arm and pointed it towards the road like a rifle. Outside the door, Chester grabbed his runners and kept walking without putting them on. I watched his right hand wiggling behind him and I was sure he meant it as a wave for me.

The next time we saw Chester, he was with his mother. She was much smaller than I remembered, and she knocked on our door as though it were made of paper. I had come in from outside to give Mother the head count report, when I heard a woman calling out hello without the *h*. Desiree heard too, and she ran over and showed Chester and his mom how to enter Maple Manor properly.

"First, take off your shoes and put them in that bin."

"Here?" Chester's mother asked pointing at the spot under the porch that was full of shoes.

"Yes, but make sure they go the right way, as if you're going to step into them."

"There," Chester said. His shoes were exactly how Mother liked them.

"Perfect. Now take off your socks and shake them as hard as you can to get off the fleas. Check the bottoms twice to make sure they're clean."

"Are we good?" Chester's mom asked, after she had put her shoes away properly and checked her own feet.

"Look in between your toes before you put your socks back on. You don't have to have pets to have fleas," Desiree said. "Sometimes *people* have fleas."

Mother came to the door as soon as Chester and his mom had their socks back on and were ready to enter. I took Chester's hand and led him back to the shoes and then into the yard where Desiree and I were playing house. We were living in a tepee that day and we were wearing our dolls inside our shirts. The boys were playing cops and robbers, but they joined our game whenever they needed a house or a woman to steal from.

"Our tepee is imaginary," I explained.

"Why?" Chester asked.

"We aren't allowed to build forts. Our mother doesn't want us to drown," Desiree said. It sounded wrong, even to me, but it was true. Neil said that one time when the twins were babies he built a fort out of old sheets and clothes pegs, and they were all sitting inside when Dad came rushing through the backyard with his garden hose and soaked it to the ground. Dad swore he didn't know the babies were inside.

Before Chester arrived that day, Neil had been stealing Desiree's baby and the twins had been driving up to our tepee on their motorcycle and making silent siren sounds by waving their arms over their heads like helicopters. I was supposed to be the nanny who managed the papooses when the mothers were killed. I told Desiree Chester could be her new baby.

"What's he doing here?" Neil asked, forgetting his whispery robber voice.

"His mom's here."

"I don't want to be the baby," Chester said. "I want to be the enemy."

"I'm the bad guy." Neil said. "I always am."

"Can't he be your partner?" I asked.

"Nuh-uh."

Just when I was about to quit the game and take Chester on a tree chair tour, Neil decided Chester would be Desiree's adopted baby Andrew, and that the cops would never solve the mystery of the missing child because Nelly ate it for dinner. Desiree whined that a baby boy would never take the place of her girl baby. She took the bonnet off her just-like-me doll and tied it on Chester's head. By the time she was finished with Chester, Giant Amy was lying naked on the ground with her blinking eyes rolled back in her head.

Chester and his mom didn't stay long. I watched them out the window as they left, half running, half walking. She was pulling him along, stretching his armpits while he stared back. He did that wave again, but from behind this time, and I was sure it was for me. Later on that day, I overheard Mother telling Dad about the visit.

"She was pregnant."

"So?"

"So, she lost the baby."

"Oh. That's too bad."

"She miscarried right before we stopped by. I wonder what she would have named the baby."

"Tell me you didn't ask. Sherry, please. You didn't, did you?"

I couldn't believe Chester's mother had lost her newborn baby as if it were a mitten. Mother was shocked, too, but Dad said some things were meant to be. All he wanted to know was why Chester had been left alone with a pig.

"She started bleeding and the car was in the shop. They tried to take their bikes. Can you believe it? This is what happens when people put their trust in a car instead of a woman who was born to catch babies, like Marie. I don't know how people think a hospital can save a baby."

I pictured Chester's mother riding around on her bicycle, searching for her bleeding baby. *What would she do if she found it—put it in her bike basket?* I knew babies were slippery at first, but I couldn't imagine how a grown woman could be so clumsy as to drop her own baby, even if it was only her second.

Dad said if it would make Mother feel better he would send over one of our chickens.

"Two," Mother said. "A boy and a girl chicken. Otherwise, it will seem like we mean it as a replacement," she said.

"For the pig or the baby?" Dad asked.

Chester started coming over a lot more after Dad left the free chickens in his parents' pig pen. His mom sometimes brought him by in the mornings, and we didn't have to bring him back until after our evening walk. Most of us didn't care that it meant skipping the Whirl Creek trail.

"We never take the trail anymore. I hate this road. It's dull," Neil said one evening when we were escorting Chester home. "Besides, it's Mother's Day, not Chester's Day."

"Not Neil's Day, either," Mother said. "Go whichever way you like. Just be back at the house before us, or Dad will worry."

"Fine," he said.

"Be careful," Dad said.

Mother was teaching Chester the names of the wildflowers.

"Sherry, why are they called black-eyed Susan?"

She didn't know why. She said God had some funny ideas sometimes.

"Who's God?" Chester asked.

"You don't know God?" Desiree said.

"He's the nature maker," Mother said. "He made the flowers. Nobody can doubt that. Look how they're all so different."

"My mum is called Sue," Chester said. "Are there any flowers named Sherry like you?"

"Of course. Somewhere. Maybe in heaven."

"What's heaven?"

"Heaven? Well, it's the palace of perfect amounts," Mother said, pointing into the sun, acting as though it were no big deal that Chester didn't know where God lived.

"Do you like butter?" I asked Chester. I talked in an upsy-daisy voice to him, bending into his face, and bouncing my head back and forth.

"I'll check," Desiree said. We raced to the grass and yanked a few wildflowers out of the ground. I ran back and discovered Chester liked butter before Desiree caught up. "I'm going to check Mother," Desiree said, pretending not to care that Chester was a butter lover.

"Do you think she is going to hate butter suddenly?" one of the twins asked.

"Yeah, since yesterday?" the other added.

I gave Chester two buttercups so he could check the twins. He was delighted to find they both loved butter, though he called it *margereen.* I didn't tell him that almost everyone liked butter in the daytime, but I could tell Desiree wanted to.

While Chester was checking the twins, Mother grabbed Desiree by her back pocket and pulled her to the side of the road. When they walked back towards us, Mother took Chester's hand and smiled. Desiree wiped her eyes and waited until Mother wasn't looking before she told me we weren't allowed to pick flowers anymore if we wanted to go to heaven.

Neil wasn't home when it was time for the bedtime story. Dad thought we should wait, but Mother started reading from *Jude the Obscure* anyway. She read in her regular voice and slipped the bookmark back in after the part where Jude thinks dirty thoughts about the woman he can't marry 'cause she's his cousin.

Dad stood by the bathroom door while we said our bedtime prayers, saying he wished Neil would stop clowning around and come home. Mother wasn't as serious about it. She laughed when Dad put his coat over his pajamas to go look for him.

"If you think you can save him, you're wrong," Mother said. "He is how he is."

"Even so, he still deserves to be looked for," Dad said.

I fell asleep and had a dream about Neil and the pig from Chester's. Neil was standing at the edge of Whirl Creek, only it was made of butter instead of water. He was wondering how to get across without walking around the long way when another pig swooped down from the sky and told Neil to hop on its back. The pig took Neil to a place called Christminster, where he fell in love with a girl who looked exactly like Desiree. Neil and the girl who wasn't Desiree had a baby, and they tried to erase its freckles with the end of a pencil. When the freckles wouldn't come off, they dropped the baby in the butter creek on the way home because they knew it was going to turn out bad, like a rotten egg. As the butter in the creek turned to blood, Neil pushed the twins out of the Star Wars bed for real and I woke up. When I closed my eyes again, we were all standing along Whirl Creek throwing flowers at a burned-up baby.

CHAPTER 6—SHOEBOX

There was a specific moment when Chester and I knew we had become more than pals. It was obvious to both of us when it happened that day in Mother's closet, though we didn't make an official declaration to each other. I was in grade five and Chester was in grade four, which didn't make any difference at our school in Mitchell since it was all the same class.

"They glow in the dark, I swear," Chester said, holding out a pack of Lifesavers. "It's some kind of weird science."

"Show me," I said.

"We need to go somewhere dark. Somewhere Neil can't find us."

"Why?"

"We have to look in each other's mouths."

I checked my watch and realized Mother was due for her washroom break. The *Little House* theme song had already started, but we knew Mother would wait until the last name rolled over the screen before she turned the TV off. We waited in the kitchen until her bathroom door shut, and then ran to her room and snuck into the closet. I pulled the light string down and closed us in. Chester unwrapped the Lifesavers, and told me to stick out my tongue.

"Don't chew it yet," he whispered. Chester unrolled one more candy and put it in his own mouth, just as someone on the other side of the house started howling my name.

"It's Neil," Chester said. "He's calling a meeting."

"Quick, hide," I said.

"Where?"

"Behind something red."

"Why red?"

"So your track suit will blend in."

I pushed Chester to the left of the closet and then hid myself behind the green clothes. Neil opened the closet door and pulled the light string.

"Whoever is in here, get out of the closet!" Mother said, from behind the washroom door. Neil turned the light back off and left the room.

"Okay, now chew," Chester whispered to me, still hiding behind the clothes. "And open your mouth." He tipped his mouth back and pointed in for me to see. His mouth was so wide I felt like I could go right in.

"Holy!" I said out loud. "I can see all the way down."

"Told ya."

"Now look in mine," I said. I opened my mouth as far as I could and waited for Chester to get closer, but I knew I couldn't get it as big as his.

"Hey, something else is glowing in here besides us," he said.

"What?"

"It's the stickers on that shoebox," he said. "Star stickers."

"What's in the box?"

"I don't know. It's too dark. Turn on the light."

I pulled the light switch and looked at my watch. We had fifteen minutes before Mother would finish.

"It's a bunch of newspaper clippings," Chester said. "Probably your dad's work stuff."

"Probably."

"This is weird. These papers are all about the same thing. Some circus in the USA. A fire in Connecticut."

"Weird. I wonder why Mother is keeping all of these. They look so old."

"They are old. 1944. July 7, 1944. Hey, look at this one with the yellow lines. It stinks like a highlighter. Holy God. Look at the names of the kids in the picture!"

"Shh. Don't say Holy God, Chester. Say gosh. Mother will—"

"Holy God, Caroline. Look at the picture on this one. This little girl. It's your mom! Your mom was in the paper. Wait, it's both your parents."

Chester read the article out loud. He kept stopping and sneezing in his elbow, and I was afraid Mother would hear us shuffling the papers to hide the sound. Chester read the headline out to me again when he was done reading.

"Brother and Sister Lose Everything. Local hero Peter Quartz saves baby sister Sherry from beneath a chair of flames." Chester sneezed again.

"Shh!"

"I'm not messing with you, Caroline. Brother and sister, it says. Brother and sister. Read it for yourself."

I took the paper out of his hands and read silently, sliding my index finger across the highlighted parts while Chester looked at the other clippings.

"Hey, look at this one. It's from a few years later. 1950. *The Flaming Indian Made Me Do It: The Circus Confession of Robert D. Segee.*" Chester said Robert with a French accent and said conversation instead of confession.

I finished the first article and then picked up a second one. Then a third. The story of the circus fire was scary and sad, but it was the date I couldn't get out of my head. The fire that had almost killed my parents was on July sixth. My birthday.

Mother's toilet flushed.

"We have to get out of here before Mother comes out," I said. There was still time for her to wash her hands.

"I can't believe this Robert guy," Chester said. "Who would admit to something like that? I wonder if he really did it?" He put the article he was reading back in the shoebox so I could put the lid back on.

"Chester. Whatever you do, promise you won't tell anyone we found these."

"But Caroline—"

"Pinky swear, Chester."

As soon as the finger promise was made, I checked that we weren't sitting on any papers, and then put the box back behind the sweater coat. We snuck out of the closet and ran upstairs to the kids' bedroom where Chester couldn't stop pacing between the beds and sighing. Every few seconds he looked at me, said *holy god,* and sneezed.

"I have to tell you something about your mom," I said to him, finally, and he came and sat beside me on the Star Wars bed. "Your mom lost your baby sister right after she was born. She dropped her and then couldn't find her. She lost her, Chester. You were only like four or five at the time. I guess she wasn't good at carrying babies 'cause she only had you to practice with. Maybe that's why she hasn't had another one. Maybe she's too scared she'll drop the next one and lose it too."

"Maybe," Chester said, not looking too surprised or concerned about his baby sister.

"Don't be mad I never told you. I found out one time when I was looking for pennies in Mother and Dad's closet. I heard them talking about the night it happened. At least it's not murder or something. Accidents happen, right? Even with babies. Promise not to tell anyone?"

"You're sure it wasn't my dad who did it?"

"I know what I heard, Chester. My mom said "she" carried the baby wrong not "he." You promise not to tell, right?"

Chester wiped his nose on his knuckles and then pinky swore harder than he had the first time.

"Now we both have family secrets," I said.

Chester tucked his chin into his turtleneck as if it were a pocket. The others had given up looking for us and were getting their boots on for the milk walk. Mother must have assumed Chester and I were with them, because she left us alone upstairs.

I wondered if Chester was in his shirt thinking about the circus, or if he was thinking about his dead baby sister. I wanted to fill the silence to make sure he didn't suggest we go and look at the papers again. I don't know what made me call the dead baby a sister. It could have been a brother for all I knew. Mother hadn't said what the baby was before Chester's mom had dropped it.

"Wanna play I spy?" I asked, and then started without waiting for his answer. "I spy with my little eye something that is…red." As soon as I said it I wished I could take it back. It wasn't his tracksuit I was thinking of, it was his lips, but I knew that red would remind Chester of the clothes in the closet where we found the shoebox.

"I think I'm gonna go home," Chester said instead of guessing.

"It's Friday."

"I know. I'll come back in a while."

I couldn't let Chester go home right then. I was sure that if I did he'd have too much time to sit and remember the date of the circus fire. He'd realize then that the circus fire wasn't just any bad day; it was a bad day that was also my birthday. He hadn't mentioned it yet, but I assumed he was probably too freaked out about the brother sister thing that he didn't even think about the actual date. If he was a real member of our family that would have been the first thing he noticed when we read the stories. Chester took his face out of his shirt and stood up.

"Can I come?" I asked. Mother always said walking alone could make you remember things, and I was worried Chester might remember my birthday if he got the chance.

"Where, to my house?"

"Why not? You're always at mine."

"You wouldn't like it there. It's not like here. There's almost always nobody home."

"Well, you'll be home if we go right now."

"I need to be alone to get my homework done."

"What homework? We always have the same homework. You have your school bag with you."

"It's for the science fair. I can't do it here. My project's on mould. The bread's at home in my sock drawer."

Chester was right that he couldn't do that kind of homework at our house. Even if we hid under the Star Wars bed to do it, Mother would smell something and come looking for us.

"Science fair isn't until the end of next week," I said.

"I need to make today's observation and then I'll come right back. I promise." He held out his pinky, and was gone for about five minutes when I decided to follow behind him. I had heard Mother going into the attic, so I knew it was safe to leave for a short time since she would have assumed that Chester and I had gone with the others on the milk walk. I put my coat and boots on outside, and pulled my hands high into my sleeves. As I walked to Chester's house, I planned how to get him off the topic of the circus if he brought it up again. If he said anything about Mother and Dad being brother and sister, I'd say something like *speaking of sisters…maybe your sister would have looked like you—only pretty. Maybe she would have been best friends with Rosie. Maybe she'd be bigger than me too.*

"And where do you think you're going, little missy?"

It was Neil. He was at the front of the pack, with the others walking behind him in a row, each one carrying a single bag of milk. Neil carried two outer bags, and one of them was full of trash that the others had probably collected with one hand along the way home. In the second bag Neil carried all of the mittens, which made me wonder who had said something to make him angry. "And where's Chester?"

"You left without us," I mumbled. I was afraid to open my mouth too wide in case he could smell the mint candy on my breath. I wished I had eaten an egg or something to get rid of the Lifesavers smell.

"Where were you when I called?"

"Looking for pennies. We couldn't come out because Mother was in the washroom. Then all of sudden you guys were gone."

"I checked in the closet before we left to get the milk. You guys weren't there."

"We were. We just didn't want Mother to hear us come out so we stayed quiet. We had a lot of pennies."

"Where's the money now?"

"Um, Chester has it. He had to run home to get something for his science project. I'm going there now to remind him not to forget the pennies. Don't let Mother see that I'm missing, okay. I'll be home soon."

Neil loved to hear that line, "Don't tell Mother." Anytime he had something to bribe one of us with he got in a good mood. As he started walking towards Maple Manor he told the others to march.

"And don't forget to moo as you walk. You're cows, remember?"

The driveway up to Chester's log house was full of puddles so I stepped in his boot tracks all the way up to the front walk. There was a doorknocker and a doorbell, and I didn't know which one I should use since Chester was usually waiting at the end of his driveway when he was expecting us. The thought of my wet socks freezing permanently onto my feet got me to press the doorbell, but my hand was so shaky I wasn't sure I had actually pushed the button in. When nothing happened, I pressed it again, this time taking my mittens off and jabbing my finger into the centre. Before I could even hear the bing-bong echoing inside the house, Chester's dad was standing over me with the doorknob in his hand.

"We don't want any, girly!" he said and then kicked the door shut so hard it popped back open. Chester's mom appeared at the door moments later. She pulled me inside and stuffed me in the closet, telling me to *shush mes amis*.

The front door slammed closed again and I watched through the crack in the closet as Chester's mom got on her knees and looked through the hole in the front door to see if her husband was gone. She didn't say goodbye, see you later, or anything like it, and Chester's dad didn't offer any kind of goodbye, especially not forty-three kisses or however many his mom's age was.

"*Je suis désolé*. What are you selling, *ma petite chou*? I'm sure we could use some. It is *choc-o-lat,* I hope. *Combien?*"

"Mom. It's Caroline," Chester said, standing beside his mom with a dishtowel in his hand. He looked older in his house than he did in ours.

"Oh, Carole. You poor dear. You're just a wee thing, aren't you?"

"Car-o-line," Chester said. "Like the song."

Neither Chester nor his mother explained to me what I was doing in the coat closet. She didn't ask which song, but I could tell by the way she nodded her head and crinkled her eyes that she didn't know Neil Diamond.

"I came to remind you that you need a sketch of the mould. Sketching is part of the science project, remember?"

"I'll fetch us some tea and buttertarts," Chester's mom said.

"We don't have time for tea, Ma," Chester said. He opened the front door and tried to pull me out with him.

"Wait, my boots." I had taken them off inside the closet. Chester's mom walked back into the hallway, looked outside, and then closed the front door as I put my boots back on.

"You best wait until the storm lets up. You'll freeze your buns off in that rain. *Très froid*."

"We'll be fine," Chester said.

"Take your boots off, *Carolynn*, dear. I've just made some hot tea."

"That will be nice," I said, taking one boot off and leaving one on, not knowing who to obey.

"No it won't, *Caroline*," Chester said. "We don't even have sugar here."

"Nonsense. I've got a little somewhere. Enough for two cups, Chesty."

"Your mother will worry, right Carl?" He used the stupid nickname one of the kids at school had given me, so that I couldn't make fun of his.

"I'm sure she'll understand about the weather, won't she dove?" Chester's mom asked.

"Mother's busy washing her hair now," I said, looking at my watch to confirm. "She won't notice us missing for...forty-nine minutes."

Chester was leaning against the wall fiddling with his hair and staring at my empty boot. He kept opening the door to check on the weather. I heard his mom pour the whistling water into a teapot and then after a bunch of opening and closing of cupboards she began scraping a sugar bowl. My feet were cold and wet, and my bum eventually slid down the wall to the floor, leaving a wet streak behind me on the purple paint.

"Chesty, why don't you show your girlfriend around while the tea is steeping?"

"She's not my girlfriend!" Chester said.

"Well, she's a friend and she's a girl, isn't she? At least take her into the family room."

"It's just rain now. I think we can go, Ma."

"Torrential rains. They just said it on the radio." She walked out of the kitchen with the teapot and cups balanced on a cutting board, and motioned for me to follow. I pulled off my wet socks and stuffed one inside each boot. Then I draped my coat over my arm and felt my way into the room with the hot tea where Chester's mom was sitting on a sofa. I sat on the floor near her feet.

"Oh dear. You'll need some socks. You don't want to catch a cold." She grabbed my coat and said she'd warm it in the dryer. "I'll fetch you a pair of my socks," she said, looking at my feet. If Desiree had been there she would have said that we don't wear socks out of the family, or that dogs are meant to fetch, not mothers or wives. *You don't catch a cold from being cold. Colds are from catching other people's sneezes.*

While I waited for the socks, I counted fifteen fingerprints on the front window of Chester's family room. Instead of wishing I had a paper towel and spray bottle, my fingers longed to reach out and connect the dots. At Maple Manor we had a living room, a dining room, and a TV room, but I had never heard of a family room.

Along one wall there was a long gray couch with a pink knitted blanket tossed over it without any concern of corners or tassels hanging properly. Chester stood in front of the window and then plunked himself in a wooden rocking chair. There was only one armrest, and his left arm looked awkward on his lap. My body moved back and forth, and I knew if his mom wasn't there I would have asked him how he could sit in a chair like that and not even bother to rock.

"Don't you think we better go to your house now?" Chester said. "We don't want to miss dinner." He stood up and the chair started rocking by itself.

"It's Friday, Chester. Self serve."

"I know, but Neil will get all the good stuff if we don't hurry up."

Chester's mom came in with two matching socks for me. They only went up to my ankles and they had little yellow pompoms on the heels. I couldn't believe they fit me perfectly. While I put them on, she passed out the tea in gold-trimmed cups of different colours and sizes. Mine had a chip on the handle, but it was the most beautiful cup I had ever used.

"Thanks, Mrs. Richards," I said.

"Oh no. Please call me Susan. Sue. And sit on the sofa, *sil vous plait*."

"Please call her Caroline," Chester said into his teacup. "And speak *Anglais*."

The weather was getting louder and the electricity couldn't make up its mind. It wasn't until his mom said she was going to get some candles for just in case that I decided I wanted to wait the storm out at Chester's.

"We better get back to your place before the power goes out," Chester said, but I didn't budge. The smell of cinnamon candles had me pinned to the floor. Chester's mom had turned the lights off and lit them even before the electricity went out. She also put on a record and let me look at the album cover. *L'amour.*

"It means...the love," she said. "It's our favourite, right Chesty?"

Chester didn't answer; he kept sighing and standing over the rocking chair. Whenever it stopped, he gave it a little push. I wanted to jump in and get a ride.

"I like your buttertarts, Susan Sue," I said instead. "I didn't know there was such a thing as brown butter. Mother always uses the yellow kind. Is this margereen?" Chester's mom looked at me like people do when they aren't quite sure if they have heard you right. Then she smiled and nodded and took one for herself.

"So, tell me about yourself, Caroline."

"Um. There's nothing to tell," I said. My voice was so ugly compared to hers, and I was sure that the French had a prettier word for um.

"When did your family move to the Whirl Creek Flats?" Chester's mom asked. She wiped a running sniffle on her knuckles and licked the crumbs from her fingertips.

"Before I was born. They moved here when Neil was a baby. They're American," I said. That sounded fancy, at least.

"Neil is your big brother I assume?"

"He's nothing like her," Chester said. "He has freckles."

"I have twin big brothers too," I said. "They kind of look like me. They look exactly like each other."

"Twins? *Très magnifique.* And what are their names?"

"Caroline has lots of brothers and sisters, Ma. You don't need to know all their names. It's not like you'll remember them."

"The twins are Les and Lee. It's from Neil Diamond's middle name, Leslie. But Lee is spelled with an e instead of an i, otherwise it would be Les and Lie. Neil sometimes calls Lee *Lie* anyway."

"I see. And Neil is named after—this Neil singer, himself?"

"Neil and the twins came along before Mother thought of using names from songs. Mine was the first song name. It's from the song about the good times."

"Oh. That's good news. And where in America did your parents marry?" she asked, taking a second buttertart and ignoring Chester's sighs.

"They married here. At the creek. Two weeks ago." I held up two fingers like a young child and then quickly twisted them together and tucked them under my crossed legs.

"How do you mean two weeks ago at the creek?"

"Not this week, last week. Whirl Creek."

"No, really? Chesty, you didn't tell me you went to a wedding, son!"

"Oh, no. Chester wasn't there. It was just family," I said. Chester stuck his head between his knees to show that he didn't care about my story.

"But why didn't your parents marry before, who was it Neil? Before the first one of you was born?"

"Ma!"

"*C'est trop mauvais.* Nevermind, dear. Well then tell me, who came to the wedding?"

"Nobody, Ma! Don't you listen? Neil wasn't even there. Geez!" I had never heard Chester sound so annoyed. His Z sounded like one that Neil would make.

"*I* was the maid of honour. I had to sign my name beside Mother's. It's not because I'm more special or anything. I'm just the oldest girl, that's all. There's an easy way to remember us all, but you don't need to bother learning it."

"The maid of honour. Oh Caroline! *Tu est vraiment spéciale!* What did you wear?"

"Blue jeans. We all did. It was the theme."

"Theme? I understand not wearing a white gown under the circumstances, but I figured a woman like this would wear cream, or at least an olive suit."

I told Chester's mom it wasn't Mother's fault about the jeans. She didn't know it was her wedding day. "Mother and Dad's wedding was a surprise."

I explained how Simon copied out all of the wedding duties from the encyclopedia, and how we each picked our parts out of a hat. "It was kind of weird because Rosie picked the best man and Simon picked the flower girl, so they switched. That's why Neil didn't come. He thought he should be the best man, but Simon already had it all written down. It was a short ceremony because Mother was leaking on her T-shirt underneath her coat during the song."

"What song? The wedding march?" she asked.

"Neil Diamond's newest one. *Forever in Blue Jeans.* It's a love song, too, like *Cherry, Cherry.* That's Mother's favourite. We memorized the new song and sang it for Mother and Dad after Desiree told them to kiss and make up. I mean, just kiss."

"What about flowers? Did your mother have a bouquet to throw?"

I told Chester's mom how the twins threw leftover Spanish rice in the air, and that it kind of marked the end of the wedding because Mother got upset over the littering and she made us all get down and pick it up with our hands. I looked up at Chester's mother and decided not to tell her about our family honeymoon.

"Something terrible happened after the wedding, though. Someone died."

"Oh, I'm so sorry, doll."

"Who?" Chester asked.

"Karl Wallenda. Dad said he wasn't really a friend. He was more like, well, at the time he said he was more like Mother's Big Bird."

"That was sad when Karl Wallenda died," Chester's mom said. "He was a legend, that one. He gave people courage to, how do you say, step onto their boxes?"

"You knew Karl Wallenda?" I asked. I didn't know what boxes she meant.

"*Mai oui! Naturellement.* The whole world knew him."

"Who was he?" Chester asked.

"A famous tightrope walker. They were all daredevils, his whole family, and it was a big family. But that Karl. He was *la crème de la crème.* Then one day he lost his balance while walking between two high-rise buildings. Died instantly."

I nodded and pretended I already knew everything she said. A snowball struck the window.

"Neil," Chester said, without even seeing him.

"*Ta frère! Oui?* I can't wait to meet him. Let him in, son!"

"Let him freeze," Chester said, staring at the window. "He's at my house now."

"Pardon?" Chester's mom asked. She had picked up the dishes right then, so it was possible she really didn't hear him, but she looked like she had heard him perfectly.

"We better go, Caroline. Your mother must have sent Neil. She'll be angry if you don't eat at the right time. I'll just wet my hair so it looks like I already had my shower."

"Let him in, son!" Chester's mom said again, as she walked into the kitchen. The moment she was gone, Neil wrote *FU Neil* backwards on the window with his finger. It was an old trick he used to get us in trouble. He didn't usually use swear words, but he wrote mean things about himself like *Neil is a jerk,* and tried to get his timing perfect so that Desiree or Simon was standing right beside the window when Dad walked in. Mother and Dad both learned Neil's trick quickly, but Chester's Mom fell for it, and she sent Chester straight to his room. Once Chester was behind his slammed door, Susan Sue went outside to try to apologize to Neil.

"He's gone already," I said. "I guess I better go too."

"Nonsense. I'll drive you. *Il fait très froid.* It is very cold, Caroline," she said, smiling through her translation.

"Actually, it sounds nicer in your language."

"French isn't *my* language, sweetie pie, but I did have a secret language when I was your age. I'll teach it to you sometime," she said. "Maybe next time you visit."

We left Chester at the house while she drove me home. Instead of going up the driveway, she pulled over on the wrong side of the street and asked if she could braid my hair. She said she always wanted a girl with long hair like mine. As she combed, and tugged, and twisted, she thanked me for something I didn't even know I did.

"You know, Caroline, I have to thank you for your little visit today. You inspired me with your Karl Wallenda fella and your blue jean wedding. Your parents moving all the way here from America. Sometimes you need to lose everything to find what you're looking for."

When the braid was done, she pulled a small mirror out of her purse, and told me to look in the rearview mirror while she held the other one up at the back.

"Au revoir, ma petite chou," Susan Sue said, as she put her arm in front of me to open my door.

"Wait, can I ask you something?" I said, and then didn't wait for her to nod. "Did you name Chester after Lucy Maud Montgomery's son? Mother is sure you did. Lucy Maud's son had a lucky birthday. July seventh. 07 07. She actually went by Maud not Lucy, but I guess you know that. Probably everybody knows, right?"

"Lucy, who?"

"Lucy Maud Montgomery. Anne of Green Gables. The writer. She had a son Chester, like you."

"Très bien. She must have been a smart woman, this book writer. I'm sorry I don't know her book."

"Book? She wrote lots of books. So you mean Chester wasn't named after Lucy Maud's lucky son? His birthday was July seventh. You're sure you didn't name him Chester for good luck?"

"I shouldn't tell you, Carole, but nobody has ever asked, so why not? Chesty was, how do you say it nice in English, conceived? Yes. He was conceived on a ...chesterfield. A lucky one, you can say, I suppose. This is how he got his name."

"You named him after a couch?"

"Oui, but this wasn't just any chair, ma belle. This was a chair a woman would never forget. Black velvet. You won't tell Chesty our secret, huh? Au revoir, Carole."

As I snuck in the back door and crept upstairs, I wished Mother would befriend Chester's mom instead of hating her because she drove a car and had hair and a job. *If God wanted humans to get all over the place he would have given us wheels, not feet,* Mother always said to herself, when Chester got dropped off.

Susan Sue looked sad as she drove away. Maybe all she needed was a grown up friend to tell her secrets to. A friend to help her look for the baby she had dropped. A friend who could offer her a copy of *Anne of Green Gables*. I vowed to never tell Mother that Chester wasn't named after Lucy's Chester— the only kid I'd ever heard of to be born on the luckiest day of the year. One day after me. What would dad think if he knew Chester was named after a chair?

"What's that knot in your hair, Caroline?" Mother called to me as I tried to escape up the stairs. "You haven't been using other people's brushes, have you?"

CHAPTER 7—BIRTHDAY GIRL

The week before Chester's mother ran away, she brought me a gift. She must have seen the pink balloon blowing out front of Maple Manor with my name written across it in magic marker, because Chester wasn't the birthday-remembering type. Mother was. She said it was a sin to forget a birthday. There was always a balloon with someone's name on it hanging from our mailbox, even though we didn't know who half of the people were. Nelson Mandela, July 18. Sigmund Freud, May 6. Hitler, April 20. She wasn't picky about who it was. There was always a pack of party balloons in the everything-drawer, and every morning she would check her birthday book and then pick out a balloon of an appropriate colour. Pink and white were proper for girls, and blue and black were for boys. Purple and yellow were okay for either. Dark purple. Not mauve. Mauve was for girls. Women. Elderly women. Women over 65. People who were grandmothers.

While Mother prepared the curly ribbons with scissors, she always hummed the birthday song and then whispered a name when it came to the part to slip one in. Mother didn't just celebrate other people's birthdays with balloons. She baked a cake almost every day while most of us were at school. Lemon, chocolate, banana cream, carrot, vanilla. Mother's cakes weren't the kind from a box where you just add egg whites; they were the start from scratch multi-layer type, with pastel coloured frosting and sprinkle toppings. Dad's birthday cake always had candy all over it like a gingerbread house. It usually said *Peter* written in cherry licorice across the top. Sometimes Mother spent a whole day making a cake just perfect. On my birthday, she always made a double-decker circle cake with white icing. It was always vanilla cake, even though she knew marble was my favourite. The vanilla cake was always the most beautiful of the year, but even still, I wished that just once she would ask me what flavour of cake I wanted like she did the others. And I wished that just once Dad would sing during my birthday song instead of looking into his lap and waiting for it to be over, like a national anthem or a dinner prayer.

"You can junk it if you don't like it," Chester's mom said to me about my present as she stepped away from the door. I couldn't believe she was going to leave without watching me open it.

"Thank you. What's the French word for thank you?"

Chester's mom waved her hand in front of her face and told me *bonne fête.*

"Bonne fete," I called out to her as she walked towards her car. She turned back and smiled. Her nose was running and she wiped it with her sleeve.

"Merci, Caroline. For more than you know."

We didn't buy gifts for each other as a rule, and Dad didn't like being showed up by a stranger. All of the other gifts were homemade and wrapped in newspaper.

"Shown up," Mother said. "You should have invited her in, Caroline." Mother always said people should have been invited in after they walked back up the street or pulled out of our driveway. Even when she did invite people in, she almost always kept them to one or two rooms. She liked the excuse that the toilet was out of order and that there was a flood, even though our washrooms were clean enough to lick.

"Can I open it?" I asked, shaking the gift from Chester's mom near my ear.

"After dinner," Mother said though I could tell she wanted to know what it was too.

By feeling Susan Sue's gift, I could tell it was a book. Maybe *Anne of Green Gables*, I thought, though I wished it was a copy of the record *L'amour*. It didn't bother me that we probably already had the book Susan Sue had wrapped up for me. Every corner in the TV room was stacked with books that Miles had brought in from the thrift shop. Mother's rule was that for every half hour of TV we had to read an hour of silent pages to *save our brains*. Neil always spent the reading hour checking if any of us were reading with our lips moving. If he ever caught any of us doing it he would roll up a piece of duct tape and stick it on the inside of our lips so Mother couldn't see it if she walked by. *Mother said read, not speak. Are you deaf? Maybe you were born without ears. Maybe you have no brain.*

I had never had a book of my very own before that birthday. I didn't know for sure that it was new, but I assumed if Chester's parents could afford two cars and suitcases, they could afford to buy real presents. I knew that since it was my gift, I wouldn't have to follow all the rules that normally applied to books. Mother believed books were sacred and not to be dragged into different rooms and stepped on. She was especially picky about the ones she spent months flattening. Sometimes it took a whole year from the time Miles brought us a book to the time we got to read it. But birthday gifts were different. A birthday gift belonged to the person whose birthday it was, and it was one of the only things in Maple Manor that didn't have to be shared.

I took a long time to finish my dinner and cake, hoping everyone would forget about my gift from Susan Sue. I didn't want all of their eyes watching me while I took my time with the real wrapping paper. Mother took my plate away after everyone was done, saying it would be bedtime if I didn't hurry up and open my presents. I saved the one from Susan Sue for last.

"Well. Don't just sit on it," Mother said, after all of the other presents were opened. I settled the gift on my lap and asked everyone to please be quiet. I wanted to hear the lip of the envelope scrape the card, the crinkling of the tissue paper, the unscotching of the tape. On the front of the book there was a young girl with permed hair in a banana clip. She had one hand over her mouth, and on top of her was a little white cloud that said *I can't believe I'm learning French!* I flipped through the pages quickly and tried not to cry from excitement.

"Whoopdie doo. A book." Neil said. "Like we don't have a million."

"Like you've ever read one of them," I said.

Nobody saw the title except Chester, and I knew he knew it was about French by the way he rolled his eyes and shook his head at his mom who wasn't even there. I didn't care. I was going to learn French. I already knew two words just by reading the cover. *Français* meant French and *Jamie* meant love. I wished I had it for a middle name, but Mother didn't believe in extra names for babies. *Bonne fête,* I said over and over to Susan Sue in my head.

That night in bed I promised God I would study French every Friday night. It seemed like a Friday thing to do because we weren't allowed to disturb Mother and Dad on laundry night, and it was the only time besides Saturday mornings that I knew I could disappear for a while without anyone telling on me.

My new French book was divided into chapters, and by the end of it I was supposed to able to count to 100, eat in a restaurant, ask for directions, and go to the zoo or the doctor *en Français.* I turned the book over and read the back where there was a list of other books in the same series, including *I Can't Believe I'm Woodworking, I Can't Believe I'm Rug Hooking,* and *I Can't Believe I'm Drawing People who Look So Real.* Inside the front cover there was a yellow box with a homework tip that said the best way to practice something new was to designate one evening a week and stick to it for at least three weeks. I turned to the back and found a tiny record tucked inside the last page. The sticker on the front said *Play Me.*

I signed the study contract *Caroline Jamie Quartz* and wrote *Fridays* in the time slot and *My Swing* in the spot for place. I wished I could write Paris or Quebec, but studying French every Friday night while swinging on a maple tree sounded romantic. I couldn't wait to tell Chester's mom my plan. I hoped my book would tell me how to call Neil a freckleface in French.

On the third Friday night, an hour after the clothes were hanging on the line, I noticed Mother watching me on my swing. She was at the chicken coop doorway staring at me through the triangle crotch of a pair of wet jeans. Her head was freshly shaved. When she saw me see her, she walked through the pants and stood directly in front of me, forcing me to jump off my swing to keep from kicking her.

"How do I say time for bed on frenchez?" Mother asked. Dad walked by the kitchen window and came out to see what was going on.

"It's *Français*, and I'm not there yet, Mother. I know bed is *lit*, and time is *temps*. But French doesn't go together like English. It's built differently. Almost like backwards sometimes. It might be *temps lit*, but I have to study harder to find out." I wished I could ask Chester's mom.

"Why are you interested in French, anyway? It's not like Chester ever speaks it, especially now—"

"I think it's in my blood," I said. I had heard contestants say that in the Family Feud intros, but I didn't understand exactly what it meant.

"It's not. I promise you there is no French in your blood," Dad said as he got closer.

"How would you know? You can't see the blood that's inside."

"That's true," Mother said, "Thank God for that."

"Why thank God?"

" Some people can't stand the sight of it. Some people faint when they see blood. Some people faint when they even talk about blood."

"What's faint?" I asked.

"Um, you start to look like you're dead but you're not," Mother said. I knew she had more to tell me but instead of finishing her thought, she started playing with my hair and then took my hand off the swing and put it to her head so I could feel the shine. Dad had already walked into the chicken coop when I got up the nerve to tell Mother there was something I needed for learning French.

"I wish I could listen to the record that came with this book. I can't be sure that my accent is truly French unless I hear it. I can't go on to book two until I hear it. I mean if Miles finds book two. I hope he does." I opened the French book and slid the small record out of the pocket to show her.

"Don't touch it like that, Caroline!" Mother put her finger through the hole in the centre and held it up into the kitchen light, staring at it for a while as if it were a diamond ring.

"Sorry."

"We do have an old record player. It's in the attic. I'll have a look for you tomorrow if you remind me. For now it's bedtime," she said, tapping her watch. She walked back into the kitchen and motioned for me to sweep off the tree chairs before I came in. She was already inside the house when I climbed back onto my swing to study one more page. I knew it wouldn't take more than five minutes because most of the words from *Le Cirque* were almost like English: *tente, trapeze, elephant, clown, maître de cirque, tigre.*

It was nearly ten o'clock when I woke up on my swing and realized I was still outside. My head was hanging so low Mother must not have seen me as she snuck into the chicken coop to join Dad.

Play me, I heard Mother say, when I lifted my head from my chin. It was almost like a whine, but not in the same way Desiree always said, *play with me.* The jeans were still hanging on the line and the back door was open a few inches. With the kitchen light on low I saw the shadow of Mother's naked head and Dad's ponytail wagging wildly above it in the chicken coop as he repeated the words *Cherry, Cherry* over and over. They didn't spot me through the jeans as I stood up on the swing to get a better look at what they were doing. I grabbed a branch from the tree and hoisted myself up as high as I could for the last few moments. When it was all over I knew it by the silence and the stillness. The only thing to see or hear was the light in the kitchen that was purring and fading in and out.

I slumped back down and kicked off my shoes, pumping the swing as hard as I could until I was high enough to jump off and land in a dark patch of grass. I ran up to the bedroom and prayed that Mother and Dad would think the thud was a raccoon or a cat jumping off the roof. I felt around in the dark to find the vacant bed, and fell asleep with my French book tucked between my legs. As I slept, I dreamt about chickens. The chickens were laying egg after egg in the attic, and after they filled up the whole floor with eggs, they abandoned their chicks and Susan Sue appeared. She climbed a long twisted rope into the attic and knocked the door open with her head. Her hands were raw and burning from the rope, and she picked up the eggs one at a time. I was at the bottom of the rope looking up as she struggled to keep the eggs in her hand. They were coated with a slippery white goo, and as they came falling down towards me I tried to juggle them. Susan Sue couldn't hold on to even one of them, but I was juggling three then four then ten, all while balancing on the rope ladder and coughing on cinnamon smoke. One of the eggs finally dropped, and when it cracked open Susan Sue's baby rolled out and its head popped off.

Mother was standing over me with my French book in her hands when I opened my eyes that morning. The others had already played the secret games in the basement and snuck back up for breakfast.

"Sorry. I slept in," I said, but Mother wasn't looking for an apology. She had pulled out the front page where I had written my French name and was tearing it up over top of me while I rubbed my eyes.

"It's called a given name because it's the name you were given the day you were born. Don't you ever think of changing your name again," Mother said. She walked away with the French book and I never saw it again.

CHAPTER 8—SHILO

I blamed myself for inspiring Chester's mom to run away. I knew why she did it, though I wished it hadn't been me who gave her the nerve to leave. What mother wouldn't go looking for a lost baby, even if it meant leaving an older child behind? We once lost Simon for five minutes down at the creek, and Mother had threatened to drown herself for letting one of her children out of her sight. Chester's mom couldn't have known that his dad would disappear days after she left, or that some dumb agent would take Chester away from us. Mother said there was nothing we could do besides pray that Chester's mom found her other kid and returned to the little house, but I knew Mother was praying for the opposite.

When weeks and then months went by, and I found myself saying the same prayer in a different city, I knew there had to be a better way to get God to listen. To win against Mother's prayers, I had to find something better than getting down to my knees.

*

It was my idea that we start worshipping God in a real church after we moved to Kitchener. Dad would do anything to get back at Mother, and taking God indoors, in the city, was a good start. When the twins complained he told them it was important for us to have a religious background so that when we called things miracles or gifts from God we really meant it. He was sick and tired of us saying *thank you God or Jesus* every time we found a penny on the corner to throw in the lucky fountain.

The church Dad picked for us was called St. Mary's, and Dad swore he didn't pick it because Mother thought Mary was the most beautiful name in the world. He said he picked it because of a man named Marvin that he met at the King Street Barbershop.

"He's the head honcho," Dad said.

"I thought priests didn't get haircuts," Desiree said.

"That's nuns," I said.

"Priests don't get wives," Dad said.

"Why do they care about having nice hair then?" Desiree asked.

"Some people do everything for God," I told her. "It's in their genes."

"Marvin says there are lots of girls your age there, Desiree. I'm hoping you can make a friend before school starts."

On the first day of church, Father Marvin asked to have a word with us in the church office. We walked in two by two with Dad at the front, and I couldn't believe we were already in trouble.

"Oh my, there are a handful of you," the priest said.

"This is nothing," Dad said and then snorted. "I mean, I've got the smaller half. I mean, I got less kids," he said, smiling at me. I heard Mother's voice in my ear. *Fewer.*

"The church frowns on divorce, you know."

"Yes, no, I wasn't aware of that. There are no official papers," Dad said, but Father Marvin didn't know that he was talking about the wedding, and how it had been arranged by us kids. I wondered what was worse to God, having babies without a wedding or with a fake wedding. Then I remembered the shoebox and the newspapers and wondered why God hadn't struck any of us dead by now. Could it be that God didn't know everything?

"The children are baptized I assume," Father Marvin said. His glasses slid down his nose and barely hung onto one ear. Desiree watched and wiggled her nose so obviously I had to pinch the inside of her elbow to get her to stop. I liked being a churchgoer. I liked the trumpets in the balcony and the way the old ladies with white gloves counted with their lips as they rung their gold bells. The trumpets reminded me of November eleventh on TV. And of heaven. Mother always said the sound of trumpets signalled the opening of St. Peter's gates. Sometimes when I looked up into the sky and the clouds were breaking away from the sun I was sure I saw heaven. I hated the idea of being kicked out of church already. I hadn't even had a chance to ask God to help me find Chester.

"Uh, not exactly," Dad said.

"Either they are or they aren't, mister—"

"Quartz. So I guess, no, sir, Marvin—"

"Father."

"Actually, they've always just called me Dad."

It was decided that we could go to Sunday school, but we weren't allowed to have the bread or the blood of Christ because we weren't baptized. If it embarrassed us to stay in our seats when everyone else was going up to the table, we could walk to the front and stand with our hands over our breasts. I couldn't believe the way Father Marvin said the word *breasts,* and how he looked into Desiree's eyes when he said it as if he knew something the rest of us didn't.

We drove to church every Sunday in our new powder blue station wagon. It had three sets of seating with the last two seats facing out the back. We weren't allowed to make faces at the people behind us, but sometimes Desiree and I pretended to be deaf, and the people in the cars behind would point at us doing our fake sign language. I couldn't help but wonder if they went to their own churches and prayed for our hearing, like I prayed for Chester's mom to hurry up and get home with her full-grown baby kid.

Desiree made the first church friend. Her name was Emily and she wore French braids.

"Stare much?" Emily asked me a few weeks after we joined the class. I turned away and pretended I hadn't heard her question. I told myself to look at the wall and count the bricks, but she was blonde, which didn't make it easy. We didn't have any blondes in our family, unless you counted the streak at the back of Neil's head, which even Mother admitted was more like grey. Besides her head, Emily's legs and arms were covered in long blonde fur you couldn't help but want to pet. One day the fur was gone.

"You look different," Desiree told her. They were colouring the same Jesus, and every time Desiree switched colours she snuck a hard look at Emily.

"Do you think Jesus had blue eyes and sandy hair? He always does in the pictures," Emily said.

"Let's give him purple hair today," Desiree said, looking at the boys beside her who were giving their Jesus a mohawk. She put down her crayon and looked closer at Emily. "What's different about you?" she asked.

"I think red eyes would go nicely with this Jesus," Emily said.

Our Sunday school teacher was Addie with two *d*s. Addie asked Emily to stand up and repeat what she had just said about *this Jesus*. "Come up to the front. And bring your pretty picture with you." The way she said pretty reminded me of Orphan Annie's Miss Hannigan. Emily picked up her picture and held it upside down while she wiggled her way up to the front of the particleboard that separated us from the kinderbaby class. Then she stood at the front and scratched while Addie quizzed us.

"How many Jesuses are there?"

"One," I answered.

"No. None," Emily said. "Duh—Jesus died millions of years ago." She looked up at Addie for approval.

"His body died, but his spirit lives on forever," I said. "At the right hand of the Father." I didn't really know what that meant, but I had heard Marvin say it a few weeks in a row, and I assumed it meant Jesus stayed close to him. Maybe the devil was on Marvin's left.

Addie was so impressed by my answer she became even less impressed with Emily. She took a Bible out of her bookbag and opened it to the red pages. When she found the right spot, she handed the book to Emily and told her to read out loud from a chapter called the *Crucifixion and Resurrection*. None of us could concentrate on the story with all of the scratching Emily was doing between sentences. At first, I thought it was a nervous thing, like biting your lips or fingers, but then I realized what was bothering Desiree about Emily.

"Emily shaved her arms," I whispered to a kid next to me. Nicholas was the one who always emphasized Addie's double d as if it were a new joke every week. He passed the message on and added the part about Emily's legs and moustache. Addie was so busy helping Emily with the pronunciation of words like *blasphemy* and *prophecy* that she didn't notice our whispers, until the message got to Desiree.

"That's it!" Desiree said.

"What's it?" Addie asked.

"Emily shaved her arms!" Desiree said.

"She feels like a cactus," Nicholas said. "I wonder what else she shaves."

"That's enough!" Addie said, putting her hands over her ears. She looked relieved when she saw the kitchen ladies walking in to put the coffee on. "Put away your crayons and Jesuses. Uh—Jesus," Addie said. "Desiree, you are in charge of presenting the good deed for the class next Sunday. Caroline, please remind your sister."

The Good Deed was like Sunday school's Show and Tell. Every week, one of us had to do something nice and then tell the class about what we did and how it made us feel. It had been Nicholas's turn that day and he made paper roses and coloured them red, and handed them out to all of the women who walked through the church. Addie wore hers behind her ear, but it kept falling to the floor, and every time she picked it up Nicholas tilted his neck to look down her blouse. When Addie asked how it felt to hand out roses Nicholas said his good deed made him feel warm and fuzzy inside.

"Did you do your good deed?" I asked Desiree the following Saturday. She had caught me looking at Rosie's diary and I had lied and said I was reading the weekly Bible reading Addie had assigned.

"What are you going to do for yours?" she asked.

"I don't know. I'll think of something when the time comes. Maybe Addie won't even pick me to do one. Maybe I'm already good."

"Maybe I'll do mine right now and get it over with. I just need to think of something good. I could make paper hearts for the church people," she said, and then walked away when I shook my head.

Desiree walked back into our room a few minutes later and told me her good deed was going to be buying Dad a chocolate bar from the corner store.

"All I have to do is ask Dad for money to buy milk," she said. I nodded and prayed that she hadn't seen Rosie's diary. When she walked out again, I tucked the notebook into the broken slat on the headboard and climbed down the ladder.

"I bought some yesterday," I heard Dad saying when I walked into the kitchen.

"But I drank it," Desiree said.

"All of it?"

While I grabbed myself a glass of juice, Desiree made up a story about how she cooked some tinned soup for lunch and accidentally poured the salt from the big hole instead of the sprinkle side. She said she had to make a whole new batch of soup and then when she tested it to see if it was hot enough she burnt her mouth.

"So I had to drink a tall glass of milk to cure my tongue from the salt and hot soup, and I finished it. So we need more milk. I'll go by myself—I just need some money."

It was a true story, except it was something Neil had done three years earlier and instead of giving him milk money Mother made him drink nothing but lukewarm water for a week afterwards.

I couldn't help but think of 'Thou shall not lie' while Desiree was gone. I wondered if God would take into consideration the fact that Desiree was about to do something good when she lied. This got me thinking about what God would do if Desiree got hit by a car and died on the way to the store right after lying to her dad, even though it was for a good cause. *Would she still get in to heaven?* I tried to unthink the part about Desiree getting in an accident, but it kept coming into my head over and over, each time with a different colour car.

Twenty minutes after Desiree left the apartment, the buzzer rang. We had been living in our new home for almost a month, but there had never been anyone at the door. The only reason we knew what the buzzer sounded like was because Dad always pressed it when he was coming home from work. He said it was so that he wouldn't give us heart attacks when he came in, even though he came in at quarter past four every day. The twins said the real reason he did it was in case he ever got stuck in the elevator. They said if he buzzed and then didn't come through our door a few minutes later, one of us would know to go and rescue him.

"Fire!" Dad yelled, when he heard the sound of the buzzer that afternoon. He grabbed his ponytail and stuffed it in his mouth.

"No, Dad. It's the buzzer."

"What buzzer?"

"Someone's at the door," I said.

"For Christ's sake! I gave your sister the house key!"

"Bonjour?" I said into the speaker.

"Uh—this is Constable Eddie Rodriguez. I'm looking for Peter Quartz."

"Oh my God. Desiree," I said.

"Don't tell me she really did it," Dad said. "She's been threatening to run away, but ever since she met Emily she—I thought she was—"

"Your kid's fine. Just a little unlucky, you could say. She was caught shoplifting at the corner store. Can you come down and collect her, please?"

Dad hung up the phone and we both ran out the door and into the elevator.

"I gave her milk money! Why in God's name would she steal milk? Maybe she *was* planning on running away."

"There must be some kind of mistake," I said. "It was supposed to be a good deed."

"You knew about it? I should have sensed there was something fishy going on," Dad said. "She had this big script ready, and I had a feeling it wasn't hers."

All I could think about on the way down the elevator was that God had listened to my prayer and that Desiree wasn't dead. We could tell she had been crying because her sleeve was all wet at the bottom.

"It said buy one get one free!" Desiree said to Dad before he could yell.

"What did?"

"The sign above the chocolate bars," the policeman said. "Apparently, she was planning on buying one of the two she stole."

"I was. For my dad, for Sunday school. I swear to God. Tell them, Caroline."

"I don't care who it was for. Your little sister here isn't going to change what the camera caught you putting in your pocket," Eddie Rodriguez said. When he smiled he had teeth like a donkey.

"That was the free one!" Desiree's nose was running again, and I wished I had something to give her so she wouldn't have to wipe it on herself in front of the policeman.

"You were going to buy me a chocolate bar with my money and then keep one for yourself?" Dad asked.

"Sounds like she has a fair bit to learn at Sunday school," the policeman said.

"It's only been a few weeks," Dad said, defending her. He was trying not to laugh and the policeman was too.

The elevator door opened suddenly and Dad jumped. Our landlord stormed towards us in a panic. He waved a pink note above his head, and then read some instructions from it to us as best he could.

"Your, uh, wife wants you to go to the uh, tree house? You need to pick up the kids because something is different with this baby. It's taking too long." He handed the note to Dad as if it had cooties.

"Mother in labour," Dad and I said at the same time. It was getting to the end of August, and I had already assumed Shilo was going to be the first September baby. I thought we might even be already at our new school by the time she came around. It almost made me happy to think that another kid in our family, besides me, was going to mess up Mother's knuckle rhyme. June, July…September.

Instead of settling the problem with Desiree, the policeman offered to drive us wherever we needed to go. At first Dad agreed, but when he heard the officer say it sounded like an emergency, he changed his mind.

"We'll need our car for getting back. Can you take the girls and I'll drive myself?"

"Sure, you kids know the way to the uh—tree house?"

"Maple Manor," Desiree said. "It our house's name."

"Oh, your other house."

"Thanks officer. Sorry about my daughter's—sin."

The policeman waved off the incident and showed Desiree and me to his cruiser. He opened the door and told us to slide in the back. When we were all in and buckled, he turned his sirens on and sped down King Street on the wrong side of the road, continuing through the intersection even though the light was red.

"Are you allowed to do that, mister?" Desiree asked.

I hit Desiree on the arm, "Say sir, not mister!"

"When there is an emergency I am. And please, call me Eddie."

I didn't understand how Mother having a baby could be an emergency, but I didn't dare argue with a policeman. After I told Eddie how to get to Whirl Creek, he started quizzing us about church.

"So, what do they teach you in Sunday school these days, anyway? Besides doing good deeds."

"We colour a lot," Desiree said. "Emily's favourite colour is blue. Peacock blue. I like baby blue, like Mother."

"We learn the Ten Commandments," I said, hoping to make us sound more grown up. I wanted him to know, somehow, that I was the older sister, but I didn't want to have to tell him.

"Oh yeah, and what are those?"

"Don't lie, don't steal, don't say God's name in a swear, don't be jealous of other people, don't work on Sundays, don't kill, and something else—I can never remember," I said.

"Thou shall not commit a-dult-er-y," Desiree said, looking at the piece of paper she had taken from her pocket. It was on the back of the instructions for the good deed in the helpful hints section. "What does that mean again?"

"Addie said that one doesn't apply to kids," I said.

"But what does it mean?" Desiree asked. "Do you know, mister?"

"I'm afraid I don't go to church."

"But you are an adult. Do you or don't you commit —it?"

"Me? No. I love my wife. I'm a one-woman man. Besides, we're practically newlyweds. Ask me again after the seven year itch," he said laughing.

Desiree and I both turned purple, and then none of us said anything for a few minutes. While we drove in silence, I started thinking about the Commandments. I realized that together Desiree and I had broken almost all of them, just since moving to Kitchener. I wondered if Mother was partially right about the city.

"So, it's my birthday," Eddie suddenly said. "How old do you girls think I am?"

"You're working on your birthday?" Desiree said, instead of guessing. She leaned forward and Eddie turned around to look at her.

"It's not Sunday! Is this another crime I don't know about?"

"It's just, well, shouldn't you be at your birthday party?" Desiree asked.

"Me? I'm too old for birthday parties."

"How old are you?"

"Desiree!" I pinched her arm hoping she'd shut up.

"Well, how old do you think he is?" Desiree asked me.

"Thirty-five."

"What are you, a psychic?" Eddie said, looking at me in his rear-view mirror.

I thought Eddie was calling me psychotic, and I didn't know if that meant he was much older or younger than I guessed. He looked at his watch and asked why our mother wasn't at the hospital if she was so close to giving birth.

"Mother always has her babies at home," Desiree said. "Like Mother Nature."

"Really? Isn't that a little dangerous?"

"There's nothing dangerous about having a baby," she said. "Unless it's early. Or late. It never is, though."

"Mother's babies never take long enough to bother going to hospitals. She's probably already had this one by now," I said.

"Well, it looks like you girls must have yourself a new baby brother," Eddie said when I pointed out Maple Manor and suggested he park a bit away from the house. "At least I assume, because of the baby blue," he said pointing at the balloon on the mailbox.

"No. That's the usual birthday balloon," Desiree said. "It's probably from this morning, before she even knew today was the day."

"Sorry?" Eddie said, looking for a better explanation.

"It's our mother. She celebrates Neil Diamond's birthday every year. She's crazy about him, that's all," I said. "His birthday is— today."

Desiree looked at me as if to say, why are you lying to a policeman, but I avoided her eyes. *Thou shalt not lie* started up in my head as Eddie got excited.

"I didn't know I shared a birthday with a celebrity. Neil Diamond, eh? I love that guy. Sweet Caroline and all those goodies," Eddie said. The way he said it, I knew he didn't remember my name. "What's that other good one?"

"Desiree," Desiree tried to say, but I covered her mouth.

When we drove up the driveway, Neil came running out with his arms whipping around his head like a helicopter, saying that we had to take Mother to the hospital.

"She's been trying for like seven hours," he said. It never happened to Mother, but she always said babies that took longer than an hour or two probably knew better than to come into this world.

"Seven hours?" I said, not believing Neil.

"The midwife says it's a big baby," Neil said. "Like a giant or something. A boy, no doubt. This one isn't going to be no runt."

"Your dad will still be a few minutes yet. Let's get her in the car and I'll take her," Eddie said.

Neil and Eddie ran into the house and carried Mother out to the police car. They spread her out in the back seat and tried to force the door closed, but it was too late to go anywhere. The head was already coming out when the midwife got in the backseat with Mother. Even with the sheet tied around Mother's body, I saw more than I needed to. A gigantic head with mounds of wet yellow hair like a chicken baby was the first thing to show.

"She's a girl," Marie said, finally.

"Fine." Mother said. "Shilo."

"That's a lot of hair for a newborn, isn't it?" Eddie asked, as he caught his first glimpse. He had turned away while Mother pushed out the shoulders, sitting down on the curb between Rosie and Simon.

It was Shilo's feet I was looking at then, not her hair. They had taken the longest to come out, and it looked like she had at least two extra toes. I was afraid to count.

"Seven hours and seven minutes," the midwife said. She wasn't even looking at her watch so I knew she made up the number to make Mother feel better about how long it had taken.

"Pretty good for a woman who almost miscarried," Marie whispered to me, while Mother checked the baby over. "I was sure she was going to lose this one in the beginning. She almost did, you know. It was probably stress from your guyses move. The whole separation, too."

"What do you mean lost?" I asked Marie.

"Babies can die in the womb from too much stress, you know. Lots of woman miscarry during stressful times." She continued on for a moment, but I wasn't listening. *Miscarried. Lost. Died.* I had been wrong about everything.

"It's his birthday," Desiree told Mother while pointing at Eddie. "I stole chocolate by accident."

"I guess a lot of people are born on the same day," Eddie said, waving his hand at Desiree to forget about the shoplifting.

"That's why at least twelve newborns a day get given to the wrong parents in hospitals," Simon said. I hoped he'd keep talking so Eddie wouldn't have a chance to say anything about him and Shilo sharing a birthday with Neil Diamond.

"Let's all go inside, shall we?" Mother said, as Dad's car came into sight. "I need to bake this man a cake."

As the others walked into the house, I stood out on the curb pretending to wait for Dad. Mother and Dad's conversation about Chester's mom took control of my mind. I looked up the street and imagined Susan Sue riding down the hill on her bicycle with an empty basket hanging from the front. *She was pregnant. So? So, she lost the baby. She miscarried right before we stopped by.*

*

On the last Sunday of the month, the church school kids got to go back up before the service was over to join the communion. A hunched-over man and his wife took backward steps down the aisle, cuing the church people to go or wait their turn for the bread and wine. When Dad pressed his back against the bench so that the couple beside could squeeze by, something made me stand up and go with them.

"I'm going up," I said into Dad's ear. I hoped people would think the couple were my grandmother and granddad.

"Caroline. You heard the rules."

"Yes," I whispered. "You have to be baptized in the name of the Lord. I am."

"No, Caroline."

"Yes, Dad. I am." I was pretty sure the look I gave him reminded him of what he told me that day at the creek, because he pushed his body back again and let me go up. I heard Desiree and the twins being shushed as I joined the couple as though I belonged to them. We walked swiftly, and nodded our heads at the stained-glass Jesus. At the altar, we kneeled on the red scratchy carpet and made cups with our hands. I was sure I was supposed to close my eyes, but I was afraid of the wine pouring through my cupped hand. Chester and I had once tried it with lemonade, and no matter how hard you closed your hands, some would trickle through.

The communion bread looked like a silver dollar, except it was made out of paper instead of chocolate. Everyone else was eating their paper so I did too. As I chewed, I tried to put out of my head how Mother said diseases came from people doing what everyone else was doing. When I finished the bread, I noticed through my squint that the wine was going right into the church people's mouths, and that everyone was drinking from the same cup. It was disgusting and splendid at the same time and it reminded me of Susan Sue, and how she licked her fingers while eating and didn't wash them after. I kneeled at the rail and prayed my usual prayer. *Please let Chester's mom find her lost baby and then come back and find Chester.* Then I remembered that there was no lost baby, just a dead baby, and a runaway mother.

An old woman knelt beside me and whispered in my ear that it was time to stand up and go back to my mom and dad. People stared as I walked down the centre aisle instead of going around the outside with my fake grandparents. The choir sang *Alleluia* over and over and I knew it was going to get stuck in my head. I wondered what it meant. Maybe *Jesus loves me in French* or something like that. I wished I still had my French book so I could look Alleluia up in the index where all of the translations were.

Some people shook their heads back and forth and held their arms out like birds while they sang. I sat down next to Dad and ignored Desiree's taps. Father Marvin stood behind the altar guzzling back a whole cup of wine and eating the paper circles as if they were Cheerios. I hoped God would take my prayers more seriously now that I had tasted his blood.

CHAPTER 9—THE SIX-SEVENS

Ms. Lizzy was the grade six-seven teacher at our new school. Mother said she was the only teacher she had ever heard of who went by her first name. "It's just for this year," Ms. Lizzy said when Mother forced me to ask her why. "I'll take Donny's name in the summer." Ms. Lizzy really meant *next summer,* but *the summer* probably sounded closer and Ms. Lizzy was tired of having a fiancé. She counted the days down on the corner of our classroom chalkboard because she couldn't wait to change the word to *husband.* It bothered me how she said husband with an s sound instead of a z, but it didn't make me like her any less. Donny gave Ms. Lizzy a gigantic ring that always got caught on her sweaters, which made her face turn purple. She kept a picture of him on her desk instead of a paper mache apple with pencils stuck in it like Desiree's teacher. Donny's last name was McDougal. He was the first person I knew with two capital letters in his name.

"My teacher has a Scottish fiancé," I said at dinner after the first day of grade seven.

"So does mine," Desiree said.

"Oh yeah. What's a fiancé then?"

"Grade sixes have to take French too, you know," Desiree said. "I'll find out."

Twelve of my classmates were sevens and half of us were girls. Lucky for me, the sevens girls stuck together during class and at lunch and recess, so I never got called the new girl like Desiree in her grade-six-only class. We had a club called The Six Sevens, and according to the rulebook no grade sixes were allowed to join. There was Kristen, Krista, Christina, Christie, Samantha, and me. I was more popular than Samantha because my name at least started with a C. In grade seven we learned subjects like social studies, fractions, and family life. Three of the grade seven girls wore bras even though they didn't have anything to put in the cup parts. Samantha showed me hers in the bathroom at lunch one day when she was untangling one of the straps. She taught me that the letter part of the bra was for how big of a pocket you needed for your boobs, and that the number part was for how fat your back was. She laughed when she told me how in grade five her sister had searched through all of the measuring cups and told their mom she needed a quarter-cup bra.

"My sister was so mad because I already needed a third cup. That's really a B," Samantha said translating for me. "You'd be like an A minus, Caroline. That's probably like a tablespoon." She laughed at her own joke while she put her bra back on and asked me to do her up at the back. "Don't tell Christina I said that or she'll say it all the time. She'll give you a dumb nickname. My sister says nicknames are impossible to shake once you get them."

Christina kept track of our stuff in the Six Sevens rulebook, which was a lost school agenda belonging to a grade six kid that we had found down by the monkey bars. She made charts for things, like which boy each of us had a crush on and if we had our period. None of us had it at the beginning of the year, but by Christmas Christina did. She made Samantha tape a maxi pad to the calendar page on the day she got it, and it stuck out of the agenda like a stuffed bookmark.

It was a tradition for the older grades to put on a Christmas pageant at Mansfield Elementary. Ms. Lizzy chose me to be the narrator of the Christmas story because I put up my hand first when she asked who knew what the *mas* stood for in Christmas. As the narrator, I had to say all of the parts that were too hard to act out, like the Immaculate Conception. Christina was chosen to play Mary. She wanted the part so bad she told the whole class that she was the only grade seven who could really have a baby.

"Fine, but just for the record," Ms. Lizzy said, "Mary didn't necessarily have her period when she got pregnant. Remember, Christina, Jesus' mother was a virgin."

Instead of using a plastic doll, Mother suggested we use Shilo for the baby Jesus. I tried to change the subject, but Mother kept calling and asking if I had asked my teacher yet. She finally called the school herself and convinced Ms. Lizzy that it was a terrific idea to use a real baby for the part. For the dress rehearsal we used the stuffed Alf doll that Donny gave Ms. Lizzy for Valentine's Day. I wondered how God felt about Christina playing the part of the most important mom in the world.

"Why isn't my real baby here for the rehearsal?" Christina asked me.

"Mother doesn't have a car," I said.

"What about your father's car?"

"Dad needs his car for work. He delivers things." I said. I wasn't ready to tell anyone that my dad accepted a job as a church janitor. It wasn't exactly a lie since he did have to deliver baked goods to sick church people sometimes.

Christina held Alf from its foot and swirled it around in circles.

"My baby better be here tomorrow. And he better not cry."

"She," I said, quietly, hoping Christina wouldn't ask me to repeat. When she looked at me strange, I promised that Shilo would be wrapped in a blue blanket so no one in the audience would know the difference.

On the day of the real pageant God sent freezing rain instead of the light snowfall I had begged for in church the previous Sunday. With only five minutes left before show time, half of the seats in the school gymnasium were still empty. Miles was supposed to pick up Mother and the Creek Kids, and he had promised he would deliver Shilo at least ten minutes early so she could get used to Christina. "Only if the weather is good," Mother had warned, even though it had been her idea to use Shilo in the pageant. "I won't risk my baby's life for some stupid show."

Dad, Les, and Lee finally walked in as the lights were dimming. They stood under the exit sign and refused to sit when the grade eight ushers tried to take them to some seats. Desiree played with the paper lambs the grade ones had made. She seemed less concerned than I was that Shilo hadn't arrived yet. Without a real baby to amuse, all she had to do was curl up and look pretty in her white cotton batten. She was the only animal in the show.

Christina was furious. "Where's my baby?"

"I guess because the weather is bad—"

"I saw your father! He looks just like you. Where's the kid?"

"Mother was supposed to be coming separately, but—"

"Separately! What kind of mom and dad come separately?"

Ms. Lizzy handed Alf to Christina and told her to behave more like a saint.

"I bet your baby sister doesn't even exist," Christina said. "Just like your stupid Chester. That's probably your dog's name or something."

We were at the part in the play where the Three Wise Men brought gifts for the baby Jesus, when I saw Mother coming in. I almost didn't recognize her because she was wearing a flowery dress instead of her blue jeans. The Creek Kids walked behind her two by two—first Rosie and Simon, then Magdelene and Melinda. Miles was at the back pushing the baby buggy. It wasn't the same buggy that folded up like an umbrella that Mother always used for her babies. This was a big stroller with wheels like a dirt bike and a special shade to keep out the sun. I assumed it came from Connecticut, because it looked too nice for a thrift shop stroller. I imagined Neil picking me up and putting me inside, and forcing me to suck my thumb and ask for a diaper change. Mother walked right by Dad and chose five empty seats in the front row.

Simon unbuckled Shilo and held her up to the stage for someone to take. She wasn't wrapped in a blue blanket like I had requested. She was wearing a frilly pink jumper with a matching ribbon in her wild hair. I wondered if she would have an English accent when she learned to talk.

Ms. Lizzy ran out from behind the curtain to collect her. She tidied Shilo's hair for a moment before placing her in Christina's lap. Christina frowned and accepted a Rubik's cube, a Jem doll, and a Chipmunk Christmas album from the wise men for a second time. I was forced to change my script a bit to make sense of it all.

"After the three kings dropped the gifts off to Mary, a disciple named Simon delivered Mary's miracle baby," I said into the microphone. It squeaked because I talked too loud. All of the kids plugged their ears, and I forgot not to say *b*s or *p*s so loud, like Ms. Lizzy had suggested.

"The baby was called Jessica," I blurted out. "God's only daughter."

Ms. Lizzy smiled and gave me the thumbs up before she signalled for the curtains to close. I glanced at Mother and noticed she was pushing the stroller back and forth even though there wasn't a baby in it. The other people in the gymnasium were laughing so hard they could hardly stand up to clap. I took a bow and asked God for forgiveness. I wasn't sure how he would feel about me changing the story up like that, especially so close to Christmas. I hoped it wouldn't get in the way of my regular prayers getting heard. *Please God, don't let anyone learn Mother and Dad's secret over Christmas. Please let the kids not think my mother and dad look the same.*

On the way out of the gymnasium, Mother handed Dad an envelope with an invitation to Maple Manor for Christmas dinner. Except for Dad, we all knew the invitation was coming. We had picked names for the gift exchange before November was even over. Mother had said there was no reason we couldn't all be together for one day.

"We'll have to celebrate in two separate rooms," she had said a few weeks earlier when Desiree said it would make God sad if we didn't spend Christmas together.

"Or we can do it like musical chairs," Simon suggested. "Like, we can all just keep moving down a seat until the music stops. Dad and Mother can sit like ten chairs apart."

"Yeah, but with Christmas carols instead of the radio," Rosie said in agreement.

"Except there are no chairs," I said.

"There are lots of chairs," Rosie and Simon said at the same time. It was the first time I had noticed them doing the twin thing. Besides finishing each other's sentences, Simon was growing his hair to his shoulders, and teaching Rosie all of the lakes in the world. She had already learned all of the boat accidents.

"We always put them away on Fridays before Dad drops you off," Simon said.

"What's the point, anyway," Neil said.

"We can dine in separate rooms," Mother said. "Or not at all."

Desiree had tried to change the subject, but it made things worse. "Emily's family has dessert before dinner on Christmas," she said. "And they open presents at Christmas Eve instead of in the morning."

"*On* Christmas Eve," Mother said. "And you don't have to come if you don't want to do Christmas the right way."

"But what about Mary?" Desiree said. "She didn't do things in the proper order. And she's the whole reason Christmas came."

We all stood at the table waiting for Mother to send Desiree outside to her thinking chair, but Mother told us all to gather on the floor around the circle stool before she started her speech.

"If God cared so much about weddings coming first, he wouldn't have picked Mary and Joseph to have *his* one and only baby. God cares about love, and love isn't something that belongs on a lousy piece of paper." She picked up the first piece of paper in reach and began to rip it in pieces. I threw up in my mouth and swallowed as the shreds floated to the floor. The sound of paper always did that to me.

"That was Dad's invitation for the Christmas dinner, Mother," Simon said.

As she gathered up the paper from the floor, Mother told us that some things aren't meant to be. Then she went directly to the craft box and pulled out materials for making a new invitation.

*

As we drove up to Maple Manor on Christmas Eve, it looked as if Mother's usual Christmas prayer had been answered. It was a rainy day, but the whole front lawn was glistening white.

"It snowed here!" Desiree shouted. "No fair. Why doesn't it snow in the city?"

"That's not snow," Dad said, realizing what Mother had done. There wasn't a trace of lawn at the front—the whole yard had been covered in white garden rocks. When we got inside, Dad didn't say anything about the lawn, but he pretended to forget the rule about taking off his shoes. Everyone was taking a bath, except Mother and Neil. Magdelene, Melinda, and Shilo were in Mother's bathroom, and Rosie and Simon were in the tub upstairs.

"Aren't the kids a little old for all this washing? How dirty do they get sitting in this house staring out the window at the great outdoors?" Dad said. We could tell by the school shoes at the front of the house that nobody had been outside since Christmas vacation started. Dad wanted Mother to look down at his feet, but she didn't.

Desiree, the twins, and I pretended not to hear them arguing as we examined the homemade decorations around the house. I fiddled with the two paper chains woven around the banisters. One chain had all of our names written on the rings, and the other had all of the names of the famous people who had the same birthdays as us. On the celebrity side where it should have had a name to match mine it said *Sweet Caroline*.

When the water turned on for the fourth time upstairs Dad said he didn't think it was appropriate for Rosie and Simon to be bathing together. He said he didn't care that they were brother and sister. It wasn't right at this age.

"Don't be ridiculous, Peter. They're wearing their bathing suits."

"But why are they taking so long?" Dad asked. "We've been here for almost an hour."

I waited for Mother to say that it had only been forty-seven minutes, but she didn't even look at her wrist to check. Her watch arm was bare.

"I think they're making more decorations," she finally answered. "They never get any homework for the holidays, so that must be what they're up to. I think I hear scissors and stuff. They like to decorate. They even take their crafts into the bath these days. "

"Tell me something, Sherry. Are we all going to get in the bath for Christmas turkey tonight, or should we bundle up and eat outside on the rocks?"

"Actually, Peter," she said, spitting as she said the P and not even wiping it off her own chin, "there are plenty of chairs for all of us. In separate rooms. Why don't you come in and have a seat with your family?"

"Let's keep to separate houses, shall we?" Dad said, after he had peered around to where the tables were set and noticed the chairs.

" Separate. It's the way you think we should have left things, right? We should have gone our separate ways in the first place. We should stop pretending we were meant to be together. Weren't those the words you used, Peter? We aren't kids anymore. Correct me if I'm wrong."

Before he got in the car, Dad picked up a rock from the lawn and threw it overhand onto the street. He was halfway down the street by the time she got outside with one of the folding chairs that had been put around the table. She threw it across the yard and it landed at the curb.

"Just because *you* didn't need Chester, doesn't mean he didn't need us," Mother shouted, loud enough for me to hear from the window. She sat on the ground with no coat on, tossing the rocks at the chair. It reminded me of how Dad had taught us to skip rocks on the water down at the creek.

"Maybe you can't remember how it feels to be separate from everything!" Mother shouted as she threw one more rock.

CHAPTER 10—BAPTISM

Mother swore she could smell the city on us whenever we came for our weekend visits. She always waited until Dad had driven away before she told one of us to wash up, and you could tell who was going to get picked by the way she sniffed the person from top to bottom, and then gagged in her elbow.

The first Friday of our first spring living as a split family, she decided I smelled like tires and ordered me into the shower to get the rubber smell off. As I walked up to the upstairs bathroom, I heard her telling the others to go out and sweep the tree chairs. I was glad Neil wouldn't be able to play his stupid trick where he forced each kid to pretend to have to pee so the person in the shower burned and then froze after each flush.

When Mother opened the bathroom door on me I thought she was going to tell me to double up on the soap, but instead she whispered for me to turn the water on full blast. Downstairs at the front door I could hear Neil doing rock, paper, matches to decide who had to carry Shilo around outside during the chair sweep.

"I lied about the tires, Caroline," Mother said, after I turned the hot and cold on full. "You smell sweet today. It's just, we need to talk."

In the space between the curtain and the wall, I saw Mother locking the door behind her, and before I could look away, she took off her blouse and grabbed the shaving foam out of the cupboard. After she had covered her head with cream, she stood staring at herself in the mirror without putting the razor near her head. I went back to washing myself and prayed it wasn't the day to learn everything.

"I need your help, Caroline," Mother said, grabbing the foam for the second time. I could almost hear her saying it like she used to do in the closet, only I imagined it sounding even worse with water on her lips. *I mean to tell you everything, and I am going to tell you everything right now. Your father and I aren't who you think we are.*

Mother's hair had grown at least two inches. I couldn't remember ever seeing it that long, and I was afraid she was going to ask me to help get it all off.

"I need you to help me baptize Shilo," Mother said. She put the razor on the counter and rinsed her head under the tap.

"Baptize Shilo? Why?"

"Because it's the right thing to do. For babies."

"Oh."

"I don't want the others involved. They'll want to make a big show about it. They'll want to know why they're not baptized. Your Dad didn't want to do it again after you. Don't ask me why, Caroline. Don't ask why, okay?"

I wasn't sure if Mother didn't want me to ask her why because she didn't know why, or because she didn't want to explain why any better than Dad did. She put the razor back in the cupboard and dried her head with a towel. I didn't know if I should turn the water off and get out, so I pretended I still had soap in my hair.

"We'll do it at Whirl Creek, just like we did the day you were born," Mother said. She opened the door when she heard Shilo crying, letting cold air fill the room. I bent down and turned the hot on higher, expecting Mother to go straight to Shilo, but instead she closed the door quietly and put her mouth against the shower curtain.

"It will be the same kind of thing, except without your dad there this time."

I wanted to say that Dad wasn't really there for my baptism either, but I stopped myself, and said something worse instead. "And without that weird man, right?" I turned off the water, but Mother reached in behind me and turned the cold tap back on. She let it run hard on my feet, and I prayed she wouldn't pull out the knob for the shower nozzle. Desiree was shouting that she couldn't find the diapers, but Mother didn't open the door. She put her whole head in the curtain and demanded to know how I knew about *the man*. I was sweating, even with the cold water running over me, and I knew I couldn't tell Mother about Dad's confession at the creek. Even if I could get her to pinky swear not to tell him, it would put all of the other secrets I had told in my life at risk. *Never share a pinky swear.* They were Mother's words, not mine.

"You told me," I lied. "Remember? In the closet that one time last year? You said there was a priest there to do the ceremony. *God, please let her not want to tell me more about her past. Please let her not say the word e-ver-y-thing.*

I tried to cover myself without making it look like I didn't want her to see something that wasn't yet there.

"I sometimes forget how old you are getting, Caroline. I still think of you as my baby. Soon you'll be able to have your own babies." She pointed at my stomach and drew a circle in the air, though she was looking lower down where my fist was.

"I had forgotten that I told you about that man," she said. She reached into one side of her shirt and adjusted herself. There was a piece of paper sticking out of her bra. Maybe a note or a newspaper article.

I turned off the water and thanked God that Mother believed my lie. She had started the story so many times, but had never gotten to the part about the man. The furthest she had ever gotten was how the stars looked that night when she and Dad left Miles to look after Neil and the twins so he could get his badge for Scouts.

I felt better about my own lie when Mother told hers. *I still think of you as my baby, Caroline.* Mother had stopped thinking of me as her baby ever since Shilo was born. She had stopped thinking of any of us in that way; you could tell by her voice and how it didn't go up like a kindergarten teacher anymore, unless she was talking to Shilo. Mother called Shilo *Angel* in the voice she used to call me *Sweet Caroline.* I didn't know what it was about Shilo that made Mother so crazy for her. I wondered if Mother thought Shilo was sent from God like some kind of saviour or something. Maybe that's why she wanted her baptized. Maybe Mother had a dream where an angel told her to have a baby with the agent and pretend he was really Dad's

119

kid. *Behold, you will conceive and bear a child who is not from your brother. She will be holy and will save your other children from your sins.* Maybe Mother thought Shilo could fix what was wrong with the rest of us. *You will name her Shilo and she will save the freaks.* According to the baby name book, Shilo's name meant peace.

The Friday before the baptism Mother asked me to go to the library and find out all I could about the procedure.

"We have to get it right, otherwise it won't mean a thing to God," Mother said. She pushed me lightly on my swing, but I held on with my hands instead of my elbows.

"I saw a baptism at church a few weeks ago," I told her.

Mother pushed the swing harder when I said the word church. She said the bulletin from the baptism might have all of the words you were supposed to say during the actual ceremony, but it wouldn't give any facts about why people did baptisms, or what God's point in them was. She wanted me to know the reasons and the point since we weren't going to be using a real priest.

I went to the library that Monday and wrote out some notes from what I learned from two encyclopedias to share with Mother. I hoped that what I had to tell Mother would convince her to cancel the baptism.

"Augustine Hippo was the one who invented it," I told Mother over the phone. "Baptism erases Original Sin."

"Which sin is that?"

"I'm not sure. I guess it depends which definition you use for original. So I guess it could be either the first sin a baby makes, or the most creative one." I had an example for the second type right away, but Mother didn't know the real story about the chocolate Desiree had stolen accidentally for her good deed. After she baked the cake the day Shilo was born she had asked why we arrived in a police car, and Dad had stopped Desiree from explaining by staging a coughing fit. The noise had startled Shilo awake. I remember the way Dad looked at Mother's lap and how he clasped his hands behind his back when Shilo howled. It was obvious Dad didn't have a clue how to shut Shilo up. If it had been any other baby he would have taken her outside after her first drink to introduce her to her thinking chair. But there were no trees left in the yard, except the big maple, and there wasn't any mention of Shilo needing a chair back then.

I asked Mother to name all of the sins Shilo had committed so far, but she couldn't think of any.

"Then maybe it's too early to baptize her," I said. I had rehearsed the line in my head seven times before making the call.

"You were baptized the day you were born. The second you were born. You had no original sin."

I nodded, even though I didn't mean it. I wished I had the nerve to tell Mother right then and there that it was her and Dad's sin that was the problem.

"But you always said I was a little early. Maybe that was my first sin. It's not that big of a deal, but it still wasn't according to God's plan, right? The nine-month plan thing? I'm still on the small side, and I don't fit in with the knuckles."

"Well, I suppose Shilo's original sin was…she took longer than usual to come out," Mother said.

I told Mother I didn't know about usual. Samantha's mom had said that she was in labour for three days before they cut Samantha out with a knife, or something like that. She said the doctors put her to sleep and when she woke up they passed her a clean baby. She said it was like it wasn't real.

"It could have been anyone's baby," Mother said. "Tell me this. Does this Samantha look anything like her parents?"

CHAPTER 11—SOCKS

No matter how hard I prayed for Mother to change her mind, the day of the baptism came. When Dad arrived for the visitation that Saturday morning, Shilo had red dots on her cheeks, forehead, and chin. Each pock had a symmetrical dot on the other side of her face.

"This one will be staying home today," Mother said at the door, holding Shilo under her arms like a football. Mother never went to the door when Dad was expected, so she already looked suspicious, even if Dad didn't notice the red marker all over Mother's right hand.

"Why, because she needs her face washed?" Dad asked, scraping his nail across one of the spots.

"Because she's being punished for getting into Simon's markers," Mother said, turning red when she realized the spots didn't look real in the sunlight. Shilo wasn't even crawling yet, and Dad would have known that none of the others would have dared draw on a baby.

Dad argued that Mother should punish the little ones on her own time.

"It's going to take me all day to get these marks off," Mother said.

"I drove all the way out here to see *my* children," Dad said. "And frankly, I don't care what they look like. I already bought the movie tickets."

Mother said she had already run Shilo's bath and that she wasn't willing to waste the water for some dumb movie that *her* baby was just going to cry through.

"Desiree will go in Shilo's place, won't you Desiree?" Mother said. It was all part of Mother's plan that the twins would ask Dad if they could stay at the apartment on their own for once, and that Desiree would offer to skip the rest of the Maple Manor visitation in order to go with Dad and the Creek Kids in place of Shilo.

As Desiree ran out the door to join the others, Mother took Shilo into the bathroom and waited for the car to disappear. She wanted the dots off before the baptism, but after scrubbing for twenty minutes, she finally gave up.

"It's not like anyone is going to be there to take pictures or anything," I said. Simon had said that Shilo had her own baby book, but I didn't think Mother would take the chance of putting a secret like this in it.

Mother wrapped Shilo in a long white sheet that had two holes in the bottom. As she cut the holes off with her shears, I realized it was a costume from the dress-up box. I pulled out the sheet of paper I had copied the words of the baptism ceremony onto and tried not to think of Shilo as the Holy Ghost. Since we had no witnesses, there were only a few lines Mother had to say.

"I don't think God will mind if I do the other parts since we don't know any priests," I said.

We started the ceremony almost as soon as we reached the water. I had never seen Mother looking nervous at the creek. Instead of calling the ducks with a soft voice and tossing bits of bread to them, Mother kept looking over her left shoulder and shooing the birds away with her free hand. She looked up at the sky as if it might poop on us. Shilo was wailing before we got to the part where you pour water on her head.

"It's normal for babies to cry during baptisms," I said. "I mean that's what the librarian said. She had all her babies baptized in a church."

"How many is all?" Mother asked, which was almost always what Mother wanted to know when the conversation ever turned to another woman's kids.

"Four or five," I said, though I was sure it was probably more like one or two, if she even had any. I didn't know of even one kid in my class that had a bigger family than six. At school, I only counted the twins and Desiree when people asked me how many brothers and sisters I had. Even five got called a big family in Kitchener.

I unrolled the notes I had and started the ceremony. "Baptism is about life and death. Water, through history has sometimes meant drowning, but it has also meant being revived, refreshed, cleansed—"

Mother heard the voices even before I did. "Someone's coming," she whispered. "Forget the pointless parts. Go down to the water part. We have to at least do the water part."

I skipped the part where the mother says that she promises to raise her child a Christian and the priest swears that the baby will enjoy everlasting life. "What name have you given your child?" I whispered quickly, dipping the measuring cup into the water.

"Shilo. Hurry, Caroline!"

I poured a cup of the creek water over Shilo's forehead as the voices got closer.

"Shilo Quartz, I baptize thee in the name of the father, the son, the holy—" It was then we realized whose voices were getting closer. We stopped the baptism without saying another word.

"What are you guys doing here?" Simon shouted as he ran towards us.

"What happened to the movie?" Mother asked him when he was close enough to whisper to. She dried Shilo's head off on her jeans, and Shilo screamed and puked up milk all over the sheet she was wrapped in.

"Dad forgot his wallet," Simon said. "We decided to come down here for a walk instead because we didn't have enough time to go back to the apartment and get it. You guys took too long fighting. He couldn't think of anything else to do for free."

Dad and the others had reached us by then, and everyone was wondering what we were doing there and why Shilo was all wet.

"We couldn't get the marker off," I said. My answer was so quick and unplanned it felt like someone else was speaking out of me. Maybe even God. Mother looked at me and nodded.

"What made you think that creek water would get marker out better than the well water at home?"

"It's not your home anymore, Peter," Mother said, ignoring the question.

"Or is this your way of punishing a baby?" Dad asked.

I stepped in again, this time with another excuse. I told Dad that Mother was feeling kind of sad about our family spending time so separately, and that I had suggested we come down to the creek where we always used to come as a group.

"It's almost like it's meant to be that you forgot your wallet, Dad," I said.

"Don't lie to your dad, Caroline," Mother said. "We just needed some air. Shilo was crying a lot from all of the scrubbing. Sometimes fresh air is the only cure for anything. We brought a sheet to sit on."

Mother threw Shilo over one shoulder and pointed towards home, meaning I should start walking with her. The paper that we were reading from was still in my hands, and I crumpled it up before Dad could ask what it was. The others started following behind in pairs, rushing to catch up with us, but Dad called them back.

"We just got here. There's no reason to go home yet. This is my time, remember?"

As Mother and I started walking home with Shilo, Dad started a loud game of hide-and-go-seek with the others, as if it was something he did with us all the time. Mother turned back and shoved Shilo into Dad's arms. "Isn't this what you were looking for?" Mother said. "Next time, bring all my kids. I don't care how old the twins are getting. They still need a mother!"

When we were halfway to the house, I asked Mother if she thought we had done it properly or not. "I mean, do you think God considers Shilo baptized?"

"I think so," Mother said. "I guess there's no way of telling for certain, but I feel better. You know, just in case."

"God's probably busy, anyway," I said. "There was that earthquake somewhere yesterday. I heard it on the radio in the car."

Mother said she didn't think God worked that way. If he didn't have time to hear us make a mistake during the baptism then he wouldn't hear us doing what was right, either. He wouldn't even know we had tried.

"We did the right thing, Caroline. It was good enough. Anyway, it makes me feel better, just in case."

"Just in case what?" Rosie had the quietest footsteps when she wanted to, and neither Mother nor I had heard her following us home.

"Aren't you supposed to be hiding?" Mother asked.

"I told Dad I was going home with you. Desiree stayed in my place. My throat hurts."

Mother told Rosie that if her throat hurt than she had better keep her mouth quiet for a while. We both knew Simon must have told Rosie what he had heard and seen when he first walked up to us at the creek. Mother and Rosie and I walked the rest of the way in silence, and when we reached Maple Manor, Mother told Rosie to get into the sick bed, which was always waiting with clean sheets outside the upstairs bedroom. Mother's closet door closed and the papers started shuffling almost at once. I went up to check on Rosie. She had stuffed the sick bed with pillows and was playing with the puppet theatre that Miles had brought over to Maple Manor the day after the move.

"How's your throat?" I asked her.

"Bright pink. Simon says it might be striped."

"I know what Simon told you," I said. "I know why you were following us. I just want you to know it was all Mother's idea." I got ready to threaten her if she told anyone else about the baptism. I was going to tell her I'd show Neil the pages from her diary where she had drawn hearts with Chester's initials all over them, but Rosie ignored what I said and started whispering wildly about the sock puppets and how they were all colour-coded, and that she was going to tell me the rules-of-the-theatre once and only once. Rosie was so good at whispering she sounded clearer than most people did when they talked. It didn't matter how fast she spoke; you could still catch every word.

"Mother is fluorescent pink, Dad is navy blue, then it goes the colours of the rainbow, so it's easy to remember, starting with red for Neil. When you run out of rainbow colours we go to the others, which are white, brown, beige, and grey. Shilo is black. You can remember her easy cause of *Black Sheep*."

"Fine. I'll be me," I whispered, picking up the green puppet and stuffing my hand into it. My heart was racing, but I knew exactly what to do even the first time we communicated this way. I wondered why Mother had never thought of colour coordinating us.

Rosie picked up the purple sock and went behind the curtains. After a few moments, the purple sock appeared and the play began. "I think someone is going to die," it said. Rosie put the black sock on her other hand and laid her palm flat out.

"Why do you think that?" I asked, moving the mouth of my green sock for five slow syllables.

Rosie picked up the pink puppet, but didn't put it on her hand. She held it up and looked me in the eye. When Neil came bursting through the door to announce that Dad was waiting for me in the car, we both sat on our puppets, and pretended to be practicing for a spelling test.

"Spell baptize again," I said.

"B-a-p-t-i-s-e," Rosie said.

"No, with a z," I said. "We're Canadian."

"So zed then," she said.

"The Creek Kids say zee, Small Fry," Neil said. "And when you're under my roof you will too."

*

"What's that video game called again?" I asked the Saturday after the almost baptism.

"Titless," Neil said. "Like you."

Mother was sitting right there, but it was Simon who shushed him for calling me a bad name. Simon explained that the game was called Tetris, and that the blocks that fell were called *tetrominoes*. "Like dominoes, only—"

"It's nothing like dominoes," Mother said. "Dominoes don't fit into each other. Dominoes knock each other down."

"It's like a computer jigsaw puzzle," Simon said, but Mother didn't like that definition either. Miles had won the computer in a raffle at *The Second Chance*, and since he didn't have outlets in his trailer he brought it to Maple Manor.

Mother sat in front of the screen staring at the shapes as they dropped from the top of the screen. She kept her hands busy while she watched by brushing Magdelene and Melinda's pony dolls, smoothing their manes over and over, always using the coloured plastic brush that matched the horse body. Neil was showing the twins how the shapes fell more quickly in the other levels, but every time he did it Mother threatened to turn it off. She liked the shapes to float naturally into position, *like leaves from a tree.*

As soon as Mother got into her trance, I went to the upstairs bedroom. Rosie was lying on the puppets, and she sat up as soon as she saw me. She picked up the purple sock and got right back into the show as if it had been a long intermission instead of a week living in separate houses.

"I have something else to tell you," the sock said in a clear quiet whisper. "I caught Mrs. Pinksock sharpening the letter opener. Again. This is the third Friday night in a row."

It took me a few seconds to get what Rosie was trying to say. I grabbed the green sock that was me and put it on my right hand. I couldn't think of how to put my response into sock language. I switched Miss Green to my other hand, but it still didn't feel like me, so I switched her back.

"Maybe we should talk to Mr. Red about this. He's the only one who's bigger than Mrs. Pink. He could watch to make sure *you know who* doesn't do anything. And stop her if—"

Simon walked in and said that involving Mr. Red was the stupidest idea he had ever heard of. Rosie tried to toss Simon his sock, but he shook his head and told her she never should have taught me the colours. Nobody trusted Mr. Red. "If anything, Neil is probably in on Mother's plan. He'll probably be the one to do the cutting," Simon said.

The next Sunday I noticed Addie kept looking my way as she spoke to one of the other Sunday school teachers during coffee time after church. I went to the closest cookie table near them so I could hear most of what they were saying. At first I thought they were talking about my size.

"What brought all this on anyway?" another teacher asked.

"One of the kids in my class wanted information last week. She wanted to know the point of baptism and I didn't have the answer."

"Well, did you look it up?"

"Yes. There's nothing in my Bible about baptizing babies. In fact, it says that only believers should be baptized. Babies don't get choices. For God's sake, they don't even get to decide between bottle and breast," Addie said.

"Oh my God, I never thought about it that way," the other teacher said. She took a sip from her empty cup, and then shook it as if more would appear.

"Did you know that other churches simply refuse to do it before the age of reason? They say it's pointless before then because the child isn't old enough to accept Christ as their Saviour."

" What's the age of reason again?"

"Seven," Addie said.

"Oh my God! Seven years old? Mia was only seven months when we had her baptized!"

When we drove home from church that day, I asked Dad what the age of reason was. He told me it was some famous book that upset the church, written by some guy who didn't believe in miracles.

"But my Sunday school teacher said it means you're old enough to get baptized," I said.

"Oh, *that* kind of reason. That's a bit tough to explain. It's like when you get that gut feeling telling you something is right or wrong. You might be like six or seven when you first get it, but it's a lot longer before you recognize it as something important. You need to hear the whisper before you can answer the call."

"What whisper?"

"At first you won't even hear it as a whisper. It'll be more like a *should* that you ignore. It doesn't turn into a whisper until you've had to face the consequences a few times. Then you'll start to hear it. It gets louder too as you age, thank God."

I was satisfied with the definition, but Desiree wanted to know more. She wanted to know why she had never heard the whisper even though she was way past seven. *Maybe it's your defect*, I thought, but I didn't dare say it. *Maybe you'll never hear your own whisper.*

"Plus, how will I know when I hear it, if it's so quiet?" Desiree asked. "I don't want someone to steal my money or something just because I can't hear myself."

"You might get more than a whisper, if you're lucky," Dad said. "The whisper comes first, but if you ignore it, you sometimes get a second chance. The second time you might hear your own voice in your ear or something. Or you'll lose something like your keys or your mitts and it will make you late, and you'll wonder whether it's even worth going or doing what you had planned by the time you find them. Chances are it's probably not."

Desiree was so frustrated she started to cry. "If this is so important, how come they don't teach us it in school when we're seven?" Desiree asked. "Why do they only teach us stupid stuff?"

*

The following Saturday, when the little ones had returned from the movie and went in to check on Neil's Tetris score, I followed Simon and Rosie upstairs. I stopped them before they could get out any puppets. "Let's play something different today," I said. "Let's play church."

"How?" Simon asked.

"You sit behind the theatre curtain and pretend you're a priest."

"Okay," he said, getting on the ground behind the curtain. "Which sock should I use for a priest. White?"

"Forget the socks. Just keep the curtains closed. I'm the church girl who comes to make a confession. The priest isn't allowed to tell anyone what I say. Got it?"

Simon got into character so easily I almost felt like I was really talking to a priest. I tried to remember how Maria did it in *The Sound of Music*. Rosie sat off to the side and listened.

"Forgive me Father for I have sinned," I said.

"Everyone sins, child. Sins make the world go round."

The word sin made me think of Mother and Dad kissing. I pictured them as kids sitting at the bottom of a bed kissing each other good night 'cause they had no mum or dad to do it to them. "My mother and I did something wrong. To my baby sister. Well, Mother didn't, really. It was more me. But it was her idea," I said.

"I saw you stopping Mother, Caroline," Simon said, putting his whole head out onto the puppet stage. "I know it wasn't your idea to try to drown Shilo at the creek that day."

"Drown? Are you crazy?"

"No, but Mother is. I saw the sheet, Caroline. I saw everything. The rocks, the sheet, the papers. Everything."

"We weren't going to drown Shilo! We were baptizing her! In case she dies before she's seven."

CHAPTER 12—FAMILY TREE

When Desiree told me she was going to have Mr. Morris for her grade seven history class I knew I had to act quickly. Mr. Morris was the teacher who made his students do family trees in the first week of school. The year before, when I had been assigned a family tree from Mr. Morris, I had made most of it up. The only part that was true was my having one younger sister and twin older brothers. For the made up branches there were my happily married parents, Peter and Suzy, and each of their parents and grandparents who were all still alive. Mr. Morris had commented on my tree in front of the whole class because I was the only kid who had no dead relatives. I hoped he didn't ask why my parents lived separately in real life, but not in the tree.

"What's your family secret? There aren't many people who can say they have both sets of great grandparents," Mr. Morris had said as he was handing the papers back. "I hope you appreciate them every day, Caroline. I never had grandparents, never mind great grandparents. Most of my relatives were gone by the time I was born. That was the norm when I was growing up. We didn't have triple bypass surgeries."

When Mr. Morris asked for a show of hands for how many of the kids in my class had all four of their grandparents, plus at least one set of great grandparents, only one other girl raised her hand, and she was one of the sixes who wasn't even doing the same project.

Besides my fake grandparents, my tree included a fake dog and cat, and a fake aunt and uncle on both sides. Aunt Betty and Uncle Fred, Auntie Barb and Uncle Barney—they were all names I had overheard other kids in my class saying when they talked about birthday presents or holiday traditions, and I figured my tree would look more real if I used the same ones. Some of the girls in my class complained that they had to talk to all of these old people on the phone to get answers for their trees. They hated the way grandparents always asked the same questions. *How's school? Who's your boyfriend? What do you want to be when you grow up?* I pretended to agree, though I had secretly enjoyed doing the project and making everything up. Each of my fake aunts and uncles had at least four kids and some of those kids had already had kids of their own. Pretty much all of the cousins' names came from songs or singers from the weekly top 40, which I was listening to while I did the project. Mr. Morris gave me 99% for my grade, and the missing mark was for forgetting to write my own name in the diagram. Mr. Morris held the tree up high above his head and shouted out all of my relatives' names before he gave it back to me.

"Hey Caroline! What about Auntie Wilma?" one of the kids in my class asked as I walked to the front to claim my paper tree. "Yeah, and don't you have a purple pet dinosaur?"

I knew Desiree wouldn't think to do the same thing for her family tree assignment. I figured she'd probably call up Mother after school, or wait until Dad got home and ask one or both of them questions she wasn't supposed to ask. Dad would lie on the spot, without blinking or thinking. The only problem with that was that he'd make up aunts and uncles with different names than Betty, Fred, and Wilma. With a last name like Quartz, Mr. Morris would quickly realize that Desiree was my sister, and he would probably remember the names from my family tree; some of the kids called me Pebbles even in grade eight. My biggest fear, though, was that Desiree would get to Mother first. There was no telling what kind of lies she'd make up, or whether she might tell Desiree the truth. I knew I had to think of a way to do Desiree's project for her.

"I know what Mr. Morris is going to make you do for your first project," I told Desiree that night as she stood behind me waiting to brush her teeth. Mother didn't approve of kids brushing at the same time, and it was one of the old rules Desiree and I both agreed to keep at the apartment. "I can help you with it, if you want. I still have mine and I got almost perfect. It's *really* hard."

"What's almost perfect?" Desiree asked. "Mother says something is either perfect or not."

"I got 99% on it. Stupid me, forgot to write my own name. But, if you copy mine, you'll get perfect. You'll have to write your own name, of course."

"Okay, so, what's the project?"

"You have to make your family tree."

"Family tree. That's easy."

"Well, it's not that easy—"

"Sure it is. I'm good at drawing trees, and maple leaves are easy to trace. You might have to help me with the swing. I'm not that good at drawing moving things. I can describe them, though. That's part of the project, isn't it? The words part. Like a speech? You used the maple tree for yours, right? I wouldn't exactly call that tiny twig outside of King's Tower a family tree. We share it with half of Kitchener, and I don't think it would even hold a baby swing."

I almost called Desiree the stupidest person in the world, until I realized that her mistake about the project would work better than trying to hand in a fake family tree without her seeing it.

"I'll help you draw the swing," I said. "And, if you want any help colouring, I can help you with that too. I actually miss colouring. We don't do that in our grade any more. Not even maps."

Desiree said she would take care of the colouring if I would help her with the description part, if she needed it. I made a deal with her.

"I'll help you with the project, as long as you don't tell Dad."

"Okay."

"I mean, don't even tell Dad about the project. If you do, he'll ask to see it, and if he asks to see it, he'll know I helped you with it."

"So?"

"So, this summer I promised I wouldn't help you with your homework or let you copy any more of my stuff. I pinky swore to Dad, Desiree." I held my finger out and noticed it looked more crooked than usual. My pinky had always had that funny bend to it, but it looked further away from my other fingers than it ever had. "If you need a parent's signature on it, I'll write it. I've been practicing Dad's."

Desiree came home on the second day of school with the project assignment from Mr. Morris.

"You were right," she said. "We have to do a family tree for history class, and it's due on Monday." She said it right in front of Dad, and he looked up from his newspaper for a second.

"A spelling bee. Oh. I bet there are a lot of hard words for a history spelling bee. I'll quiz you if you want. Let's go to our room where it's quiet," I said.

Desiree followed me to our room where I pinched her and said she had promised not to talk about the project in front of Dad. "He's going to want to see it, remember?" I said.

"Stupid me, I forgot."

"That's why I changed it to a spelling bee. He can't ask to see a spelling bee, and it's not something you can copy from me."

"What if he wants to quiz me on the words?" Desiree asked.

"We'll make up pretend ones. We'll need to think of some history words."

Desiree looked at me funny, and then asked one of the smartest questions she had ever asked.

"What do trees have to do with history anyway? Drawing trees seems like a project we should have in science class. Or art."

I couldn't think of anything smart to say back, so I shrugged.

"I guess I could ask my teacher," Desiree said.

"No. Look, I think it's because Mr. Morris hates history. He told my class last year he'd much rather teach science, but he can't because the school already has an intermediate science teacher. He made us study other things that weren't very historyish, too."

"Like what?"

"Pistols and stamens," I said. "It's like sex for plants. You might have to learn it. Anyway, I wouldn't ask him about the drawing project, if I were you. You'll make him feel worse about hating his job."

That night I dreamt that Desiree drew the maple tree for her project. She wanted to show it to me before she handed it in, only every time she called my name to come and see it, I couldn't get to her. I'd either have pins and needles in my feet, or I'd be stuck on the phone with Mother who wouldn't let me go, or I'd be standing at a traffic light that wouldn't turn green. In the dream, Desiree gave up and decided to show it to her class before handing it in. I was finally able to move, and I stood in the doorway of Mr. Morris' classroom as Desiree presented her picture to the class. Instead of asking why she had drawn a tree rather than labelling it with her family members, Mr. Morris asked why she drew half a tree instead of a whole one. All of Desiree's class members sat at their desks waiting for the answer. Then my own grade eight classmates walked in, each one choosing a desk to sit at. There was two of everyone, and they all sat and stared at Desiree while she held up her half tree. When everyone was settled and the room went silent, Desiree finally spoke. *The reason there's only half a tree is because we only have one side of the family.*

The Saturday before Desiree's tree was due I caught her sitting in the yard with a pencil and a sheet of paper on her lap. The paper was blank except for a pile of pink rubber bits from her eraser, and a hole near the centre of the page where her jeans showed through.

"I'm trying to rub this out better. Mother said she can still kind of see the lines of my first tree."

"You showed it to Mother?"

"So?"

"What did she say?"

"She said she could still see the lines. She wants me to put the trunk more in the middle of the page, but I don't know how to make it perfect."

I showed Desiree how to fold a new piece of paper in half gently and trace the crease. I told her she had better not show Mother a second time because Mother would insist that each side of her tree had the exact number of branches and leaves, and she would make us stay at the house until it was right.

TARA BENWELL

"And the Miss Teen USA pageant is on tonight," I said. "If Mother asks, tell her you don't have to hand it in until Tuesday, so you're going to do the rest on Monday night. And say you forgot that you're not supposed to look at your model while you draw."

"What model?"

"The thing you decided to draw for art class. The tree."

"You mean history class," Desiree said. Then she pinky swore to keep the promise she had already broken.

The day Desiree handed her family tree in, I got my first assignment of the year from Madame Castles.

"Today, we're going to write letters. Letters that we're never going to send," our Social Studies teacher.

Madame Castles told us to think of something we really wanted to tell someone, but that we knew we would never have the guts to say. It could be an apology, or a confession, or a secret. "Maybe something you need to get off your chest. Think of it as a healing process."

Madame Castles put her timer on and told us we had fifteen minutes. A lot of kids sat at their desks twirling their pens or tapping their feet and staring at the ceiling. All I could think about was Mother standing at the kitchen window, writing Chester's name in her own breath. I could still hear the sounds that came out of the room that day. *There might be a way, babycake.*

"If you can't think of anyone to write to, but you know what you want to write, write to me. I won't read it. I promise."

"So how are you going to mark our letters if you aren't going to read them?" one kid asked.

Madame Castles turned off the timer and lectured us about how not everything in life gets a mark and that her class was about learning life lessons, not getting a piece of paper with a big checkmark for our parents to tack on the fridge.

"There are starving children in the world. You kids are going to have bigger problems to solve when you grow up than knowing whether *i* comes before *e* or not. Now get writing." She reset her timer.

The bell for lunch rang even before the timer went off. In the homework box, Madame Castles wrote that we should either tear up or bury our letters when they were done.

"Can we burn them?" Samantha asked.

"No. Unless you do it in a fireplace. Whatever you do, don't put them in your underwear drawer for your little brother or sister to find."

Most of the kids were already sharing their letters before pulling out their brown bags for lunch, and some of the popular kids were even getting cans of pop or pizza slices in exchange for a secret letter. I shoved my letter into my sock and pretended I didn't write anything.

As soon as Madame Castles said that we were going to write letters without sending them, Chester's name had shown up on that window in my mind and I couldn't wipe it off. I knew my letter would be to him, and that I would bury it rather than burn it, but it took me a few days to figure out how to write what I really wanted to say.

The next Saturday when we were out for a visitation with Mother I lied and said I had to get some rocks at the creek for an art project. I told her I needed rocks of all colours and sizes, not just white rocks like the ones out front.

"Why don't you use Desiree's brains?" Neil asked. He was playing Tetris, but he always had one ear waiting for something he could insult one of us with. He could get away with saying anything when his video game was on because all Mother did was stare at the screen and brush the pony dolls.

Desiree didn't take Neil's comment in a bad way. She thought he was calling her a good artist or something. "I already made art this week," she said. I looked at her and shook my pinky at her, reminding her not to bring up the family tree project in front of Mother. We sometimes forgot Mother was even in the room when Tetris was on.

"For science class," she added. "That dumb Mr. Morris. He hates history even though that's his job. People should take job quizzes before they go and be something like a teacher, hey Caroline?"

I walked out of the room quickly before any of the Creek Kids could ask to come with me on my walk. Before I left, I dared Neil to beat his best score before I got back, hoping it would give everyone a reason to stay put while I buried my letter to Chester. At the front door, I grabbed the pencil out of Simon's shoe and twisted it into my hair.

I took the parent way toward Whirl Creek, and as I walked I kept my hand on the letter inside my pocket. At the halfway point, I looked behind me and then tucked the letter into my sock. With the letter down by my feet, my legs walked a different way, and within minutes I was standing outside of Chester's old house wondering how and why I was there. I walked towards the empty pigpen and turned myself upside down trying to get the old memory of him back into my brain. It felt different there, and I couldn't even remember Chester's face when I tried. Candy bar wrappers and chip bags were stuck against all four corners of the fence, and the house looked as empty as it always had.

There was no sign anyone had moved out or in since Chester's parents disappeared. I wondered what I would see if I walked up to the window and peered in. *Would there still be a rocking chair by the window? Would it still be rocking?* I flipped back over to my feet and pulled my letter out. I read it over silently one last time, tracing the words with my pencil, but not changing anything.

> *Dear Chester,*
> *I wonder where you are these days. Hopefully you've found a normal family to live with. I have to tell you something about our secret. Desiree almost found out about Mother and Dad this week. She had a project to make a family tree. I had the same project last year, but I just made up fake relatives. Desiree isn't smart enough to make stuff up like I did, but then again, she doesn't know what we know. She never will, because guess what? Mother ripped up all of those articles from the shoebox the day I told her I was moving to Kitchener to live with Dad. You should have heard the sound of the ripping. I can still hear it when*

I look at a newspaper. Desiree thought all she had to do for the project was draw a tree from our yard. I guess we know where her stupid comes from. Maybe I'll grow an extra finger or something. If it's just a finger thing I can deal with it. I wish everything was still the same like normal with all of us. Not just my family, but yours too.
From your old neighbour, sort of like sister, best friend, Caroline.
P.S. This letter is being buried alive.

I used my footprints to measure the exact centre of the square pigpen and then marked it with a star. I folded the letter as many times as it would go, and dug a hole in the dirt with my pencil. I dug so deep that when I reached in to touch the bottom I was all the way up to my armpit. I threw the note in and covered it up with dirt. If Desiree had been there she would have worried that some Chinese kid might find it on the other side.

I was about to get up and walk home when I had a special feeling come into my writing hand. I dug up the note with my fingers, and erased the word *From.* In the empty space before my name I wrote *Love,* using a heart for the circle like Rosie did in her diary when she wrote Chester's initials. I took out the words after love and kept my name. When I was done, the last line before the PS just said, *Love Caroline.* I changed the heart back to an o, tracing over it until it was twice as dark as the other letters. You could still see the heart a bit, but it didn't matter because I was burying it alive. I read it through one last time and then added a PSS:

There's something about your family secret too. Your mother didn't drop your baby sister. It might not have even been a sister. It could have been a brother for all I know. Whichever it was, it wasn't her fault. It wasn't your dad's fault either. Sometimes babies just die before they come out. Maybe God saw the future and didn't want two orphans in your family.

When I looked back at my footprints they looked bigger than I thought they would be. I looked at my hands and they looked bigger too. I was like Pinocchio, only with big fingers and toes instead of a big nose. It was too soon to go back to Maple Manor. I needed to collect some rocks to make it look like I really had a project to do, so I ran to the creek and stood at the water's edge for a few minutes. I tried to imagine myself as a newborn baby. I tried to feel my own self getting smaller and younger, but again the image wouldn't come to me. The youngest I could picture myself was at my fifth birthday party where I kept asking Dad why I couldn't have candles or chocolate or rosebuds like the others. I had cried when he told me to shut up the questions, and Mother had stood up and taken my perfect vanilla cake with her to the closet.

The birds came out of the creek and paced around my feet. They were looking for bread, but all I had in my pocket was Simon's pencil. I took the pencil out and wrote *Sorry* in the sand. As I walked home, I wondered who I was sorry to and what for. *Was it the hungry birds? Was it Chester? Mother and Dad? Was I sorry to myself for being born? Sorry to God?* I took Neil's Passageway home, and as I walked I imagined all of the things that could go wrong with me because of Mother and Dad's secret.

Once I was inside our backyard, I walked towards my thinking chair to set down the rocks I had collected on the way home. Even before the back gate clicked closed, I saw the tiny paper circles blowing around the yard. I recognized the paper right away—blue lines on white paper, like the kind we used at school. Not the kind of school paper the kids used at the Mitchell schoolhouse, but school paper we pulled out of our notebooks back in the city.

When I got closer to my chair, I found the large piece that the holes had come from, placed underneath a rock. Two words were left untouched by the hole punch, and I threw up in my mouth as I saw the trace of my own heart turned into the *o* for *Love*. I heard the voice of Madame Castles in my head. *Whatever you do, don't put your letter in your underwear drawer for your brother or sister to find.* Why hadn't she reminded us to watch our backs if we planned to bury our letters alive?

CHAPTER 13—PIGS

Desiree's class got their family trees back faster than I had expected. When she came home from school that day, her cheeks and neck were as red as the big F written in one of the branches on her paper. Mr. Morris had written a comment in a speech bubble, and it looked like the tree itself was doing the talking. *Can we read instructions, Desiree?* An arrow pointed to the back of the paper where the instructions for the family tree were written, but it was too late. Even Desiree knew Mr. Morris didn't believe in second chances.

The drawing of the tree was perfect; it looked like the tree behind Maple Manor. Anyone in our family could have identified it, even without the tree chairs in the background. Beneath the photo Desiree had written a description that was so simple and true it almost made me apologize for not pointing out the instructions in the first place.

> *This is our family tree. It's a maple tree, and it stands for us. We used to be the trunk but now we are the branches. My family is like a stack of pancakes. You can take us apart but we'll always be sweet because of Caroline.*

I asked Desiree if I could have her tree picture to tack above my bed to remind me of *the good times*. I said I'd change the F to Fantastic and cut off the note from Mr. Morris so that Dad didn't see it. I kept talking because I was afraid Desiree was going to ask me why I didn't tell her what a family tree really was.

"Maybe you'll get Madame Castles next year, like me. She teaches grade eight socials. She doesn't believe in marks."

"I hate Mr. Morris," Desiree said. "I hate his stupid projects."

"At least you don't have to do speeches," I said, as she walked out to find the tape and scissors. "I have to stand up in front of my whole class and talk like a teacher," I said, loud enough for her to hear me in the hall.

*

There was a grade eight rumour going around that if you failed your speech you got put back into grade seven instead of going on to high school. The topic alone was worth twenty-five per cent of the grade, which was supposed to stop us from talking about our summer cottage or pet hamster. When I asked Samantha how she picked her topic she said she let fate handle it. She wrote the first twenty things that came into her head on little pieces of paper and pulled one out of a hat.

"And you picked moods?" I said. "Like good moods or bad ones?"

"There are a lot more than two moods," Samantha told me. "For example, right now I'm in a *blah* mood, which is probably 'cause I'm getting my rag. You look like you're feeling kind of blah too. Are you? I wouldn't be surprised, you know. Before I got mine, my sister said she and mom always got theirs at the same time. That's what happens when girls live in the same house or spend a lot of time together. There's no reason it wouldn't happen to best friends. It's like God's way of saying sorry for making us have to have it so we can make babies. If you get yours today maybe I could use the example in my speech. You really do look blah."

I told Samantha I was feeling frustrated, not blah. I pictured her sitting in her mother's closet, tearing perfectly good paper into long strips, and picking one out of her mother's pink beret. There was no such thing as scrap paper at Samantha's house. "I can't think of a good topic. Did you throw out your other papers?"

I didn't want anyone, including Samantha, to know I had already decided to do my speech on pigs. How could I explain that it was almost like the pigs had chosen me? The feeling was so strong I wondered if it was how Mary felt when God told her she was going to have his son. It was like someone's life depended on my doing the speech. But whose? Some pig?

"Pigs?" Ms. Lizzy said when I brought her my speech topic proposal. "What about pigs?"

"Like what they mean. What they stand for."

"Oh, you mean in literature?"

"I mean just everyday pigs."

"And what do they mean? Stand for?"

"Different things. You know, like green can be for good luck and jealousy, right?"

"Right. And greed," Ms. Lizzy said.

"Well, pigs are like that. They're more than just meat for sausages. You know like woman are more than just machines for making babies."

Ms. Lizzy wrote a checkmark on my paper, which meant my topic was accepted. She said she'd go against her own rules and wait to assign the actual topic mark until after I delivered the speech. It was my second year in Ms. Lizzy's class, and it was hard to get used to calling her Mrs. McDougal. After she got married she switched from the split to the grade eight class, and she kept all six of us grade seven girls. I didn't mind being in Ms. Lizzy's class two years in a row, but Samantha thought Ms. Lizzy secretly wished she was one of us, or that she thought she was our keeper or something.

*

"What are you reading, anyway?" Desiree asked as she traded me the scissors for the tape. I cut Mr. Morris's note off the tree and placed it inside my library book for a bookmark.

"Just a book," I said. I taped her tree above my bed and smoothed it out to make sure it stuck.

"A book about what?"

"Pigs," I said. Desiree handed me a red pen from her schoolbag and I turned her F into Fabulous.

"You stole the pig book?" she said, coming halfway up the ladder to look at it.

"Not *the* pig book. It's just a book from the library about pigs."

"You're doing a pig project?"

"It's not a project, it's a speech. And you don't have to tell anyone," I said looking up at her tree.

Desiree cut her toenails with the scissors while I took notes from the book about all of the kinds of pigs.

"I miss the pig book. Is there a part about Zeus in that one?" Desiree asked.

"No."

The Zeus chapter was our favourite from the pig book because it showed the piglets, and Mother was always in a happy mood when she read it. *Pigs symbolize fertility. Legend says this is because of their fruitful mammary glands*, Mother would say without looking at the words. *So, baby Zeus drank juice from the pigs?* Desiree always asked, even though she knew it was wrong. Mother would shake her head and explain, *Pigs have milk just like I do. It's just that they have more. So much more. And they breed so quickly.*

Desiree threw the scissors on the floor and ran out of the bedroom. Her wind knocked the family tree off the wall.

"What's wrong?" I shouted after her, but she was already behind the bathroom door. "Did you cut your toe?"

"Caroline! Something gross is happening to me."

All of the blood in my head felt like it was rushing somewhere down in between Desiree's legs. I had always prayed it wouldn't happen that way. I knew Mother would be devastated if Desiree turned into a woman first.

"What do you want me to do? Should I come in?"

"Yes! Come and look."

I opened the door and walked into the bathroom, expecting to see Desiree squatting on the toilet trying to figure out the maxi pads. Instead, she was standing on the seat looking in the mirror. Her T-shirt was in the sink.

"I have boobs, Caroline. Look." Her hands were covering up what she said she had so I couldn't see a thing.

"All I see is your hand, Desiree."

She let go of herself and turned to face me.

"Oh my God," I said, staring at her in the mirror instead of straight on.

"I know," she said, half bragging, half whimpering.

"When did that happen?" I pointed at them with the red pen that was still in my hands.

"They started a few months ago, but today I can actually feel them growing and it hurts. It's like there's a marble taped to the end of them."

I was still staring in the mirror when I realized Desiree had put her T-shirt back on and walked back to the bedroom. I flipped up the toilet seat to make sure there wasn't any blood. Then I checked the cupboard for the package of maxi pads that Dad had put there the day we moved into the apartment. I had taken the package out many times to read the instructions on the back, and I was sure Desiree had too. The last thing I did before I left the bathroom was hike up my own shirt for the usual inspection. Nothing.

When I walked back into the bedroom Desiree was rolling back and forth on her bed as if in pain. I sat down on the floor beside her and tried to think of something nice to say. I wondered how she had been hiding them.

"Des, can I tell you something? I think it will make you feel better."

"What?" She held the scissors to her chest and pretended to snip herself.

"It could be worse. I mean, I thought you got your thing."

"You mean my period?"

"Well, you never know. You could get yours before I do. It doesn't always go by age."

"I already got mine, Caroline. Last year."

"What?"

"You thought the boobs came first? Mother doesn't always know the proper order of things. She's not God, you know."

"I know, but—"

"Those pads Dad keeps in the bathroom are for when you get yours, Caroline. I use tampons. I have been ever since I got blood all over the carpet in Mother's closet. I wasn't used to having to pack pads for the weekend then. Mother gave me her thingies to try and that's what I use every time."

"You mean Mother knows?"

"She told me to keep it a secret. She wants everyone else to think you get yours first. Including you. "

"Oh."

"You know, you really should stop praying for yours."

"What makes you think I—"

"Sometimes you pray so hard you're actually whispering."

I climbed up the ladder to my bed, and we both stayed silent for a while. After a few minutes, Desiree climbed up beside me and tried to braid my hair. She divided it into two sections and twisted it around and around, telling me she was sure I would get mine soon. She said Emily told her that women who wanted babies really bad sometimes couldn't have them because they were trying too hard. I stared at the family tree and ripped at the corner while she talked and twisted.

"Maybe it's the same with periods."

"You told Emily I don't have mine?"

"I had to. She was crying when she got hers at Sunday school and I had to say something!"

"Like what?"

"I said she should be glad she got it 'cause it's worse waiting when you are already halfway through grade eight."

"Thanks a lot, Des."

"Maybe it's because you were born two months early, Caroline. I mean, maybe since you weren't born on your real birthday your whole system got messed up, and that's why you haven't got it yet."

"I was born on my real birthday, stupid. How can you be born on a day that's not your birthday?"

I knew Desiree had fallen asleep before me that night because I felt the sun coming in our room while I was still awake. I had spent the whole night worrying about Desiree and her body, and wondering why mine wasn't changing. I didn't even want to fall asleep because I was afraid to have a dream about my future self. *Caroline can't have babies until she gets her thingy,* Simon had said to Neil when he saw me walking around holding my stomach a few days earlier. It was the same day my letter to Chester was dug up and shredded, and I kept feeling like I needed to throw up. I could tell that Neil was trying to tell me something, but he never once grabbed my wrist or told me to be on my thinking chair at a specific time. *Maybe she already has it,* Neil had said to Simon, making sure I could hear them talking. *You can't tell if a girl already has it unless you see the red toilet water.* Simon shook his head at Neil and said *uh-uh. Mother says you'll see the little ant hills under her shirt first.* Neil shrugged. *Not if she's some kind of freak of nature. Maybe she'll never grow out of her baby body. Maybe Rosie will crack hers first. Maybe God's punishing Caroline for something.* It was Neil's way of telling me he was the one who had found, and destroyed, my letter to Chester in the pigpen. He nodded his head up and down while I shook mine back and forth. *We're all freaks,* I wanted to say as his hands made a writing motion. *Not just me.* He mouthed the words *you better shut up* as he tore up the invisible page. Something about his eyes told me he would never tell another soul about Mother and Dad's secret, or the fact that I had written the word love before a boy's name. I wondered if it had something to do with his deformity, whatever his was. Maybe he had already discovered something weird on the inside that none of us could see. Something weirder than a face full of freckles that made you want to play dot-to-dot. I couldn't think of any other reason why Neil wouldn't tell everyone about the letter he had found in the pig pen.

On the day of my speech I dressed in pink and put pigtails in my hair. Before I walked out of the apartment, I stuffed my underwear with toilet paper, just in case Neil was right when he said that if you think bad thoughts they come true. A few minutes before the lunch bell Ms. Lizzy smiled at me and pointed to the front of the class for me to take my turn. I grabbed my cue cards out of my sock and walked to the front of the room.

> *What do you think of when you imagine a pig? Do you think of bacon or dirt? Do you think of ham or pennies? You know that we eat pigs and that we put pennies in pigs. You know that pigs roll around in mud. But did you know that pigs are also lucky? Did you know that in some parts of the world pigs are like rabbit's feet?*

Mrs. McDougal, boys, and girls, today you will learn three new things about pigs, and I promise you will never look at these animals the same again. Many of you probably have a piggie bank. But did you know that pigs are a symbol of wealth? To many people around the world having a pig is like having money in the bank. Pigs give families food to eat or money to buy food. If you have a pig dream that means you will probably get rich. Fortune tellers say babies who are born in the Year of the pig are destined for wealthy lives... Another thing you probably don't know is that pigs have good intuition. Good intuition means you make the right choices in life. I don't mean you eat a carrot instead of a chocolate bar. Intuition is about more important choices, like ones that can change your life.

We should all be more like pigs, by listening to the whisper inside us. Like, if you have to go to the bathroom, but something inside you says don't go to that bathroom, then you should listen to that whisper and go to a different bathroom, just in case.

Pigs also have great smell. You think pigs are dirty, right? People say things like he stinks like a pig or she sweats like a pig, but pigs are actually cleaner than most of us. Did you know pigs don't even sweat? The reason they roll in mud is to cool themselves down, but pigs are some of the cleanest animals around. They go into a corner to poop because they don't want to eat near their toilet.

Would you keep a pig in your house as a pet? If you want to have a baby, maybe you should. Pigs are symbols of fertility, especially white pigs. Women who want to have babies in Greece keep pigs nearby.

One type of white pig is the Chester pig. This pig is common in Canada and the United States. Chester White pigs are known for having lots of babies and for being very good mothers. To Native Americans a pig is a reminder of the things we have to be thankful for in daily life. If we want to succeed in life we need wealth, intuition, and fertility—

The lunch bell rang before I had time to finish my speech, and Ms. Lizzy made everyone sit and wait for me to say my closing remarks and review the three things about pigs they had learned. "Her fake boyfriend's a pig!" Christina blurted out, and Ms. Lizzy excused the class for lunch.

At lunch, Christina came up to me and said she knew Chester didn't really exist. *Who names their imaginary boyfriend after a pig?* Right after she said it Marty Munson came up behind us and looked up my shirt and down my jeans to check if I was really wearing pink everything. Samantha held the bathroom stall closed from the outside while my face cleared up from crying. When the lunchroom teacher came in to check on what was taking so long, Samantha lied and told her it was a girl thing and then accepted a dime for the machine on the wall. She pocketed the free pad and then told me what Marty did was more of a grade seven thing to do than a grade eight.

"Forget about it. Change your mood. We only have a few more months at this school anyway, Caroline."

"What if he goes to our high school and tells everyone what he did?"

"He can't."

"Why can't he?"

"He's going to fail after his speech about plain old shoes, Caroline. Besides, my sister said that in grade nine the boys only tease you if they really like you. It's a kind of sign. If Marty tells everyone in the high school that you were wearing pink underclothes, they'll say that he is in love with you. It might even be true. That might be why he did what he did today. "

That wasn't the part I was worried about. I was afraid Marty Munson would tell everyone I was wearing a pink undershirt on my baby body instead of a pink bra. Either that, or Christina would tell everyone I stuffed my kid-sized underwear with Kleenex.

CHAPTER 14—KYLE

If there was anything that changed my mood or helped me forget I didn't have my period the summer before high school it was watching the letters on Kyle Fitzpatrick's jersey at the twins' baseball games. There were so many loops and lines the letters had to wrap around underneath his armpits, and when someone on the team got a run Kyle would lift up his arms and spin around in a circle so fast you could see a line of hair going down to his belly button. One time when he was in the outfield and a player on the other team struck out the coach had to go all the way out to remind Kyle to stop twirling and tuck his shirt in.

It didn't matter to me that Kyle was the worst player on the twins' team. The fact that he was never out running bases meant I could watch him from up close for at least half of the game. Sometimes I sat right behind the batting cage and listened to the boys smacking their gum and talking about the World Wrestling Federation. That was how I found out Kyle and I were about to become school mates.

"I'm starting at Kitchener Collegiate this September, eh boys," Kyle told the twins during one of the last games of the summer. "Got any hints about subjects. Or girls?"

"Take Nine Typing," Les said.

"Don't forget Coed Gym," Lee added.

"Typing? Is it easy?"

"It's a cinch," Les said.

"Do lots of…chicks take typing in Canada?"

"Dude," Les and Lee said together. The boys shook the metal fence, and I could tell by how hard it rang that Kyle was going to enroll in typing as soon as he got home.

That night I unstuck the envelope I had addressed to Kitchener Collegiate and changed my cooking class to typing. I made the change right in the wet liquid paper and spent the rest of August praying that the secretary would be able to make out the bumpy words.

Everybody brought a bagged lunch on the first day of high school. The garbage bins on the way to McDonald's were full of them.

"I don't have any money, either," Samantha said. "But my sister said you don't even have to order anything at Mceydees as long as you show up."

We ate our apples on the way to McDonald's and then sat on the grass near the front entrance as if we had already enjoyed our cheeseburgers. Samantha pulled someone else's burger wrapper closer to us with her foot.

"Tomorrow we eat in the cafeteria, right?" I asked.

"Yes. And one of us has to get there right after the bell rings so we can get a good spot. We'll have to keep that table for the rest of the year, you know."

"I want a good spot for typing class," I said. "I'm going to head back to school a few minutes early to make sure I get a window seat."

I stood by the water fountain across from Room 101 waiting for the typing students to head into class. Kyle was the fourth person to enter. I counted to seven, taking extra long breaths between the numbers, and then took another gulp from the fountain before following him in. The seats were set up in pairs and I pretended to inspect the room before I took the spot next to Kyle.

"Hey," I tried to say, but only the *h* came out. Kyle wiggled around in his desk and tapped at the keys on his typewriter with two fingers. He didn't seem like the kind of kid who would show up early for class, and I prayed that the rest of the seats would fill up quickly so it didn't seem weird that I had sat right beside him.

"Best seats in the house, right?" Kyle said. He pulled a Paula Abdul notebook out of his knapsack and rested it face down on his lap.

"Yeah. I like the back."

I turned towards the aisle and started pulling pen after pen out of my backpack. As I lined up the last one beside the others, I looked up for a moment and remembered I was in typing class. Instead of putting the pens back, I pulled a piece of paper out of my binder and pretended to check which ones were working. I felt Kyle watching me as I wrote my full name in seven colours for the pen test.

"Hey, girly. You got twin brothers?"

"How'd you know?"

"They're on my baseball team. I seen you there. I mean, I seen you watching us. Them."

"The Junior Zees?"

"That's my team."

Mother freaked when the twins told her the name of their baseball team. She wanted to know what kind of Canadian team was called the Zees. She never came to a game, but once wrote a letter to the coach saying if he didn't change the name to the proper zed spelling she'd pull the twins from the team.

"Dad made us go to every game. You know, family support and all," I said, and Kyle nodded.

Our teacher, Mrs. Wu, came in and told us to make sure we were sitting at a typewriter that felt comfortable. "We have a mishmash of desks and chairs this year. It's important that you can reach all of the keys without straining or feeling cramped," she said. "Some desks are meant for longer arms."

"How's yours?" Kyle asked me. He shifted his back from left to right and rolled his shoulders. He didn't stand up, but I noticed he was looking around the room.

"Don't move," I told him. I pulled my chair in closer and held my hands on the keys of the typewriter in case. Mrs. Wu was scouting for someone who would switch desks with a tall kid at the front.

"Huh?"

"Please don't switch seats. There's a guy in here who's—in love with me. If you change seats, he might come and take your spot. I'll kill you if you move, I swear."

The class scrambled around. Almost everybody changed seats just because they could. Kyle was eyeing an open seat beside a girl with a blonde bob and a Florida tan. She wore a red blouse and white jeans, and looked as though she had jumped right out of a Sunkist commercial. A chubby kid with braces slid into the empty spot beside her before Kyle had the chance to abandon me.

I watched the orange juice girl while Mrs. Wu took attendance. Kyle watched too, and he made a kissy sound when Chantal Berish held up one finger to indicate she was present.

"Hey you. Tap your desk when the creepy guy gets called," Kyle whispered to me. Mrs. Wu was on Ms by then and I looked around the room for the guy I should say. It couldn't be someone Kyle knew, so I had to pick a kid from my own elementary school. I expected to see Marty Munson since he had been haunting my typing dreams all summer, but there weren't any guys from my school, as far as I could tell. I considered saying the guy with the shiny teeth, but I didn't want any more attention directed that way.

"Is there no Caroline Quartz here?" Mrs. Wu asked.

"Girly, isn't that you?" Kyle said, shoving his elbow into mine. He was looking at the paper with my name written all over it.

"Me. That's me. Here," I said shooting both of my arms up at the same time.

"Hmm. Barely," Mrs. Wu said. I could tell by what she did with her pen that she wouldn't have any trouble remembering my name. Standing out on day one was not on the to-do list in high school, according to Samantha's sister. *But don't worry. You'll probably have the opposite problem,* Samantha had said.

"You didn't tap," Kyle whispered after all of the names were called.

"His name was at the beginning, before you said to," I whispered back.

"Oh. Then I know the guy you mean," Kyle said.

"You do?"

He looked all around the class and nodded his head. "Yeah. Aaron Asta. A lot of girls from my school were in his arse club and they didn't even know it."

"His what?"

"Don't worry. He never actually touches girls. He's too chicken. He just walks behind them and gives their arses and diddies a score of 1-10. He keeps a list in his pencil case. I seen it once."

I didn't know who Aaron Asta was, but I was sure Kyle would be expecting me to look at the guy with disgust.

"I'll watch your back, Quartz. If you want me to. If I see him poking around you, I'll let you know somehow. I'll say something like Zee."

"Zee?"

"Like short for Zees. The baseball team? Plus, we're in typing class, so, it's a good code word, right?"

I nodded my head yes and thanked God for everything so far.

Kyle started calling me Zaroline, and some days he paid more attention to me than he did Chantal. He liked to flick me on the back with his finger right at my bra strap, and one day he did it so hard the safety pin came undone. It wasn't until two weeks before school that I had found a bra in a used clothing bag in Miles' truck. Instead of stuffing it every time, I sewed up the straps an extra two inches and closed the back up as tight as I could with a safety pin. Every night before bed, I handwashed it while I brushed my teeth. It was still damp most mornings because it didn't have enough time to dry fully underneath my pillow, and I used the wetness to remind myself to say a prayer. *Thank you, God, for this bra, now please give me something to put in it.* Kyle must have known he broke my bra, because the next day he stuffed a maple seed in my jean pocket and said he hoped I'd accept a helicopter as an apology. Samantha called it a sign and she didn't even know about Maple Manor and how our whole backyard was full of those keys.

In the fifth week of class, Mrs. Wu announced a typing pairs contest. "Each sender has to type a letter with lots of questions. Think *who, what, when, where, and how* okay? When I yell *switch*, everyone has to pull the paper out of their machines and type up an envelope for the receiver."

We all groaned. Envelopes were the hardest thing to type and for this test we were being blindfolded. Chantal Berish put up her hand and asked her question. "What if we don't know our partner's address?"

"Memorize it. I'll be checking the contact records for spelling and numbers, so don't be tempted to write something like 100 Main St. There'll be no talking allowed."

When the class quieted down Mrs. Wu said that when the envelopes were sealed we would take off our blindfolds, read the letters, and respond. "You will be judged on how many words you type perfect," Mrs. Wu said. "As a pair."

"Here's my address," Kyle said, without even glancing at Chantal. "We'll ace this contest tomorrow as long as you remember my address. Then you can send me flowers on my birthday. I like Marigolds."

"When's your birthday?" I asked.

"July seventh."

"Liar!"

"Easy, Zaro! Who lies about their birthday?"

I told Kyle mine was July sixth, but as soon as I said it I wondered if he knew what that day meant. *What if people from his country had heard about the Connecticut circus, and what if he thought I was the unluckiest girl at the school? The unluckiest girl sitting beside a guy who was born on the luckiest day of the year—the seventh day of the seventh month. The same day as Ringo Starr. The day after the unluckiest day.* I made Kyle show me his student card to prove that July seventh was really his birthday.

Simon called after school that day as I was memorizing Kyle's mailing address. We talked about the weather until he made the clicking sound with his tongue that meant Mother was finally leaving the room.

"Rosie caught Mother sharpening the letter opener three times this week. I lost count of how many times I caught her staring out the window at the maple tree with that sad look on her face," he said.

"What does the letter opener have to do with anything?" I asked.

"We don't know exactly how she's going to do it, but we're pretty sure she's going to have the maple tree cut down. She's been writing letters to someone, and someone is writing back. She can't stand that Shilo doesn't have a thinking chair. She'll probably engrave Shilo's name with the letter opener on the stump. It could be worse, right? She could have been planning something else with the letter opener."

"How do you know she's going to have the tree cut down?" I asked. "It's the last tree. I can't see her doing it. Besides, she can't do it alone. Who's she gonna call to help? Miles?"

"Well, she wouldn't ask Dad to do it, that's for sure. I don't know why I'm even telling you this, Caroline. I just had to tell someone. I can't sleep at night. Rosie can't either."

Desiree heard the phone beeping in my hands and hung it up on the cradle for me.

"Earth to Caroline. You promised you'd paint my nails, remember? Just the left ones. I did the right ones perfect myself."

I sat down on the kitchen floor and opened the polish. My stomach started to rumble and cramp. *What kind of family would we be if all that was left of our family tree was a stump?* I thought about calling Mother and offering Shilo my tree chair. I could help her sand it down and change the name on Saturday. Then I remembered how she had torn my French book to pieces when I changed my middle name to Jamie. *Don't you ever think of changing your name.*

"It's called *grape dream*," Desiree said. "It's goes perfect with my new sweater. Makes you hungry, huh?"

"It smells like cough syrup," I said. I hated nail polish because of how it drew attention to my puny fingers. My stomach rumbled when Desiree held the bottle near my nose. I didn't make it to the bathroom before half of my Alpha-getti came spewing out. The rest made it into the toilet, and the letters swam around in orange circles. I couldn't help counting the *K*s and *F*s. Dad heard the mess and came out from under his newspaper to help with the clean up.

"Sorry, Dad."

"Don't be sorry, Caroline. You have a bug." He flushed the toilet and handed me a warm washcloth. Whenever one of us got hurt or upset that was always Dad's cure. I draped the cloth across my face and felt the steam seep into my skin. I thanked God I was in the apartment with the flu instead of at the house. There were rules about the flu at Maple Manor, and it was hard to keep them straight with a fever. Dad tried to help me up, but my foot was asleep and I fell back down and rolled my ankle. I transferred the cloth to my foot while Dad prepared me a fresh one.

"I think it was the nail polish that got me."

"Did you swallow some?"

Desiree came in and put her hand on my forehead like Mother always did with teething babies. "She's burning up!"

"A match burns. A house burns. A human has a temperature!" Dad said.

"I'm fine."

"Get to bed. I'll bring you a fresh washcloth."

"After that can you do my nails?" Desiree asked Dad.

I wobbled to bed and prayed for a twelve-hour bug instead of the usual twenty-four hour kind. I dreamed it was Kyle's birthday and I brought him a basket of grapes. We played pin the tail on Paula Abdul until it was time for presents. Desiree gave him a Barbie doll and he kept pinching it and calling it Chantal. The real Chantal was there too and she was wearing the tops of Kyle's pajamas. Mrs. Wu came to the party and told us on your mark, get set, go for the typing contest. We all had to go to confession and say how many mistakes we had made on our envelopes. Mother jumped out from behind the partition with an axe. She told me her plan. She said the maple tree was dead anyhow. It needed to come down. It wasn't worth anything anymore. It'd be worth more as a piece of furniture. When I pointed at the green leaves, she shoved a bowl of Alpha-getti into my mouth so I couldn't speak. She said being treeless wouldn't be so bad. Not like being motherless. When I swore at her Dad appeared and asked me not to pick on his sister. *The show must go on*, he said.

I woke up, puked in the bucket, and went back to sleep. In the morning, Dad came in and touched my forehead with the tip of his finger.

"Go back to sleep, sweetie."

"I have to go to school today. I have a test."

"You can write it another day."

"It's a pair test. I can't let my partner down."

"She can write it another day, too."

"It's a typing test, and it's a he."

Kyle forgave me for missing the typing contest after I offered to share pretzels with him underneath our typewriters. I brought the stick kind, and he pretended they were cigarettes when Mrs. Wu wasn't looking. The next week I brought in a baggie of the kind that look like lips.

"Can I ask you something? Why do some guys in the hall call you Pinky?" he asked. He put one of the lip pretzels on his face like a moustache.

"Oh, it's dumb," I said.

"Just tell me," he said. His pretzel dropped to the floor and he quickly covered it up with his foot because we weren't allowed to eat in class.

"It's dumb."

"Just tell me. I won't tell anyone else, I swear."

"Pinky swear?"

"On my mother's grave."

I held out my little finger, but Kyle didn't stick out his to lock with it. I didn't care because I had no intention of telling him the real reason.

"A few years ago I asked my friend Samantha to pinky swear something with me and one of the kids from our class heard us and gave me that dumb name. It stuck."

"That's gay, Zaro." Kyle went back to his drills, looking disappointed as if I had told a dumb joke.

"I know," I said.

While we typed I thanked God for helping me think of such a quick lie. White lies had become so easy for me to think up it felt as though they were being sent down from angels. I could have told Kyle that the name was because of my crooked finger, but that idea didn't come to me until class was already over.

On the last Monday of the last week of typing I noticed Kyle walking to class with a big grin on his face. He was wearing a polo shirt instead of a turtleneck, and his short sleeves were rolled up to his armpits, even though it was December. He stretched his hands up over his head and let out a macho groan when he saw me.

"What's with *you*?" I said. I tried not to smile or look at the parts of him I had never seen.

"Oh nothing."

"Yeah, right," I said, hip checking him into the closest locker.

"Well, since you're dying to know…I have a date tomorrow night. I think."

"Hmm." It was all I could think to say. I hoped maybe it was his nervous way of asking me out.

"Don't you want to know with who?"

"No. Not unless you are dying to tell someone."

We walked into the class and sat down at our desks. Kyle fiddled around in his backpack for a while and then asked me to guess who his date was. He slid me a baggie of popcorn, but I didn't take any.

"Chantal Berish," I said. Kyle had asked me at least ten times if I thought she was hot, and I always said she had nice hair.

"I wish. Guess again." He rubbed his palms together as if he was waiting for some good gossip. Then he pulled out his notebook and finished off the popcorn, licking each of his fingers separately.

"Paula Abdul."

"Come on. Are you motherless?"

"No, she just lives in a different house."

Kyle laughed and told me motherless meant drunk. I wished I could take back my confession, but he didn't seem to care that my parents were separated.

"Is it someone I know?" I asked. I was beginning to think it might not be me.

"Hot. You're getting hot. It's someone you know well."

"How well?" I asked. My smile stuck to my teeth. I was sure Kyle was calling me *hot* and I was ready to say yes to my first date. I took a pretzel out of my pencil case and pretended to smoke it.

"How well do you know your sister?" he asked.

"Which sister?"

"Desiree. I met her at the mall yesterday. She was with my cousin, Emily. Emily set up the whole thing, said Desiree has had a crush on me since baseball started. Funny I never noticed her staring at me."

"Emily's your cousin?"

Kyle took one of my pretzels and nodded. "Desiree's in grade eight, you know."

"I know. Nice dibbies for a grade eight." Kyle laughed and drew two finger circles around his own nipples. "I thought she was older than you at first. Sorry, she's just a bit—bigger."

"Desiree's not allowed to go on dates."

"Ah shit. You're not gonna tell your mother, are ya Zaro?"

Kyle explained that Desiree was planning to say she was going to the movies with Emily, and maybe even sleeping over.

"Sleeping over where?"

"At Emily's. Just in case we end up going to the late show. Emily's gonna keep her bedroom window open for her. Don't look at me like that, ya sap."

"Like what?"

"Like you're her mom or something. Emily's room is on the main floor. She can't fall."

I didn't speak to Kyle for the remainder of class, even though he kept asking me how many sisters I had and promised that he wouldn't stop tapping my back until I told him. When his grin didn't go away I began to pray for a miracle. God knew all about Kyle. I didn't even have to say his name by then. I just said *he*, and I assumed God knew who I meant. When we first started going to church, Addie had given us a few pointers about how to pray. She said if you wanted to ask God for a favour you should think of something to thank him for first. *Lord, thank you that Kyle has blond hair and dimples; please let him fall in love with me before the school dance.* The day Kyle told me about his date, I thanked God Desiree almost never went through with anything on her own, followed by an *and please let her catch poison ivy.* I didn't even ask for forgiveness or take it back. Instead, I thought of worse things she could catch before her date.

*

"How was last night?" I asked Desiree in front of Dad when she walked into the apartment looking healthy as could be the morning after her date was supposed to happen.

"Emily and I went to a movie."

"Any good?"

"I could have waited for video." She turned on the TV and started flipping through the channels, passing two of her favourite commercials.

"Maybe you should have looked at the screen instead of sticking your tongue in Kyle Fitzpatrick's ear," I said and started to cry in my throat.

"Who is Kyle Fitzpatrick?" Dad said, looking up from his paper.

"Nobody," Desiree said.

I took a deep breath and tried to change my mood. "An actor on TV," I said.

"Hmm," Dad said. "I thought I recognized that name."

"Desiree wants to marry him. She wants him so bad she licked the TV yesterday. She wants to put him in her family tree," I said, and ran out of the room.

CHAPTER 15—EMILY

Emily wasn't really Kyle Fitzpatrick's cousin.

"His mom's my aunt," Emily said during Sunday school, "but not the kind of aunt where it's your mom's sister." Addie had just walked out of the cubicle to get something from the craft cupboard.

"What other kind of aunt is there?" Desiree asked. I wanted to say that there were ants that lived in dirt, but I was pretending not to listen to their conversation.

"Our moms were in the same pregnancy class when my sister was on the way," Emily said. "They got close because they had to pretend they were half naked sometimes."

"You mean Lamaze," I said, and then wished I had kept my mouth shut.

"What's that?" Emily asked.

"It's French," I said.

"Who cares about French? What does it mean?" She swirled her finger around her ear and made cross-eyes at me. Even when she did that she looked pretty.

"It's for making births feel painless." After I said it I knew it was going to be one of those sentences that made me feel stupid inside for the rest of the day, and I knew Emily would get me back for making her look stupid in front of the boys in the class.

"How would you know?" Emily asked. "You couldn't have a baby even if you tried."

"She studies French every Friday night," Desiree said. "Well, she used to. At Maple Manor. I guess when Chester left she didn't need to anymore. Chester was French, so Caroline wanted to be French too. Like his mom. Maybe she wanted to learn how to give French kisses."

"Who's Chester?" Emily asked Desiree, but by the smile on her face it looked like she already knew.

"Caroline's boyfriend," Desiree said pointing at me. She said it loud enough for everyone in the Sunday school class to hear. I looked up to make sure Addie was still out of earshot and then told Desiree to dream on.

"Why else would you draw hearts around his name all of the time?" Emily asked.

"I don't." For a second I didn't get what they were talking about, but when I pictured pink hearts with Chester's initials inside I realized they must have found Rosie's diary and mistook it for mine.

"You don't anymore because you think he's never coming back," Desiree said. "Maybe he died."

"Yeah," Emily said. "Or maybe he ran away." She looked at Desiree and bit her lower lip. Then she looked back at me. "If it's not Chester, then who do you like?" she asked. I knew she wanted me to say Kyle, but I refused.

"Chester is like a brother," I said, and then wished I could take it back just in case Emily ever met Mother and figured out that she looked like Dad. I didn't think they looked anything alike, but Emily was the type who would figure something out like that. If she ever said anything I knew I would say what I always planned on saying to anyone who asked. *Brothers and sisters don't always look alike. Neil is the only one of us who's pigeon-toed.*

"Mother is still looking for Chester. She won't give up till the day she dies," Desiree said.

"She gave up a long time ago," I said. "He's probably in another country or something by now. He would have called us otherwise. He probably doesn't have long distance."

"Where's his mom and dad?" Emily asked, forgetting that she wasn't supposed to know who Chester was. "What kind of a mom up and leaves her kids?"

"Kid," I said.

THE PROPER ORDER OF THINGS

"Beats us," Desiree said. "Mother says Chester's mom ran off to be with her true love. You can't blame her. True love only comes around once in a life time."

"True. And speaking of true love... Kyle is cute, but he's not my *type*." Emily giggled and looked at me. "Period."

"You're right," Desiree said. "He's much more like me. Exclamation mark."

Addie walked back into the class and started putting stickers on our weekly quiz. I flipped loudly through the Bible I was reading, searching for the crossword clue for the baby boy God promised to Abraham even though he was one hundred years old. I got Emily's stupid jokes about typing, even though Desiree didn't. Emily didn't know that I knew she knew I didn't have my period yet. At least not unless Desiree had told her that she had told me, but she had pinky sworn that she wouldn't and I didn't think Desiree even knew how to break a pinky swear.

"Desiree, does anyone in your family snore?" Emily asked.

"I don't know, I'm a deep sleeper," Desiree answered. "Dad says I won't even wake up to a fire alarm."

Addie looked at her watch and told us it was time to head back up for the communion. When she walked away to tell the other classes it was time to go up, Emily folded her quiz and placed it in her back pocket.

"Say, *your dad*, not *dad*," Emily said. "He's not my dad. You make it sound like he's my dad when you say it like that. And I hate how you two say, *Mother*. What is she, a nun?"

"No. Mother doesn't even go to church," I said.

"She prays," Desiree said. "Especially lately. She probably prays more than a nun."

"Where does she pray if she doesn't come to church?" Emily asked.

"Outside," I said. "In the real world."

"Or in her closet," Desiree said.

"Anyway, I was just wondering if your brothers and sisters snore, because I've heard that *eep-slay alkers-tay* usually do."

"Let's go, everyone," Addie said. When the others started filing out I grabbed a crayon and wrote in Pig Latin on the top of my quiz. As we started up the stairs, I shoved the paper in front of Emily and pointed at my response.

I ont-day alk-way in y-may eep-slay.

Emily read it and waited for Addie to look away.

"Not alk-way, alk-tay," she said spitting the *t* so hard she got my face wet from two steps up.

Instead of going up for communion, I sat in the pew between Dad and Desiree and thought about how Mother taught us Pig Latin before we even learned the alphabet. *Ash-way the alls-way. Ean-clay the oors-flay. Ust-day the eets-shay.* Desiree never figured out how to turns words inside out.

When it was her family's turn to go up, Emily looked over at us and her eyes locked with mine instead of Desiree's. She mouthed the word *sleeptalker* and I understood. Using Pig Latin was Emily's way of telling me how she and Desiree had figured out my crush on Kyle.

"Emily thinks we should look for Chester ourselves," Desiree said. It was the summer before grade eleven, and aside from when we were visiting Mother on the weekends, Desiree and Emily had spent the whole time sleeping over at each other's places. I couldn't stand another night of them talking about cramps and red underwear in front of me, and I was relieved when Samantha finally invited me over for the night.

"It's too bad you're not going to be here," Desiree said. "We're going to work on stage one of our plan tonight. Emily has an idea."

"Why does Emily care about a person she's never even met?" I asked.

"Emily thinks there's going to be a reward for whoever finds him. Besides, she wants to be a detective when she grows up. It's her dream job."

"She's never going to grow up," I said. I shoved Rosie's diary in with my pajamas, even though I was sure they had already read it.

"She's more grown up than you," Desiree said, and we both knew what she meant. "Besides, she's read things," Desiree said.

"What do you mean she's read things?" I asked.

"In a newspaper."

"What kind of newspaper?" I asked, but I almost didn't want to hear the answer. If I had talked about being in love with Kyle in my sleep, I had probably dreamed aloud about the articles from the shoebox in the closet. But even if I did, and even if Emily had sent Desiree looking for them at Maple Manor, she couldn't have found anything but a bunch of torn articles. *Unless Mother had left one of the articles intact?* I wished I had checked to make sure they had all been destroyed that day when I heard the ripping. *Maybe one had fallen out and Desiree had found it and showed it to Emily?*

"There's a boy missing from his foster house and Emily thinks it's Chester. It's in the papers. He's the right age."

"Papers lie," I said, but I didn't know what made me say it. "Besides, who even knows what Chester looks like nowadays? We don't even have a picture of him from before."

"Mother does," Desiree said. "She keeps it in her bra."

"How would you know?" I asked.

"It fell out when she made me try her bra on a few weeks ago. She said the one Dad bought me was too small, and she doesn't like the way I hang out at the sides. She made me go in her closet and try hers on. When I was walking into the closet, she undid her bra from the back and pulled it out of her sleeve. The picture fell out from her armpit."

The story sounded too real to be made up, and I didn't think even Emily could have imagined it. I thought about the time when Mother watched me in the shower. How she had reached into her bra and shifted something around that had poked her.

Desiree pulled the neckline of her shirt down to show me her bra, and I recognized it instantly as Mother's.

"It was a baby picture, but Chester is one of those people who will always look the same. Mother didn't see me see it. She stuffed it back in, and now she wears it in my bra 'cause we switched. She doesn't even take it off at night, you know."

Desiree had never asked me how I got my own bra, but I was pretty sure she knew I had one even though I mostly only wore it at school.

"Emily has an uncle who draws pictures for the police. She says he can turn the baby picture into a teenager in like five minutes."

"How?"

"It's his talent, Caroline. We all have one, even if we don't know what it is."

I tried to picture Chester as a teenager but couldn't get it right.

"Emily thinks Chester's good-looking. Or at least she thinks the missing guy from the paper is. His picture is on a milk carton too. She stares at him while she eats her breakfast."

The next day Desiree called Mother and asked if it was okay if she brought a friend to stay over night at Maple Manor. I don't know what she said or did to make Mother say yes, but the twins were happy they got to stay behind at the apartment.

Emily and Desiree sat in the back of the station wagon facing out at the cars behind as we drove out to the house. I sat in the front with Dad and tried to ignore their voices.

"If we ever got in an accident sitting like this, we'd be goners," Emily said.

"How do you know?" Desiree asked.

"That's what my dad said when he first saw you and Caroline in these seats in the church parking lot. He thinks it's irresponsible. Don't worry, I won't tell him you let me sit here Mr. Quartz," Emily said.

Mother was standing at the door when Dad dropped us off, but as usual she went out of sight while Dad opened up the hatch and passed us our bags. As the car drove away she came back and held the door open for us.

Emily gasped when she first saw Mother.

"Where's your hair?" She reached out a few fingers to give Mother's head a feel. "Did someone die?"

"You must be Emily," Mother said, ignoring the question.

"My grandma cut off all her hair when my great-grandma died. She was part Indian. It's a sign of mourning, you know. When grandma's hair grew back, it was curly and great-grandpa disowned her because there were no curly-haired people in the family. It was kind of like he lost his wife and his daughter at the same time."

"Really," Mother said. "I'm sorry to hear that."

"Don't be sorry," Emily said. "I never met any of them. I never even met my grandma. It's just one of those stories you hear over and over about your family is all. When we're being bad my dad sometimes jokes that we're related to Crazy Horse."

Mother touched her own scalp for a moment, but then put her hands at her waist. She looked like she was about to call a meeting around the circle stool, but she must have sensed another question coming.

"Where's your grass?" Emily asked Mother.

"No lawn mower," Mother said. I waited for Desiree to say that Dad took the lawn mower after Mother filled the yard with rocks, but she looked too nervous to say anything. Emily accepted Mother's excuse and walked into the kitchen. She looked around for a moment and boosted herself up onto the counter where the cutting board usually sat. I thanked God for the chairs around the table, even though a few of them were still folding camping chairs.

"Down!" Desiree shouted as if her friend were a dog that had jumped on a brand new couch. I pointed to the chairs, but Mother said Emily was fine where she was.

But we just came from the city, I wanted to say. *She wore those pants in Dad's car.*

"Why are there balloons on your mailbox?" Emily asked.

"It's Mary Shelley's birthday," Mother said. She walked over to the cake and cut three pieces away from it. Banana cream with pink frosting—Dad's favourite.

"Which one is Mary?" Emily asked, looking at Magdelene, Melinda, and Shilo who were staring up at her as if she was a celebrity. Mother put my and Desiree's plates on the table and handed Emily her piece to eat while she sat on the counter. She didn't give her a fork.

"She's the one who wrote the story about Frankenstein," Mother said and smiled.

"Frankenstein isn't the monster," Simon said, speaking to Emily for the first time. "It's actually the guy who made him. You have to read the book to understand."

After Emily asked Simon which one *he* was she finished her plate and put it beside her. Before she asked her next question, she licked each one of her fingers and wiped her wet hands on her pants.

"How come you got a divorce, Sherry?"

Simon pulled Shilo out of the room, and Magdelene and Melinda followed him to where Neil was playing Tetris. I put my plate in the dirty side of the sink and motioned for Desiree to show Emily where to wash her hands. While they washed I went to the front door to grab the backpacks. As I headed for the stairs, I listened for Mother to avoid the question. Instead, she offered Emily another slice of cake and told the truth.

"Sometimes people just want different things, Emily."

"Or different people, right?" Emily said.

Emily hadn't told Desiree her plan to get the picture out of Mother's bra, and I assumed it was going to happen in the morning before Dad arrived for his visitation with the Creek Kids. On Friday night, when I thought everyone was asleep, I heard rustling in the corner and an unzipping of a backpack. I pretended to be sleeping, and even said a few words, hoping it would convince Emily I was really asleep. *You can come to my house next week, Samantha. I pinky swear it's your turn.* The rustling stopped for a few minutes and then started again after I pretend snored. After Emily pulled something out of her bag, she walked out of the room with it. I listened to her footsteps from my pillow until I heard the pots clanging around in the kitchen.

"Can't sleep?" It was Mother. Emily hadn't made any effort to keep quiet downstairs, so it must have been part of her plan to wake Mother up. I tiptoed out of the bedroom and closed the door behind me. From the top of the banister I could see their feet standing close together near the oven. I positioned myself behind the empty laundry basket and watched through the holes. Mother had Shilo with her, and they both looked wide awake.

"I'm hungry," Emily said. "I can't sleep when I'm hungry. Sorry for not liking your shepherd's pie."

"We call it shepherd's cake. You don't like corn. It's okay."

"I like popcorn," Emily said, holding up the bag. "I hope it's okay that I brought my own. My mom says we can never go to a sleepover empty-handed."

"You don't have to bring anything when you come here," Mother said, and I imagined her snapping the bag of popcorn kernels away from Emily and putting them in the outside garbage.

"You want some? It's hard to make popcorn for one. My mom says I always make too much."

"That would be nice, Emily," Mother said. She opened some cupboards and pulled a few things out and I wondered how she even knew what popcorn needed. Mother's head appeared for a moment when she bent down to pull a pot out of the oven drawer, and I closed my eyes as if it would make it harder for her to see me.

"I'm glad I didn't bring the microwave kind. Do you guys use oil or butter for popcorn?"

"You choose," Mother said. "Just watch you don't burn yourself."

When Emily started shaking the pot over the element, I had to get closer to hear what they were saying. I moved down to the middle stair and held my body as flat as I could against the wall.

"I couldn't help notice you keep a picture in your—nightgown," Emily said. "Sorry if it's a secret. I sort of saw it when you bent down to get the pot. It's weird to see a square—there."

"It's no secret. I just like to keep it close to my heart," Mother said. She reached into Desiree's bra and took the picture out and held it up for Emily to see.

"You miss him, don't you?" Emily asked, shaking the salt on.

"Yes," Mother said. "Don't you want the butter on first?"

Emily shrugged to show it didn't matter. "Desiree says Chester was like a son to you. Even though you have all these other kids, you liked him best."

"Chester?"

The popping stopped.

"Yeah. How old is he there? He looks like a newborn. Still a bit ugly."

Mother passed Emily the bowl to put the popcorn in and put the picture back in her bra. I closed my eyes, afraid of what would happen to Emily for calling a baby ugly.

"It's not Chester," Mother said. She took the picture back out and held it up in front of her own face. "It looks like him, yes. That was one of the first things I noticed the day we met Chester. Maybe it was the innocent eyes." Mother put the picture back again and took the first handful of popcorn. A piece of popcorn fell to the floor and Emily reached down to pick it up. When her head dropped down she saw me hiding against the wall. I shook my head, and begged her with my eyes not to tell.

"Well, who is it then?" Emily asked. She offered the piece of popcorn from the floor to Shilo.

"My brother," Mother said. "Can't you see the resemblance?"

CHAPTER 16—NICHOLAS

Samantha said that the goal in grade twelve was to go with a guy from another school.

"Another town would have been better," she said when I told her about my crush on a kid from church school. I pretended to be madly in love with Nicholas even though he smelled like potato skins. He was the only guy I knew besides Chester who didn't go to our school. I wrote his name inside pink hearts all over my binder.

I knew it was Emily who told Nicholas I liked him. He asked me out on the back of a note a guy could have never folded. On the front it said *Caroline Quartz is in love with you* in grape coloured ink. I had found purple notes folded exactly the same way in Desiree's pockets, though I was always too afraid to read what they were telling each other. On Nicholas's side of the note it said to nod three times for yes if I would go out with him. It didn't say what to do for no.

The week after my nods I told Dad I was going to hang out at church with some kids from my Sunday school class to listen to the choir practice.

"We're thinking about joining, but we want to make sure it's fun," I told him, using the exact excuse Nicholas had suggested. "Plus, if they're going to make me stand at the very front because I'm one of the shortest, I'm not going to join." I had purposely waited to until after Emily and Desiree had walked out to the parking lot to ask Dad if I could stay late after church.

"It's a long walk home," Dad said before agreeing. "Don't do anything I wouldn't do."

I didn't mean to lie in church. Nicholas had told me that we really were going to watch the choir in the basement, but when they started holding their stomachs and getting into their scales, he pulled me upstairs and showed me how to crouch low in the back pews so no one could see us. He talked in his normal voice, which made me think he knew that nobody was around.

 "What do you mean you don't know if you can have guys over?" Nicholas asked. "Either you can or you can't. I can't have chicks over."

"I think it's okay, probably."

"Well, do you have a basement?"

"A basement, yeah."

I wanted to ask him how he knew he wasn't allowed to have girls over, but Nicholas's mom was deaf and I didn't know if that had anything to do with it. Emily said that's why Nicholas talked so loud, and you had to put up with it and try not to back away. I didn't know if Nicholas had a dad. I had never seen him at church with the family, but then again, Nicholas had never seen me with Mother. I was pretty sure he knew I had one, though.

"If it was Mother's house, she might not let me," I said, making sure he knew I had a mom.

"My mom's dumb about chicks, too. She never used to care. Emily and I used to run through the sprinkler half nude, and all my mom did was laugh. But not anymore. She put a stop to that the day Emily got pubes. I'm a bastard, in case you can't tell. When I'm eighteen, I'm going to find my fuckin' dad. My mom says he's around. She sees him in shop windows and stuff."

Neither of us talked for a minute after Nicholas said the F-word; we just stared up at the church ceiling fans and held hands. I wondered if Nicholas was praying for forgiveness for swearing in church. I said some prayers for him just in case he wasn't. Our fingers were locked awkwardly, with two of my fingers stuffed in one of his finger slots instead of two. I wanted to fix it so badly, but I was worried he would think I wanted to start kissing or something.

Nicholas finally spoke again after I accidentally yawned. "Have you ever been all the way?"

"All the way to where?"

I realized as soon as I said it which way he meant, but it was too late. He was already laughing and pointing between his crotch and mine.

"No. Not really. I mean, I don't even want to. Not yet," I said.

"Me neither. How about halfway?"

"Half. Yeah. I've been there," I said, which wasn't a lie if it meant holding hands in a church beside a guy who said the F-word.

"Do you want to go to the prom?" Nicholas asked. He moved his other hand closer and then jammed two of his fingers into the little front pocket of my jeans. I had always thought it was a pointless pocket until Samantha told me it was her sister's best place to keep tampons.

"You're graduating this year?"

"No, but you are, right?"

"Well, grade twelve, yeah. My dad wants me to take one more year, though," I said. I didn't tell him Mother didn't believe in grade thirteen.

My thigh started to twitch and I could feel a charley horse coming on. I tried to pray it away, but I knew God wouldn't be taking requests at that point.

"So you want to go with me?"

"I thought we already were… going."

"I mean, your prom, dummy."

When I agreed to take Nicholas as my date he said he had to show me something. He grabbed my hand and pulled me out of the pew and down the stairs into the men's room. When the door shut behind us he got on his hands and knees on the bathroom floor and looked under the stalls to make sure they were all empty. He picked the furthest one from the door, kicking it open, and pulling me inside with him. He nudged me up against the side wall and stood with his back against the door while he secured the latch behind him without looking at it. When we were locked inside, he pulled me into him by my back pockets and stuck his tongue in my mouth, swishing it around the inside of my cheeks and up and down my front teeth. It reminded of the ratty washcloth Dad kept in the car for wiping the windows when they fogged up, and I tried not to throw up in my mouth. I can't remember what I did with my own tongue while he licked my mouth, but I mustn't have done much because he kept asking me if I always kissed like that or if I was nervous because we were in church. He tried to put his hand up the front of my shirt, but realized he needed both arms to keep my face close enough so his tongue didn't fall out. When I tried to squirm away, Nicholas said not to worry about sinning. When he was a kid his mom told him God didn't watch over people in bathrooms or bedrooms. She said God didn't believe in looking at other people's private parts. It felt like hours before we finally heard footsteps.

"Jump on the toilet seat, Emily!" Nicholas said to me. Instead of correcting his mistake he told me not to breathe. He flushed the toilet so that the person coming in wouldn't hear me climbing. I crouched and balanced and held my breath while Nicholas stood and took a pee right in front of me. It was the first time I had ever seen a guy go in a toilet standing up. I wished I really was Emily and not me.

When the man came in and went into another stall, Nicholas plugged his nose and laughed silently, reminding me of how Simon acted when Desiree and I taught him how to use the potty. Then suddenly, without any warning, Nicholas opened the latch and ran out. I waited to hear the tap running and Nicholas washing up at the sink, but he was nothing but a drop of pee left on the toilet seat. From my squat I reached for the stall door, pulled it closed, and silently locked it. The choir man must have thought he was alone, because his business got louder. It took him six minutes and what sounded like a full roll of toilet paper to finish, and he hummed the Halleluiah chorus the whole time.

After the man left, I counted for seven minutes and then snuck out of the stall and ran into the ladies room. There was no soap in the pump except the crust caked on around the nozzle. I turned on the hot water and held my hands under as long as I could stand to. When I was sure they were clean, I switched the water to cold and stuck my mouth under the faucet. It was the first time my tongue had ever felt tired. High heels clicked outside the door and I jumped into one of the women's stalls. I stepped onto the toilet and locked the door silently once again.

"I can't believe you missed the service last night. Ellen got the gift of tongues," a voice said.

"She didn't!" another answered.

The women took stalls on either side of mine and continued their talk. I held my hand over my own mouth.

"Yep, right in the middle of Father Marvin's sermon," the one to the left said.

"What on?"

"The sermon? Jesus in the wilderness."

"Of course."

"At first it was just a quiet murmur, you know. But then Ellen stood up and held out her arms and started chirping like a bird. Then she started chanting a whole bunch of sounds," the left one said.

The toilets flushed and I changed positions slightly.

"What do you mean sounds?" the woman on the right said as she opened her door.

"It sounded like that Walt Disney tune, you know the one with the dwarfs *hi hoing?* It was so embarrassing."

The taps turned on and the women washed as they gossiped.

"Dear, God. Imagine how Ellen felt."

"Oh heavens. She didn't mind a bit. She even stood up during the announcements and said she would hold a little meeting in the chapel for anyone who wanted to ask questions about her experience after the service."

I looked through the crack in the stall and saw one of the women pinching her cheeks in the mirror to make them red.

"Did you go to the meeting?" the other one asked.

"Are you kidding? Alice did though, and she said Ellen said it was like having a dream. She said it felt sort of like singing, but she couldn't control what she said. Afterwards, she just kind of woke up."

"What do you mean, sort of singing?"

"You know, like you do in a dream. It sounds good to you, but not to anyone whose listening. That's what Alice said. Not to Ellen, but to me. And Alice usually knows what she's talking about when it comes to these gifty things."

"True. But I don't altogether believe in it, do you?"

"Believe in what?"

"Talking like that. In tongues."

"So long as I don't get it, I don't have a problem with others getting it. Or saying they have it. Ralph would have a fit if it was me."

"So would Frank. I don't think we'd get it anyway. We're not the type, you and me."

"No, we're more the singing type."

The women pulled paper towels out of the dispenser and dried their hands.

"I guess they're some sort of chosen people. Do you think it's just the luck of the draw?" the red cheek one asked.

"What?"

"You know, being one of the..."

"The lucky ones? The tongue people."

"More like unlucky, if you ask me." They both laughed and walked out together.

I waited in the stall for another fifteen minutes before I was sure I didn't hear anyone else in the church. The front door was all locked up and I had to undo the bolt on the inside to let myself out. Before I headed towards home, I tugged on the door and realized there was no way to lock it behind me from the outside.

My tongue hurt as I walked, and when I looked up at the clouds they seemed angry. I could almost hear God's voice inside them urging me to go to the home behind the church and tell Father Marvin that God's house was unlocked. Maybe God would forgive me for what I'd done in church if I did. I convinced myself that if the first stoplight I saw was red I'd go back. If it was green, I'd go home and pray for forgiveness.

When I reached the church house I thought about writing an anonymous note and sticking it on the door, but I was afraid Father Marvin might not notice it until after his church got destroyed. Then he would probably blame the person who wrote the note and demand a confession the next Sunday. He'd make everyone submit a handwriting sample in the wooden plate where the people put their envelope money. I had no idea what kind of things God's employees really knew about the rest of us. Addie said sometimes they got messages in dreams or from scriptures.

I knocked on Father Marvin's door. Some furniture scraped across the ground inside and the front door opened a crack.

"Miss Quartz. Are you okay, peaches?" Father Marvin asked. He opened the door wide and pulled me inside.

"Yes," I said, staring at his feet. He had no socks on, which seemed weird for a minister.

"What do you need, love?" He licked his lips and blinked a few times while he waited for me to answer.

"Well, I just wanted to tell you that the church door isn't locked."

"Sure it is. I locked it myself after choir practice."

"But I was still inside," I said. My throat was dry and he asked me to repeat myself.

"Inside? Whatever were you doing inside the church so late?" he asked. He was grinning, and I felt as though my skin was invisible. Maybe my tongue was hanging out with the word sinner written all over it in invisible ink, and only Father Marvin could see because God gave him special powers. I held it between my teeth and prayed that it wouldn't start talking on its own.

"Were you praying for your mother?" he asked.

"My mother?"

"Sherry, right? Emily called the office this afternoon looking for prayers for your mom. She said she was calling for you and Desiree because your family isn't good at telling people stuff. Poor doll. I'm sorry we missed her today in the prayers for the people. She'll be at the top of the list next week, I promise you that."

CHAPTER 17—ENVELOPES

There was no telling exactly how long Desiree knew Mother had a problem. She said she wouldn't have told me if stupid Father Marvin had kept his mouth shut. Desiree never said anything bad about Emily, but I could tell she wanted to kill her for talking to Father Marvin. Maybe they had pinky sworn not to tell anyone.

Mother stared at the bumps underneath my T-shirt when I asked her about it. She avoided the question for a while.

"Are you wearing a bra, Caroline?"

"I'm seventeen, Mother."

She yanked my collar down over my shoulders to check for straps and then buried her face in her elbow and cried until her sleeve was so wet she had to change arms.

"It's not about your age."

"Then what?"

"I don't know if your Dad ever told you."

Mother put her head back down and held her eyelids closed with her fingers. Even after six years, it still felt awkward sitting on chairs at the table at Maple Manor. I wanted to run out of the room. I could feel Mother's story coming on. I had felt it before, but never this strongly. She really did want to tell me everything.

"Your dad. Did he ever tell you the importance of —checking?"

When Mother finally lifted her head, a few strands of her hair got caught in some sticky juice on the table. Her usual stubble had grown to at least three inches long. It was shortly after Emily's visit that Mother stopped shaving. She'd go a few weeks and then shave it all off and then start growing it again. It had been a few months this time, and I planned on calling it bronze if she asked the colour, even though it was more like salt and pepper.

"It's a small lump," she finally told me. She picked up her left boob like a squirt bottle.

"A lump? Did you see a doctor? Did you tell Dad?"

"I just don't want any of you to get it. You. Desiree. Rosie. Who's going to inherit my bad luck?"

"Who else know about this? Does Neil know?" Neil was working for Miles by then. Miles had used his savings to pay for Neil to go to truck driving school. He said he wanted someone to drive with him on long trips to the USA, but the furthest they ever went was Niagara Falls, and that was just the Canadian side.

Mother said nobody knew about the lump except me.

"And Desiree," I said, but Mother shook her head and said *nobody knows*. I wondered how Desiree and Emily had figured it out if Mother hadn't told them.

"You can't hide something like this," I said, but it didn't sound like my voice. It sounded like something an aunt or a sister should say, not something from a daughter to a mother. I should have been the daughter, standing at the doorway watching two women come up with a plan.

"You have to see a doctor, Mother. We'll borrow Dad's car. I can drive now."

"Leave your dad out of this."

"We don't have to tell him where we're going. I'll just say it's woman stuff. He'll think it's about me."

She didn't think it would work. *He was always better at that stuff. He had bought me my first bra, hadn't he?* She pulled at a strap under my shirt, and I avoided the question.

"He won't follow us. He'll be watching Shilo. Trust me. I'll tell him I heard a whisper inside myself that I don't want to ignore," I said. It was even true about the whisper. I had heard it loud and clear somewhere between my temples. It was my voice, only a deeper version. *Go into the closet and pack a bag. Get your mother to a hospital.* Mother and I latched pinky fingers. Her straight one curved prettily around my crooked one, as it had so many times before. *Pinky swear you'll double brush your teeth. Pinky swear you'll never pick flowers. Pinky swear you won't tell your dad.* I had kept them all, but I knew this one had to be broken.

As soon as the little ones came back from the matinee, Melinda came in and said Dad was waiting in the driveway. I ran out to the car and put my head in the window.

"You can drive home," Dad said, sliding over to the passenger seat.

I shook my head.

"What is the point of you having your license if you never drive, Caroline? I'll drive to the end of the street, but then we're switching places," Dad said, moving back to the driver's seat. "We can put a phonebook in the car if you want. I'm sorry the seat doesn't go any closer. Where's Desiree?"

"We can't go home yet. Mother and I need the car for a while."

"Your Mother wouldn't get in my car," he said, turning on the ignition.

"She will today," I said. "She's sick. Please don't ask any questions."

"Sick? What kind of sick?"

"You and Desiree should plan to stay overnight at Maple Manor. Just in case."

Dad turned the car off.

"In case of what?"

"Like if we need to go back for a second opinion or something in the morning. It's probably nothing," I said, but I knew it wasn't true.

Dad got out of the car and passed me the keys. While I walked back inside he headed toward the chicken coop, and the way he did it so fast told me he heard a whisper too. *Give her the keys. You'll regret it for the rest of your life if you don't.* When I got to Mother's room I realized I had forgotten to remove my shoes. She noticed them and looked away, but didn't say anything.

"We'll need to pack you an overnight bag, just in case," I said, looking around the room.

"In case what?"

"In case we have to wait until tomorrow for an appointment. We'll sleep there if we have to."

"There where?" Mother asked.

I wanted to say we could stay at the apartment, but I knew she wouldn't go for it. Maybe the hospital had overnight rooms. Maybe we could sleep in the car.

"I told Dad we're going to look at prom dresses at a shopping mall," I said, changing the subject.

Mother lay on her stomach and her boobs hung over the bed while I gathered some items to put in a bag.

"How do you know where everything is in my room?" she asked. She didn't seem to have the energy to question my story about the prom dresses.

"You aren't the only one who keeps your underwear in the top drawer of your bureau."

"Dresser," she said. "You still wish you were French, don't you?"

Mother looked at her bare wrist and got up to use the bathroom. I checked my watch. It wasn't her usual time. I went into the closet to find a bag. Mother had filled the open space where Dad's clothes were with floral dresses I had never seen her wear. The pen still hung on the inside of the door, and the same green bag where we always kept the clothes pegs was on top of the shoeboxes. The only other thing that looked different was the circle stool on the floor.

I picked up the bag to dump out the pegs and was surprised how light it was. When I turned it upside down, a stack of brown envelopes wrapped in a rubber band fell out onto the stool. They looked like they were still sealed, but when I looked closely I noticed that each one had been slit open perfectly with a letter knife. The return address was the same on all of them, and I pulled the elastic off and started counting them. Ten, twenty, thirty, one hundred. Inside each envelope was a short letter typed out and addressed to Mother. Aside from the date and the signature, each one was practically identical.

Dear Sherry Quartz,

We regret to inform you that our agency has denied your request for the adoption of Master Chester Richard. Please contact one of our agents for further information regarding your application.

Each letter was signed by a different agent. The one at the top was dated from a few weeks earlier, but at the bottom of the pile there were some from 1982. The last letter was handwritten and addressed to Peter and Sherry Quartz. When I held it up closely, I noticed small trails running up and down the page, and I had to flip the letter over to see the Scotch tape. It had been pieced back together so perfectly I might not have noticed it wasn't a single sheet if I hadn't taken it in my hands and smoothed the folds out with my palms. I took the second last letter out of the pile and felt it. All of the letters from the first few years had been operated on. The sound of paper filled the closet as I remembered the tearing. I could hear the ripping and shredding and breathing as if I was still a twelve-year-old hiding underneath the bed. Mother called my name.

"Sweet Caroline?"

The bathroom door opened. I checked my watch. Only four minutes had passed.

"What are you looking for?"

I shoved the most recent envelope down the back of my pants and looked behind myself to make sure no paper was showing. Then I stuffed all of the other letters back in their original envelopes in the green bag and poked my head out of the closet.

"I'm just looking for an empty bag, Mother."

She joined me in the closet and pulled a knitting bag off of its hanger. She dumped the needles and yarn on the circle stool and handed me the bag. As she walked back to the bed, I recognized the unfinished project. It was the same three rows of baby blue blanket she had been knitting before Melinda was born. I filled the knitting bag with slippers and a nightgown and three pairs of underwear. I grabbed the book from Mother's bedside table and tossed it in.

"*What Masie Knew.* By Henry James. Is it any good?" I asked.

"Terrible. Poor child always put in the middle of things," Mother said, grabbing a pillow to cover her face.

"You have to stop crying, Mother. Dad will worry if he sees your face."

"I'll just say I'm sad to see you growing up so fast," she said. "You and your brassiere."

"Mother."

"You and your prom."

As we drove to the hospital, Mother stared at my toes on the pedals. I couldn't get the envelopes out of my mind. At the stoplights, she whimpered and held on to her breasts. First one. Then the other. Then both.

"It's probably nothing," I said. I wanted to ask if there was any history of cancer in the family, but I knew she didn't know. The doctors would ask. I hoped they didn't ask me.

I drove until I saw a blue H and then followed the directions into St. Mary's. Mother said I should wait in the car to save on paying for parking, but I was sure she would go and have a tea somewhere and then come back and say everything was fine. There were a few coins in the ashtray and I plugged them into the parking metre. It spat out a ticket that said we had one hour and three minutes. As we walked in through the Emergency entrance, I prayed that would be enough time.

"My mother needs her breasts…checked," I said to the lady at the Patient's Registration desk. I knew Mother wouldn't know what to say. I prayed my voice would sound more grown up for once.

"I'm sorry?"

"She felt a thingy in one. Or in both maybe."

A man who looked like he had been attacked by a window came up behind us, and I grabbed Mother's wrist to make sure she didn't run out.

"Who's her family doctor?"

"She doesn't have a doctor."

"Did you bring your health card, Mam?" Mother was too busy peeking down her own shirt to answer.

We followed the purple arrows to Radiology and I walked twice as fast as Mother. Whenever it was time to turn a corner I had to stop and let her catch up.

"Do you feel okay?" I asked.

"Lightheaded."

"I think that's normal for a hospital."

"Oh," Mother said, then her ankles buckled and she fell to the floor. Three nurses rushed to Mother's side and hoisted her up on a stretcher. As they poked things into her, they asked me questions they thought I should know.

"What's her illness?" the nurse in blue asked.

"A lump in her breast."

"Which breast?"

"I think both," I said pointing back and forth at them. I almost hoped it was both. I knew Mother wouldn't let anyone chop off one of anything that was supposed to be two.

"What stage is she at?" the nurse in green asked. She shook her head when I didn't know and told me Mother shouldn't be walking. The wheelchairs were lined up like supermarket buggies at the front entrance. I should have got one for my mother. I should have held her hand at least.

The polka-dot nurse helped me wheel Mother into the elevator and up to a cold white bed in room 13B. I waited for Mother to resist, but instead she curled up like a caterpillar and asked for another blanket. It took four hours and twelve minutes for the first tests to come back. I called Dad from a payphone and told him all I knew about Mother's condition.

"She has stage 4," I said, reading from the paper that the doctor had given to me. "Advanced Met-ast-at-ic breast cancer."

"Cancer?"

"The doctor wants you to come down to discuss the options. You're still her husband," I said.

"What kind of options?"

"I think a bone marrow transplant," I said. I had overheard some doctors talking about it in the lounge while I was waiting for

Mother's door to open. "I think it's when one of your children donates part of their good bone to you. Probably the oldest. Neil—"

"No, Caroline. That wouldn't do her any good."

"You don't think he'd do it? He would for Mother. He'd do anything for her."

Dad didn't speak for a few seconds. When I asked if he was still there he spat out his reason.

"It can't be Neil. Neil doesn't have her blood. He doesn't have our bones."

"What are you talking about?" I asked.

Instead of answering my question, Dad pretended like he hadn't told me anything. He said Miles would drop him off at the hospital. Miles could take the Creek Kids and Desiree to the apartment so we'd all be closer.

When I got back to Mother's room she was lying on her side staring at the bags of coloured liquid flowing into her.

"What did Dad say?" she asked. I had told her I was going to get tea, but all I came back with was the quarter that the phone had spat back to me.

Neil's not your son. "He's on his way," I said. "Sorry."

I stood looking at Mother and thinking of Neil. I wondered who and where Neil's mom was if not right in front of me. *Maybe she was looking for her one true love.* The nurse told me to sit down.

"She's whiter than the sheets," Mother said. "Maybe you should get a doctor for her."

"She's in shock," the nurse said. "It's normal. She's your child."

Dad arrived smelling like the chicken coop, and as soon as he walked in he pulled up a chair and sat down beside Mother. He took both of her hands and called her *Cherry Love*. The air began to taste like candy.

"The nurse said you can sit right in the bed," I said, but Dad didn't look up at me. He looked so natural sitting there at her bedside, as if he had been doing it for years.

"I brought you a new razor," he said, patting his front pocket and then touching Mother's hair with his hands. Mother smiled and nodded, and Dad began to cut it off right away.

The doctor came in as Dad finished shaving Mother's head. He sat at the edge of the bed and introduced himself as Dr. Maxwell. *You can call me Mack for short,* he said. He wore white all over, and his yellow teeth stood out as he smiled through his bad news. On his lap was a three-ring binder with giant silver rings, and it was already filled with papers. Mother's name was written in block letters up the spine. Seeing it written that way reminded me of one of the headlines from inside the shoebox. ORPHAN QUARTZ CROWNED LOCAL HERO. Then I thought of the envelopes again—all those torn letters. That's what she had been ripping.

"I'm afraid I don't have much in the way of comforting news," the doctor said.

"He means I'm going to die."

"You'll be fine, Cherry."

Dr. Maxwell told us we all had a right to the truth. There were almost no healthy cells left, and he didn't just mean in her breasts.

"What is the success rate? After the surgery?" Dad asked.

"We don't see any reason to remove the breasts at this time. Truthfully, it's gone beyond that."

"I mean the bone transplant," Dad said.

I shot him Neil's you-weren't-supposed-to-tell-anyone eyes, but Dad was fixed on the doctor.

"It hasn't spread to the bone, but it has metastasized to the liver. Do you mean a bone marrow transplant, sir?"

"Yes. She'll have to have one, right?"

The doctor explained about the new research in stem cells. How American doctors were experimenting with self-transplants in breast cancer patients.

"It's fascinating, but it isn't used in Canada."

"She's American," Dad said. "Born in Connecticut."

"It's still in the research stage."

"I don't care about which stage it is," Dad said. His face went purple and he made a fist. I grabbed his arm before he could punch the wall.

We're going to start her on chemotherapy first thing tomorrow. If Sherry agrees."

TARA BENWELL

"Of course she agrees," Dad said.

"Your wife has to make the final decision, of course. Are there any other children besides Carolyn?"

"Nine," Mother said. She was still staring at the liquids that were pumping into her, and didn't seem to care that the doctor was biting his nails before touching her, or that he had said my name wrong.

"Nine-year-olds can be sensitive to this type of thing. I have a ten-year-old and last year his grandma was given six months. Anyway, I'm sure big sister here will be a big help, and we have some great psychologists at the hospital. Is it a boy or a girl, Sherry? Your other child."

"No, nine as in nine other children," I said. Dad looked down at his feet and then stood up.

The doctor stared at his notes and tapped his fingers on the chart in front of him as if he were counting.

"How old is your youngest, Sherry?"

"Six," I said, before Mother could give the number in months.

"And when did you stop breastfeeding?"

"How is she supposed to remember that?" Dad asked.

"Approximately."

When Mother didn't answer, Dr. Maxwell looked at Dad and then me and then back at Mother. He asked her one more time before he smiled his yellow smile and said he *got it.* Two puddles were forming on the front of Mother's gown.

"Well, if you got it, then give it to us," Dad said, and the doctor did.

"Women who develop this cancer often notice changes in their breasts earlier than this. Not right away, but by now, yes. I suspect you've had these for a while, Sherry."

When Mother refused to nod or agree, the doctor began to lecture Dad. He said early detection was the key. He said lactating women are less likely to notice something the size of a pinhead turning into a pearl.

"Or in your wife's case, ping pong balls."

"Why?" Dad asked.

"Because her breasts are constantly—engorged."

I tried to excuse myself to go pay for parking, but Dr. Maxwell told me visiting hours were over and we'd have to come back in the morning. Before he walked out of the room, he gave Mother a gentle tap on her head like you might do a child. Then he looked at dad and offered a speck of hope.

"Not all patients lose their hair, you know. She might be one of the lucky ones."

"She's alive, isn't she," Dad said, but the doctor was already in the hall.

"That's only because of you," Mother said to Dad, and reached her hands out to him.

I knew they were talking about the day at the circus, and by the way they didn't hide their smiles it was almost as if they knew I knew too.

Dad pulled his lip balm out of his pocket and applied some to Mother's lips. He kissed it off and then told her we'd be back before sunrise. Even though he spoke softly, and his voice sounded squeaky like a girl, I was almost sure he called her something other than *Poor Sherry* or *Cherry*. I was sure he called her something with one syllable like *Nel*.

"After ten," the nurse said. She was changing a bag on Mother's IV pole, and I saw her check the name on the door of Mother's room and look at Dad with squinty eyes.

Dad and I walked towards the car without speaking. I could tell by how he walked ahead of me that he hadn't forgotten about Neil.

"I know what you're thinking," he finally said.

"What?" *My Dad's having an affair. Neil's not my real brother. Mother still wants Chester. Shilo must be getting thirsty by now.*

"You think she's going to die."

"Oh."

He let me in the passenger side and closed my door.

"Caroline. You have to be strong for your brothers and sisters. You're the one they're going to go to, not me."

"Okay, Dad. Just one thing."

"What?"

I didn't want to ask, but I knew I had to. "Which ones are my real brothers and sisters?"

CHAPTER 18—LIBRARY

We were sitting in the parkade of King's Tower with the keys still in the ignition and the headlights shining on the concrete wall when Dad told me the short version of Neil's adoption, and how it all happened before they came to Canada. He didn't say Neil was *why* they moved to Canada, but he did admit that the move happened shortly after he became their son. Dad said he never would have told me if it wasn't a medical thing.

"It's not my place to tell," Dad said.

"Does Neil know?"

"Of course Neil doesn't know."

"But what if it was Neil having a medical thing? You'd have to—"

"It's not Neil's thing," Dad said. "It was the right thing to do at the time. End of story. Now, what are we going to do about Mother?"

I looked at the back seat and wished I could ask Dad how a story could have an end without a middle. The buttons on Mother's overnight bag stared back at me, and I remembered that I still had one of the letters stuffed down my pant leg. I wondered if I should mention the pile of envelopes to Dad. *Did you know she never gave up on Chester?*

"When are you going to tell Neil?" I asked instead.

"In the morning, I guess. He's going to take it the hardest, I think. Besides Shilo. There's no way of keeping it from him, though."

"You have for over twenty years, haven't you?"

Dad looked confused for a moment and then waved my question off. "Not that, Caroline. I thought you meant tell him about

Mother." I grabbed Mother's bag from the back seat and decided not to mention the letters.

In the apartment, Shilo was asleep, as if dead on top of Desiree on the pullout. She was sucking two fingers and her thumb, and Desiree's eyes and mouth were parted half open.

"Where's Mother?" she asked.

"Hospital."

"Knocked up again," Desiree said. "Emily predicted it when I described how Mother was holding herself like that in the closet. She said women get sore boobs when they get pregnant. I didn't believe her, though. I still don't believe it. It's dangerous having babies her age, you know. People can die having babies. It's not always the babies that don't make it. That's what Father Marvin said when Emily told him."

"We'll talk about it in the morning. Take your sister to bed," Dad said.

"The beds are full. We don't have room for another sister."

"There isn't going to be another sister!" I said, but I didn't say there wasn't going to be another brother either. I inched in beside Rosie and prayed that the night would last forever. That none of us would ever wake up, and if we did that it would all be a dream. I dreamt that the mail kept coming and coming. All of the mailboxes in the lobby of the apartment were ours. The envelopes were addressed to me, and instead of paper, each one was stuffed with milk. Brown milk. But it didn't taste like chocolate. After a while it turned into blue milk and green milk. Then pink milk with red polka dots. The mailman was Neil in disguise. I told him to stop pretending he had an important job. He only had one leg. The twins pushed him in a red wagon all over the country trying to find different hospitals. He told them where to deliver the mail. Shilo rode on his lap. It was Shilo, except with Mother's head. The doctor arrived in Dad's car and put Shilo's head back on. Then he tried to take mine off and give me Mother's. At the end, we all took off our heads and threw them in the TV box for Miles to take back to America.

It felt like a minute had passed when Dad came in to wake us up in the morning.

"What do you mean, wake up?" Desiree said. It had been years since anyone had told Desiree and me when to sleep and when to get out of bed. The Creek Kids got up instantly and stood in line for the bathroom, oldest to youngest. None of us were wearing pajamas. Dad took me aside and told me that Neil and Miles were on their way to Kitchener, but he didn't think we should wait before we told the others.

"What did Neil say?"

"I'm hungry," Shilo said from the back of the line. "Where's Mummy?" She shoved her toothbrush in her mouth and started sucking.

"Caroline and I have something to tell you all," Dad said. He shut the bathroom door and we followed him to the pullout, and formed a sloppy circle around him.

"Where's Mummy?" Shilo said again, punching herself in the mouth this time after she said it. Desiree looked at me and mouthed the word *Mummy* and I drew a question mark in the air beside my ear. Dad told Shilo to go to her room.

"I don't have a room in the city," she said. Dad motioned for Simon to take Shilo out of the circle, but when he tried to pick her up she kicked him in the ear. Dad pointed to the twins and they got up and dragged her down the hall by her underarms.

"Put her in the top bunk and take down the ladder," Dad said.

There were screams, then foot stomps on the wall. Then silence.

"Mother is ill," Dad said when the twins returned to the circle. He looked at me, even though I was the only one who already knew.

"What's wrong?" Desiree asked. She coughed and held her stomach like she did when she had her period cramps.

"Cancer. Probably."

"Not probably. For sure," I said, thinking of the binder with Mother's name.

"Cancer! Where?" Rosie asked.

"Up top," Dad said.

"In her breast," I said. "Breasts."

Desiree got down on the floor and spread out like a jellyfish, and the other girls collected closer to Dad.

"Cancer is hereditary," Simon said, standing up. "Maybe we should look into things. Like maybe she had some brothers or sisters or something. People find people these days, you know. "

"Who do we have here? Another Emily?" Desiree said to Simon. Desiree never believed Emily about the baby picture in Mother's bra being her brother. She thought Emily changed her mind about the missing boy being good-looking. *I think we'd know if we had an uncle,* I had heard her say.

"She already has cancer," I said. "It's us we have to worry about. In the future, I mean." *Us, not including Neil.*

"Who's going to tell Shilo?" Simon asked with a finger pen to his palm.

"It won't make a difference," Dad said. "She doesn't know the word cancer."

"Maybe not, but she knows the word breast," I said. Nobody spoke for a few seconds until Shilo screamed again.

"Mother should have been born a snake," Simon said, lying back down on the pullout.

"True," Rosie said, lying beside him. "Snakes don't have them."

"Have what?" Dad asked

"Breasts," I said. I knew Rosie wouldn't have the guts to say the word out loud. Her ant hills were growing and it was obvious she was doubling up on T-shirts.

"I meant snakes don't get cancer," Simon said. "They're immune."

When Shilo started eating toilet paper and stuffing rolls of it down her shirt, we knew it was time for one of us to explain Mother's disease. None of us volunteered.

"I need my milky," she told Neil after his attempt at an explanation. "You're gonna make me die."

"You never should have used the d word," Dad said. "Now she's going to say it all the time."

"Die? Fuck! How do you talk about people who are going to be dead without saying die!" Neil said.

Shilo shoved her fist in her mouth and wiggled out of my hand as soon as she saw Mother through the hospital room doorway. She climbed onto Mother's lap and pulled at the hospital gown trying to get at her drink through the wide armpit and then the V-neck. Mother grabbed a carton of milk from her hospital tray and forced the bendy straw into Shilo's mouth. "Milky," Mother whispered, but Shilo shoved Mother's hand away and threw the carton towards the curtain that separated Mother from her roommate. Dad walked into the room with a get-well-soon balloon, even though Mother was only allowed two visitors at a time.

"Could you take your daughter out of here, please?" Mother said. "She's being a baby."

Mother's roommate pulled the curtain open and put on her glasses.

"Did you say baby, Sherry? Let me get a look."

"Shilo, this is Mrs. White. Say you're sorry for waking her," Dad said.

"Milky," Shilo said pointing at Mother's wet spots.

"Cancer's no fun, is it?" Mrs. White said. "So, where's the baby?"

Dad looked at Mother's roommate and then at Shilo.

"She means the baby *baby*." Mother said. "You just missed it. Peter took it into the nursery, didn't you sweetie pie? They say my milk is too dangerous for the baby now. The nurses are going to teach him to take a bottle."

"Him? I could have sworn you said you had a baby girl." Mrs. White said.

"No. It's a boy. Chester," Mother said.

Dad and I looked at different walls when Mrs. White said it must have been all of the shit she was taking that got her all muddled up and thinking that Mother had said she had a baby girl. The part about the baby girl didn't surprise me. What I couldn't believe was that Mother had called a baby an *it*, even if it was a make-believe baby without a Neil Diamond name. Mother detested announcements that welcomed babies to the world that way. The midwife learned to say it the right way after Rosie was born. *She's a girl,* Marie said, each time she passed a new baby to Mother.

When Dad said he'd take Shilo back to the apartment, Mother asked him to give Chester a kiss for her on his way past the nursery.

"Give all the kids kisses," Mother said.

"What do you mean all? How many kids have you got?" Mrs. White asked.

"Ten," Mother said. "Five boys and five girls." She held out both hands and wiggled them in front of her as if she had freshly painted nails.

"In an apartment. Shit!"

Mrs. White said she needed a cigarette and rang her bell to get one of the nurses to wheel her outside. When everyone else was gone, Mother motioned for me to get up and close her door. She patted her bed and closed her eyes when I sat next to her. Before she fell asleep, she told me it was important to humour the dying, that it didn't hurt to tell a white lie in times like these.

As Mother napped, I ate everything on her food tray and counted in my head what colour of lie it really was. I scraped the skin off the oatmeal and ate it with a plastic fork. When I was done, I ate the dry scone and washed it all down with Mother's pineapple Jell-O. As I ate, I couldn't stop the math equations from popping into my head. *If you took away Neil and added Chester you'd still get four boys and six girls. If you kept Neil and took me away then added Chester, and if Melinda never happened. You could take away Shilo, maybe. Half of Shilo?*

Mother woke up with tears and slobber dribbling down her chin and neck.

"What's wrong?" I asked when I realized she wasn't just snoring.

"I'm dying and nobody even bothers to bring me flowers," Mother said. "Look at all of hers." She pointed at Mrs. White's windowsill. "She probably has a flower for every colour God made. All I get is this dumb balloon." Mother pulled the balloon down to eye level and punched it as hard as she could. Then she pulled it down a second time and traced the words with her finger. "What's the point of getting well when all you're going to do is die anyway?"

The second time we met Doctor Maxwell he pulled a blank page out of Mother's binder and wrote a six inside a circle and held it up for us to see. Mother closed her eyes, and neither Dad nor I dared to ask if he meant weeks or days. Mother said she didn't care how much time she had to live. What she cared about was getting things in proper order for the future.

"I'll need your help, Caroline," she said holding her pinky out to me. I assumed she meant help getting things right with God, but I didn't know where to start. I figured I should probably go to Father Marvin so he could change his prayers. Desiree had asked Emily to tell him she was wrong about the pregnancy, but Emily said she didn't want to say the word *breast* to a priest, and she was sure he would ask what kind of disease it was.

Instead of walking to the house behind the church, I went to the library, and when the librarian asked me if there was something particular I was looking for, I chickened out and told her I needed a book on sewing.

"Fantastic. What are you making?" she asked. "I was afraid sewing was a lost art."

"A dress for the prom," I said.

"For whom?" she asked.

"For me," I said.

"Isn't it a little early for that?" the librarian asked, looking at her watch, instead of a calendar.

"I'm graduating this year. My mother already has the material," I said. "I just want to make sure she does it—properly. She doesn't usually use a plan."

She looked at me from top to bottom, and then asked me what colour it was going to be.

"Red," I said.

"Scarlet or candy apple? Or barn?"

"Scarlet."

"How risqué." She took me to the fashion section and picked out a few pattern books, licking her finger before she flipped through the pages. After she had pointed out some of her favourites, she told me to swing by her desk if I had trouble finding what I needed. I wondered if she had favourites in every book in the library, and I wondered what was risky about wearing red. The only reason I had said red was because Nicholas said red was the sexiest colour on earth and he wouldn't be caught dead with a prom date in yellow or purple. I was still thinking about wearing yellow because if I did then Nicholas might catch on that I didn't want to be kissed or touched by a guy who peed on my foot and couldn't even remember my name. *You're still going with me, right chicky? I already got my tux, so you better not change your mind, chicky.*

I thanked the librarian and watched her return to her desk. I pulled the sewing books out one after another and pretended to browse through them. I felt her watching me, and when our eyes met, I was sure she knew I had lied about needing a sewing book.

I decided to photocopy a page from one of the books to make it look like I was finished looking. Even though the librarian was nowhere near the photocopier, I tried to find a pattern that had at least one red dress on it, just in case she asked to have a *look-see*. The only red dress I could find in the whole book was one that was short at one side and had one sleeve. I was about to photocopy it when I realized that the photocopier was black and white. It didn't matter what colour dress I printed, even if the librarian was going to ask to see the one I picked. I turned the pages until I found a long white dress with puffy sleeves that looked like clouds.

The word *will* came to me while I was photocopying the poofy dress. I knew Mother didn't need a will since she didn't work or have any money of her own, but I figured a book on wills would be in a similar section as the ones on dying. I went to a library assistant this time. She didn't look much older than me.

"My grandmother wants to make a will. Can you help me find a book on it?" I asked her.

"Sure, but you know the rule, right? No taking out books for other people."

"Oh okay. I'll just photocopy the pages Grandmother needs." I looked around to see if anyone was listening to us. It was the dumbest rule I had ever heard. *Was the library checking fingerprints now?*

"Doesn't your grandmom have a library card?"

"Ah, no, she doesn't have much money."

The library assistant put her hand on my shoulder and whispered, "Library cards are for free, sweetie."

"Well, she can't always pay the fines 'cause she can't get a ride to the library to take things back on time. My dad is sometimes too busy. She can't hold her cane *and* her books." After I said it, I wished I'd said my mom instead of my dad. I wasn't sure, but I figured it was probably more of a mom's job to look after grandparents.

The assistant nodded and went to the librarian's desk to find out about wills. When I realized she was talking to the same librarian who had helped me the first time, I made a stupid decision. I ran out of the library, forgetting I was still holding the dressmaking book that I hadn't checked out.

Dad picked me up at the library and blamed my stealing on Mother's cancer.

"We knew she was lying when she said the book was for her grandmother. Kids always use their grandmoms when they're making excuses. Even when they don't have grandmoms," the library assistant said.

"I think it's amazing that your mother is still going to make your dress, even though she is living in the hospital," the librarian said. She scratched her chin with my confiscated library card.

"Speaking of the hospital, we have to get there now," Dad said. "Sorry about this. Again."

We started walking out of the library, but the librarian called me back. "You forgot something," she said and handed me my library card. She also handed me a book on wills, and said it was due back in three weeks.

I chose the very back seat in the car and looked out at the drivers behind us and wondered how many of them had dead parents and how many had been to the prom. I wondered whether or not the library kept a file on people who broke the rules. If it did, it might also keep a list of the books everyone had taken out over the years. *Maybe library helpers used the list to do cross-checking. They're probably told to check on people like me who accidentally steal books.*

TARA BENWELL

By the time we got to the hospital I had convinced myself that the librarian had reviewed my library history, including the book I had taken out in grade nine before my first boy-girl party. Samantha had invited me to sleep over at her house, saying we should practice games that her sister talked about. She told me we might have to play a game like Truth, Dare, Double Dare, Promise to Repeat. For Truth she said you had to tell something about yourself that other people might not believe. "It could either be true or made up, and everyone else at the party will have to guess," Samantha said. She also said Kyle Fitzpatrick might be there.

"My mother and dad are actually—cousins," I told Samantha in our practice session for the Truth Dare game. "Weird, huh?"

"First?"

"First what?" I asked.

"First cousins."

"Yes, first they were cousins. Before they were our parents, I mean."

Samantha said she didn't believe me, even though I told her twice without blinking or flinching. When I started to say it a third time, I could tell she was starting to change her mind.

"If that's true, then you're... then you can't have kids, Caroline. Not ever."

"Why not?"

"Cause if you do your kids will turn out to be freaks or something. It's like really, really bad for first cousins to do *it*. It's like one of the worst sins or something. I forget the word."

"Incest!" Samantha's sister said from the doorway. It wasn't the first time we caught her listening to us, but this time Samantha looked happy to see her. Samantha told me she had to go to the bathroom and when she came back she was with her mom who said Samantha wasn't feeling well and that she was going to drive me home. As I packed my knapsack, I told Samantha I hoped she felt good enough to go to the party the next day. I told her I was just kidding about the cousin thing. "I'm the best liar I know," I said. *It's in my blood.*

Samantha's mom wouldn't let her go to the boy-girl party the next day, and since I didn't want to go on my own I went to the library instead. I must have looked over my shoulder twenty times while I sorted through the card catalogue until I found a book called *Kissing Cousins.* I hid the book between ten others I randomly pulled off the shelves, and while the books were being stamped I turned my back on the librarian and pretended to look at a brochure about literacy. I had tried to read bits of the book in bed at night, but it was mostly about a lady who grew up hating *Grandpapa* and there was nothing on brothers and sisters in the index. When it was time to bring the books back, I slipped *Kissing Cousins* in the after-hours slot, even though the library was still open.

*

The librarian wasn't the only one who felt sorry for me for having a parent with cancer. Samantha's sister offered to lend me her prom dress when she heard that Mother was maybe dying. She said it was the least she could do.

"My little sister said you were planning on wearing red," she said on the phone.

"Yeah, I think so."

"Well, I'm not convinced it's your best colour, but it's mine, and that's what I wore, of course. You're welcome to borrow it. Actually, you don't have to give it back because my mom shortened it for you."

"Thanks."

"You'll have to stuff your bra and maybe pin up the straps. Sorry. It just came out. I didn't mean to talk about bras."

"It's okay," I told the dead air. Vanessa had already put the phone down on the counter.

Before Samantha came back on I heard Vanessa in the background telling their mother how she had accidentally said the b word to me and how she felt god awful about it. Their mother thought she meant *bitch* and Vanessa got sent to her room for it.

The last Friday before the prom Samantha brought her sister's dress to school in an empty cereal box.

"Do you want me to try it on for you?" I asked Dad when I got home.

"Wait for Mother. She'll want to see it too," Dad said.

I reminded Dad that the prom was in one week, but he hadn't given up hope that Mother was going to get out of the ICU. I unstuck the maxi pads from where Vanessa had stuffed the cups, and tried it on for him anyway. It was the kind that was supposed to go down to your ankles, but Samantha's mom had shortened it so much it went just below my knees.

"Maybe I shouldn't go," I said, standing in the hall with the dress on. I figured he'd at least tell me I looked like a princess, but he didn't even look up.

As I changed into my pajamas, I noticed Dad going up to the rooftop patio. He said he was taking the garbage out, but he didn't take any bags with him. What he did have was the circle stool. Rosie and Simon had brought it to the apartment in case Shilo needed timeouts. They said Mother used it as Shilo's thinking chair since she didn't have her own tree chair. Instead of making Shilo get into her snowsuit and sit outside on a tree chair when she did something wrong, Mother let her ride the circle stool to the closet to do her thinking. Simon said half the time Mother ended up joining Shilo in there and that they sometimes fell asleep on top of the shoeboxes.

When Dad closed the front door behind him, I looked out through the peephole and saw him rolling the stool towards the rooftop stairwell. Simon saw me watching and came to look.

"What do you think he's going to do?" he asked. "Chuck it?"

"Let's go find out," I said.

"I'll get Rosie," Simon said, turning around.

"Forget Rosie for once, Soolaimon," I said. Simon looked more afraid to leave Rosie out than he did to spy on Dad, but he tiptoed out of the apartment and up the stairs without arguing. The door to the outside was cracked open with a triangle of wood, and Dad was sitting on the circle stool at the edge of the building, striking matches. As each tiny flame disappeared over the edge of the building he whispered a single phrase. It was hard to hear with the wind, but after a few minutes Simon and I turned to each other and mouthed the words.

"She loves me. She loves me not."

CHAPTER 19—LAST WISH

Mother told Dr. Maxwell that if he didn't let her go home to die in her own room she'd burn herself alive. The doctor told Dad not to worry. He said that Mother barely had enough energy to wake up and eat, but Mrs. White told me Mother was feistier after dark. She said Mother had already convinced three of the night janitors to help her go through with the suicide.

"I keep my lighter in my bra," she told me. She pulled down her gown to pull it out, and then asked me if I had even noticed her scars.

"She must *want* to live," one of the nurses said to another as she taped up a note on Mother's door that said not to give patients matches. "She can't possibly expect *him* to look after all those kids."

"The one in there now is older than she looks," the other whispered. "Surely she'll help out when things go south."

After a week of hearing Mother's threats, Dr. Maxwell gave in. "We can't keep her here if she's going to refuse treatment," Dr. Maxwell told Dad and me in the hallway. He walked into the room and told Mother there was a lot of paperwork to do before she could go home. "It's not like I can just send you on your merry way this minute. I'll have to pull some strings. But I promise we'll get you home, Sherry. If not soon, by your birthday at the latest."

Birthday? I wondered if Mother had written her real birthday when she filled out her health form. Dr. Maxwell always held on tightly to his binder, and I didn't know how I'd ever find a way to look inside it to find the date she had given. *If not soon, by your birthday.* Maybe it was his way of saying that if she didn't start telling them more information that he would keep her there until the day she died.

Something about the way he said *promise* made me think he really was going to unplug her, though. The following morning I convinced Dad I needed to borrow the car to shop for shoes with heels and straps for the prom.

"But what if they release her today?" Dad asked. "What am I going to do with her until you get back? It's not like she can take a taxi with me back to the apartment."

I offered to call the hospital from a payphone, but Dad told me not to bother. We both knew that *a little* in hospital time meant *a lot*.

I didn't need a new pair of shoes for the prom. Samantha's cousin already had a pair of flats she said went perfect with Vanessa's red mermaid dress, and they were kid size. The reason I needed the car was to go to Maple Manor and return the letter from the agency I had stolen from Mother's closet. Something told me it would be one of the first places Mother would go when she got home, and the last thing I wanted was for Mother to go to bed angry with me one night and never wake up again. I wished the agency would call and say, *Here, take him. He's yours for the rest of your life.* Even if just for one week.

The circle stool had left a ring on the carpet inside Mother's closet, and I sat in the centre of it and looked around. Everything was the same as we had left it the day we left for the hospital. The clothes were still hung chromatically with the blue jeans in the middle and the unused dresses on the right. Mother's shoes were arranged along the floor. Winter. Summer. Fall. The Spring ones were outside on the front porch with the others. The only thing that looked out of place was the knitting needles and the baby blue yarn Mother had ripped out when I asked her for a bag.

I took the envelope out of my sock and removed the letter. I tried to read it one more time, but my version of what it should have said kept popping into my head.

Dear Sherry. Give it up. You're never going to get the kid. There's more to raising kids than cleaning and walking them. Besides, no kid deserves to lose more than one mother. Concentrate on just living, why don't you?

I put the letter back on the top of the pile in the clothes peg bag and tried to imagine what Mother and Dad's mother would have looked like the day she took them to the circus. I wondered if the shoebox that had the newspapers in it was still in the closet where Chester and I had left it. I had been too afraid to look since the day I heard the ripping and tearing. The day Mother found out I was moving to the city.

I turned off the light and got on my belly to look under the dresses. The shoebox glowed from behind the sweater coat where it had always been. As soon as I had the box in my hands, I knew I had to get out of the house. I heard the whisper that was my own voice, only wiser. *Take it with you. Get the box out of this house. Go now, before you chicken out.* I unlocked the back of the car and placed the box on the rear facing seats. I wished I had a marker to write BOX on my hand so I didn't forget to take it inside and hide it from Dad. It wasn't like a regular shoebox. It was old and crushed and had American spelling. *Family Favorite Footwear.* I didn't know if Dad would recognize the box or not.

I drove back to the apartment and glared at anyone who drove close to my rear. *What if a cop pulled me over to check the car for drugs? What if I got into an accident and the articles blew all over the road? Why didn't I belt the box to the seat?* It wasn't until I started to pull into the parking garage that I realized I had forgotten to call Dad to make sure Mother wasn't being released from the hospital. I half expected to see him pushing her in a wheel chair at the front entrance of King's Tower, but as I pressed the button to open the gate it was Desiree's ponytail that caught my eye in the side-view mirror. She was standing over by the front doors throwing pennies into the fountain. There was a person standing directly behind her, and I recognized the tennis shoes instantly. I heard Desiree laughing and squealing even with my windows closed.

"Stop it, Nicholas! I need to make one more wish!"

As Nicholas kissed her behind her ear and across her shoulder, the parking gate came down on the hood of the car and the next thing I remembered was Dad sitting beside me at the end of Desiree's bed telling me that a car was just a thing. *Your mind is probably somewhere else, right now, Caroline. You shouldn't blame yourself.*

Everything came back to me quickly when Dad said the word *car.* The closet. The shoebox. Desiree and Nicholas. The kiss that didn't look nearly as bad on someone else. The only thing I didn't remember was the parking gate narrowly missing my head.

"Do you want to show me your new shoes?" Dad said, pointing to the shoebox. "I found this box in the car."

*

The phone rang twice, three times, four.

"Desiree! Pick it up," I shouted from behind the bathroom door.

Samantha's sister had pinned all of my hair in a blob on top of my head, leaving two loose corkscrews dangling in front of my eyes for sex appeal. My painted toes were separated with little sponges that she said would help keep my nails from petting each other when I drove home to get dressed.

"It's not for me!" Desiree said.

The ringing stopped. Then it started again, this time louder. I stepped into the dress and zipped it up while I walked towards the phone. Desiree and I both reached it on the eighth ring. She picked it up, put the receiver to my ear, and walked away. I held the phone against my cheek with my wrist, trying not to crinkle the paint on my fingernails, which I had decided to do on my own even though Vanessa had told me not to. The prom was starting in two hours and I had decided at the last minute to go in a group with Samantha and a few other dateless girls.

"Hello?"

"Caroline. Sweetie?"

"Dad?"

"We lost her."

That was all he said. Then he listened to me wail into the phone, telling me to hush, but not at all in a *be quiet* kind of way. I pushed the warm tears into my ears, dragging sticky polish against my cheeks.

My first cry was over faster than I had rehearsed in my head. When I was done, I looked up at the ceiling and wondered whether Mother was flapping above me, staring down at my dress and makeup. *Would she think she ruined my prom? Would she approve of the red shoes even though they weren't the same shade as the dress? What sign could I make to tell her it was okay?* I didn't want to go to the stupid prom anyway.

"Dr. Maxwell says if you guys want to see her—I mean, you know, if you want to say goodbye — you'll have to come down now. I mean, soonish."

"How?"

"Take a cab. Use the emergency Visa."

"We could maybe get the limo to drop us off," I said, looking at my watch. It would be pulling up in less than fifteen minutes.

"I'm sorry Caroline. About the prom I mean."

"We'll call a cab."

"Can you put Desiree on?"

"I'll tell her. You go back to Mother—Mother's room. Is she still there?"

"Yes. It just happened. It's been less than five minutes."

Desiree heard me crying and skipped into the kitchen as soon as she heard me hang up. She sat down beside me on the floor against the fridge and put her I'm-sad-too face on.

"I have an announcement to make," she said, grabbing my hands to inspect my self-manicure. "I am truly sorry for everything that happened between me and Nicholas."

"Forget about Nicholas."

"No. You would be going to the prom with him instead of those geeky girls if it weren't for me. I just really wanted to get invited. It's not easy being the one who gets everything second. Well, most things. But I'm turning over a new leaf. I swear."

"Desiree."

"And I've decided that to punish myself for stealing Nicholas I won't go to my own prom next year, no matter how many invitations I get. And, on top of that, I'll fix your nails. Free of charge." She dug a nail into my polish to see if it would scrape off easily.

"Desiree, that was Dad on the phone."

"So?"

"Desiree, Mother is—"

"Oh no. Not again."

Mother had been having mini strokes all week. Her brain would cut out while you were talking to her and she would sit in her hospital bed staring at you with her fork ready to dip in her pudding.

"It's not that, Desiree.

"Oh, thank God. Those things creep me out." She pulled some tissues out of the box on my lap.

"Desiree."

"Give me your right hand first. God, we'll have to get the remover out and start all over."

"Desiree. It's Mother."

"What about her?"

"We lost her."

I took Desiree's hands and sat facing her like we did as kids when we played cats cradle with a piece of string.

"I thought they weren't going to change rooms on us anymore."

"She's gone."

"What do you mean gone, Caroline?"

"Dead, Desiree. Mother is dead."

Dad knew all of the proper language to use around death because of his old job at the newspaper.

"It's called making the arrangements," Dad said to Neil who kept asking what was going to be done with the corpse. Desiree chose a funeral home by doing eeny meeny miney mo in the yellow pages. She said she wanted to be part of it all, but she didn't want to actually go to the building with the dead bodies.

"If you're making me come you could at least let me drive!" Neil shouted from the rear-facing seat of the station wagon. He had started in the passenger seat beside Dad and had crawled back three rows until he felt settled. He and Dad and I took up all three rows of seating.

There was a sign in the lobby of the funeral home that said to *Please Be Quiet* because there was a service in session. An easel was set up beside a table of tea and goodies. The dead woman was Ethel Cranberry. There were snapshots of her from various stages of her life. Ethel in a brass band. Ethel's graduation. Ethel as a Brownie pack leader. Ethel with her husband and child. Around the easel was a border of wallet-sized school photos in colour. *We love you Grandma* was written in children's writing across the bottom.

A set of doors swung open in front of us and a hoard of people filed out holding each other in threes or more. The funeral director spotted us and whisked us away from the mourners. We followed him down a long corridor and into a silent room with white walls. The ceilings had blue clouds and silver doves.

"Welcome, Mr. Quartz, Caroline, Neil," the funeral director said. "My name is Oscar Brown. I'll be assisting you with the arrangements."

"Thank you for taking us on such short notice," Dad said as though these things were usually planned. Neil and I stood behind like little children. Oscar handed us each a business card to look at while he grabbed a third chair. Neil and I took the two leather high backs that faced the desk.

"I'll stand," Dad said.

"Oh no," Oscar said protesting.

"Oh yes," Dad said in a way that convinced Oscar to leave the chair in the corner.

There were a number of decisions to make, Oscar said, some we might not have even thought about. Burial versus cremation. Casket or urn. Flowers or birds. Public or private. Programs and death announcements. He put his papers in order and said we should get started.

"You'd have to kill me first before you burn my wife," Dad said, concerning the first item on the agenda.

Oscar paused and straightened his papers again before he spoke.

"I understand your hesitation. However, cremation is common procedure. And the most economical."

"I don't care what it costs."

"Perhaps the three of you would like to discuss it. More privately."

Oscar turned his chair away from us and continued with the paperwork, as if he had found another room. Neil and I swivelled to face Dad.

"You don't mean to bury her whole, do you?" I said.

"I do."

"Dad. She would freak."

"It's not our place to, you know, do that. It's not how it's meant to be. If it were, then we would all spontaneously combust when we die," Dad said. "And we don't."

"You are talking about a woman who spent half of her life washing her hands," I said. "You want to put her in the dirt?"

Oscar's chair jiggled and squeaked.

"There's nothing cleaner than ashes," Oscar said.

"You try eating them," Dad said.

Oscar tried the religious angle, explaining the significance of the circle of life. How a human gets the chance to complete the full circle when the body goes from to ashes to dust. He even managed to call the whole procedure beautiful. It sounded like a recipe. Dad sat down in the third seat and gave in.

We chose a corrugated cardboard crate from the cremation catalogue.

"Paper burns faster than wood. That's what your Mother would have wanted. We don't have to be there, do we? To watch it go up?"

Oscar shook his head for no and invited us into the display room. One of the small caskets had a doll in it. It was the kind of doll that should close her eyes when you put her on her back, but instead hers were open and staring. It took all of my will power not to reach in and poke them closed.

"Keep in mind the urn *will* be visible at the service," the man said when he noticed Dad comparing price tags.

I felt Dad saying in his head that there wasn't going to be a goddamned service. *Services jinx you.* Neil picked out a ceramic pitcher that had a large marigold on it, and Dad said, fine, she loved flowers.

I knew it wasn't the right kind of flower, but I didn't want to prolong the meeting.

"There's just one last thing," Oscar said as he took us back into his office. "Perhaps we should have attended to this first. The death announcement."

"Oh. That won't be necessary," Dad said.

"It's all part of the package. Package C," Oscar said. He circled a square advertisement on one of the pamphlets and slid it over to us. Dad stood up and explained how he used to work for the obits in Mitchell and how one of the perks was free ads for life. "Just bill me separately," he said, as though it were a McDonald's combo.

"It's actually cheaper to go with the package, Mr. Quartz."

"I am not paying for something I'm not going to use."

I could tell Oscar wanted to say something along the lines of a freebie, like you wouldn't order your Chinese food separately because you were allergic to fortune cookies. "You could always go with two obituaries," he said instead. Like for different newspapers.

"I don't need two. I only have one wife." I expected him to change his *have* to had, but he didn't. Simon said it took humans different amounts of time to feel comfortable with the past tense.

"Let's just sign it and go," Neil said. "F'in Package C."

I looked down at my pants while he said it and noticed a dark spot in the crotch of my jeans where I thought I had just been sweating.

"I feel like I'm going to faint," I said, and Oscar asked if I wanted a glass of water.

"I'll grab a wet paper towel for my face," I said and ran out of the room, holding my arm in front of me and pretending to scratch my leg.

As I sat in the cubicle and stuffed my underwear with toilet paper two women walked into the washroom and started testing out each other's makeup.

"Mm. Smell this one."

"Oh, I don't like vanilla. It doesn't belong in a lip gloss. It belongs in a cake. Try my hand cream. It's winter rose. Your hands'll be soft as a baby's bum."

"You know, I still think Ethel must have had a brain tumour."

"I wish they'd agreed to the autopsy. Then at least we'd know what our own risk was."

"I hear you. Mind if I take this one home? My daughter loves anything peppermint. I'll replace it on bingo night."

Part of me wanted to call out to the women. *Help. I don't have a mother. I don't even know how to put lip gloss on.* I wished it was my mother bringing home scented cream for me, or someone else's mother who knew what scents I liked. I wished one of them would pass me a pad or a tampon, and maybe even offer advice about cramps if I ever got them. Samantha said some women didn't get cramps, even though all women bled.

When the women left, I took my long-sleeved shirt off and tied it around my waist, letting the arms hang down in front of me to cover up my spot.

"May I ask why you are having the funeral in Kitchener if you are all from Mitchell County?" Oscar asked as I walked back into the room. Dad was filling out his credit card information on a form, and Neil was staring out the window. "Is it because this is where most of her family lives?"

"Yeah, Dad?" Neil asked. "Is it?"

"I hadn't thought about an actual funeral."

"What about the trail?" I said.

"What about it?"

"Don't you think she would rather be sprinkled in Whirl Creek than trapped in some Kool-Aid jug under the ground?"

"In the town that made her go mental," Neil said.

Dad told Neil to smarten up, but then started thinking and nodding his head in a maybe and yes kind of pattern. When he realized he was losing his sale, Oscar tried to take back his question.

"Oh, I'm afraid spreading ashes in public is, kind of, illegal. You could always have an additional service there after, though. At this waterfall you mentioned."

"Creek," Dad and I said, together.

"Right. One of our priests would certainly follow a procession to your beach for a blessing. The extra fee would be nominal."

"Who's going to stop us from putting her where we want her?" Dad said, ignoring the suggestion. "The government?"

"How would they even find out?" I said.

"Maybe this guy will tell on us," Neil said.

Dad put his coat on and motioned for Neil and me to do the same.

"Looks like we'll be shopping around," Dad said. I passed the man his jug back and we walked out.

The Campbell funeral home was on Montreal St. in Mitchell, next to the fire hall. It was the only one in town, and Mother's body was waiting there for us when we arrived to make the second set of arrangements. I pictured the black zipper bag being carted from the hospital to the first funeral home, and then to the second, before she finally got unzipped and burned. Whenever I thought of Mother I imagined her as a see-through paper-thin version. She was like a tracing paper cut-out, sitting on her dead stomach, looking bored, yet peaceful, with a My Little Pony doll and matching brush instead of her hospital fork.

Mr. and Mrs. Campbell remembered Dad's name from his days at the newspaper. They agreed to prepare the remains and didn't ask any questions about the service we hadn't yet planned.

"She'll be ready Friday, Peter," Mrs. Campbell said. "Any time you please."

CHAPTER 20—CAPTAIN SUNSHINE

We buried Mother on a Saturday night a few weeks after school let out for summer. Miles and Marie joined us in a ring around the maple tree before we marched two by two down the path to the water's edge. Dad walked a few steps behind at the back, holding the velvet bag. We had talked about maybe passing Mother back and forth as we walked, but the midwife was worried that some of the girls might not be strong enough for the relay.

"She's heavier than Caroline was as a newborn," Marie said to me as we started walking. I quickly changed the subject.

"Chester should be here," I said. I wondered if anyone else had noticed that there were thirteen of us in the line.

"And Emily."

"Why Emily? Emily barely knew Mother."

"They had a connection," Desiree said, but I sensed she didn't know the full story about the midnight snack.

Dad insisted we use the word *bury* instead of *scatter*. Before we left the house he had asked each one of us to place a rock from the yard into the bag because he didn't want his last memory of Mother to be a pile of ashes floating on the water's surface. Besides, he thought the ducks might see us coming and start nibbling on the ashes thinking mother's remains was their daily bread. At the bottom of the creek she could *seep out any time she pleased.*

"I don't want any of you to have bad dreams," Dad said, after he had kissed the bag and threw it into the creek. "Your mother is in a better place now, just dream about that."

In my dream I was swinging from the maple tree in my prom dress, and when I jumped off I landed in a circle of tiny dolls. At first, I couldn't open my eyes wide enough to see their faces, but eventually they turned into matchstick Simons and Rosies and Shilos. They helped me up to my feet and brushed the dirt off my dress, which was now a sweater coat. Simon and Rosie took my fingers in their hands and led me back to the tree where I had been swinging only moments before. All that was left was a tree stump, but it wasn't for Shilo. It had been carved into a chair like the others, and the word MOTHER was engraved in capitals on the back. The tiny children sat me down in the Mother chair and told me it was time to tell Dad God's plan for me.

"I got a letter from the college today," I told Dad, when I came up from checking the mail the morning after my tree dream. I had decided to tell him the fake bad news as soon as I saw him so I didn't chicken out or change my mind about what the dream meant. I forgot I had the mail in my hands.

"Well? Let's see."

"No. It's bad. I didn't get in." I folded up the grocery store flyers and put them under my armpit.

"What do you mean you didn't get in? Your marks were fine."

I told Dad that the letter said it wasn't about my marks. Too many people applied for the languages program and there were only so many seats in the classroom. I figured he'd tell me to contact the school and say I'd stand at the back, so I kept talking as quickly as possible. I told him it was probably meant to be.

"You mean the whole everything-happens-for-a-reason crap," Dad said, which was his way of reminding me Mother was dead.

I explained how I wanted to live at Maple Manor with the Creek Kids while he worked on selling the house, or whatever he decided to do. He knew we couldn't all live in the apartment forever, and that the Creek Kids had to go back to the old school, and that they were too young to look after themselves. He also knew he needed to stay at the apartment if he wanted to keep his job and make sure Desiree finished high school and didn't make an accidental baby. She was already eating lettuce on top of her cereal, and all of us knew that lettuce was one of Mother's old tricks. Desiree told Dad she was trying to lose weight for her prom, even though it wasn't until the following year.

Dad stretched his neck in all four directions and I could almost hear him saying a silent thank you prayer. He tried to say it was a bad idea, but nothing he said made more sense than my plan.

"Suit yourself, Caroline. But this is for one year. After that, you're either going to college or finding a job. I'm the dad. I'm the one who's responsible for raising these kids, not you. I don't know why you won't stay here and do your grade thirteen like all the other smart kids."

*

It took four trips in the station wagon to move back to Maple Manor. Dad thought we should wait until Miles and Neil got back from their cross-country delivery, but I knew my moving day had to be the seventh of July. I think Dad and I both had a special feeling about it, though we didn't say so to each other.

"Let's take stuff instead of people in the first load," I said to Dad on the morning of the move. I wanted to get settled before the Creek Kids got there. Dad said he wanted me to take Mother's room He said that way if Shilo had hospital nightmares, she would know where to find me.

"It will also help the Creek Kids get a feel for who's in charge. Especially now that Neil has moved in with Miles."

Dad had cut off the water and electricity at the house during the summer when Neil refused to live out at the apartment. It had been Mother's idea. She said it was a waste to pay utility bills for one person in that big old house, especially since Neil and Miles were away on their delivery trucks half the time.

When Dad and I drove up to the house, it looked as tired as we did. You could tell by looking at the outside that someone had died. Dad helped me carry the bedding and bags to the front hall and then he went back to the apartment for the second load. I walked up to the window in the kitchen and stared out into the backyard. The maple tree seemed to be twice its size, and the branches waved at me.

My swing looked happy as could be with no one sitting on it. I tried to say a prayer for the house, but I couldn't think of anything to say. Instead, I turned around and went back into the hall. I grabbed my pillow and sleeping bag and walked toward Mother's room. When I reached for the doorknob, I imagined Mother's finger poking out and inviting me to join her in the closet. I ran back out to the driveway and gulped the air, filling my lungs, and stretching my arms out just as Mother used to do on our walks.

When I got back in the house, I couldn't bring myself to open Mother's door. I went over to the table, grabbed a chair, and dragged it up the stairs. Somewhere between standing at Mother's closed door, and taking a deep breath of God's air, I decided my bedroom would be in the attic. *New beginnings*, I told myself. *That's why you're here.*

"We're home!" Simon yelled even before he opened the front door all the way.

I had heard the car coming up the driveway, and had scrambled down the ladder in time to stand in front of Mother's bedroom door and make sure no one went in to mess it up.

"Bring your stuff upstairs," I said to Simon and Rosie, who had dumped the circle stool on the floor and were walking around opening the windows with their backpacks still on.

"In a minute," Simon said. "This house smells like a barn."

"Someone forgot to flush upstairs last time you all left. Take your shoes off, girls. You need to leave them outside before you come in."

"What for?" Magdelene said.

"Mother didn't make us," Melinda said. Shilo nodded in agreement. She looked down at her shoes and shook her head from side to side.

"Caroline does," I tried to say, but only my name came out. The girls looked at me and snickered. At first, I thought it was their way of saying, you're not our mother, but after a few days I sensed it was their way of saying, you're not our Caroline.

Dad had told us to keep the curtains closed even in the day so that nobody could look into the house and see that we were living there alone. When the girls played outside they did it in the backyard, on the grass and trees and swing rather than out front in the dirty white rocks. We had to be careful of phone calls too, Dad said. If anyone asked to speak to the head of the house we couldn't say he wasn't home or our mother was dead. Dad said to tell people our parents were taking a nap.

When the first knock came, I went looking for the baseball bat Mother kept in the umbrella stand in the front closet. As I shuffled around for it Rosie reminded me it was Halloween and it was probably some kids looking for candy. It was still daytime, but Simon grabbed some apples to hand out just in case. Mother kept fruit by the door on Halloween night, even though the only kids that ever came by were ones too old for trick-or-treating. Dad used to say they were yahoos looking for pumpkins to toss, but I once heard Miles saying that wasn't it. *There's a rumour that you got yourselves a haunted house.*

I assumed the reason Chester was knocking on our door after all those years was because he noticed one of the death announcements. The newspaper had been printing the notice of Mother's death every Saturday for weeks. Dad thought it was to make up for the typo in the original one. They had misspelled my name, and I tried to tell him it wasn't a big deal that they used a y instead of an i in the survived by line, but Dad said it didn't matter that it didn't bother me. *It would have bothered Mother. She would have wanted all of our names perfect,* he said. *That's not how it's spelled in the song.*

"Hello, my friends, hello," Chester sang, through the crack of the door. I opened the door wider when I heard the familiar voice. Chester wore a backpack on his shoulders, and his hands were full of dirty white rocks from the yard. He threw them back onto the ground when he saw me looking at them, and reached for an apple from Simon's bowl.

"Happy Halloween," Simon said.

"Yeah," said Rosie.

"Who's the man?" Magdelene asked.

"Happy Birthday," I said. "Chester."

"Captain Sunshine?" Shilo said, pulling the door open as wide as it could go. Chester was like a celebrity to the ones who didn't remember him. I thought Chester would looked puzzled when Shilo called him by his Neil Diamond name since Mother hadn't given it to him until after he was gone. Instead, he smiled and said, *Here I am.*

*

None of us had seen Chester since the day the agent dragged him out of Maple Manor with his yellow balloon. Mother had told us to hide that day. She didn't say why, but I knew by her eyes that she had heard the blue minivan with the faceless angels on it coming up the road.

"Caroline, you go with Chester. And hold each other's mouths closed so nobody can hear your breathing."

"Where should we hide?" I asked.

"Wherever you feel most secretive. The best place you know."

Mother told the others to hide too. "But don't find good spots," she said to the others. As Chester and I ran out of the room, we heard Mother calling Simon back to be the seeker. She asked for his notepad and wrote out the instructions while she recited them aloud slowly. *Whatever you do, don't find Chester.* Her British accent was already coming on before the agent came in.

I took Chester's hand and led him into Mother's closet.

"Stand behind Dad's blue clothes so your jogging suit will blend in," I said. I piled the shoeboxes around his feet and climbed in beside him, covering his mouth and nodding that he should do the same with mine. We waited and listened.

"Ready or not, here I come!" Simon shouted.

"Let's look at the glowing shoebox again," Chester whispered to me. "We're stuck in here anyway."

"No way," I said.

"Come on. It might be our last chance."

"No way."

"Do you think your Mother would notice if I took one article. There's a whole pile of them. Do you think she counted them?"

I whispered to Chester that I was sure Mother knew exactly how many there were, and that we needed to stop talking.

"I can see the shoebox. It's right here. It's glowing again," Chester said, pointing into the red clothes.

I heard the agent wipe his feet at the front door, and I knew Mother would make him do it at least one more time.

"Ready or not, here I come!" Simon said a second time.

"They're clean," the agent said. "I just put these socks on in the car for God's sake, Sherry. For your sake."

Mother talked in a nice, slow voice. She offered the agent every kind of drink that existed, including ones like pop and Kool-Aid that we didn't have. We heard Simon find Magdelene and Melinda. Then Rosie.

"Someone else is hiding in this room," Chester said into my hand. His breath was hot.

"Shh," I said, accidentally kissing his palm.

"I see you, Desiree," Simon said.

"Where am I?"

"Behind the circle stool."

"How many fingers am I holding up?"

The twins were found next. Their pretend screams sounded more like a horse's neigh.

"You know I didn't come for a visit," the agent said. "The faster I do this the easier it will be on everyone, including us, Sherry."

"Just let the children finish their game," Mother said. "Please. They don't know it's their last."

"Chester!" the agent called out, using his kiddie voice. "Come out, come out wherever you are, lad."

Simon was down the hall asking Desiree if she had seen Neil.

"He's not supposed to hide good," Desiree whispered.

"I know, but I've looked everywhere."

Doors and cupboards began to creak open and slam closed all over the house. Simon came into Mother's bedroom and opened the closet.

"Neil?"

I pulled Chester's hand off of my face for long enough to whisper to Simon that it was us and that he wasn't allowed to find us. He slammed the door shut and ran out of the room.

"Not in Mother and Dad's room. That's for sure."

"Please. Just one more look," Chester begged me. "We didn't get a chance to read them all. Maybe there's something else important we'll never know." Chester felt his way through the red clothes and found the box, even though I never said yes.

I can help you look for everyone, Simey," the agent said.

"Thanks, but that's cheating. I'll check upstairs again, and I'll probably find the others. By the way, my name is Soolaimon."

A stampede followed Simon back to the upstairs bedroom.

"Psst, orphanage man. In here," Neil said.

Two new footsteps entered Mother and Dad's room. Chester opened the box and felt through the papers. I heard him grab one and crumple it into his pocket. We heard the *psst* again, then nothing for a minute because you can't hear pointing. The closet door opened before Chester could make it back behind the blue clothes.

"Game's over, sunshine," the agent said. "Get your shoes." Neil came out from under the bed and got close enough to whisper in my ear, "I guess there is a Chester's Day after all?"

At the front door, Mother had a frayed piece of green ribbon in her hand, and she pulled a yellow balloon out of her pocket. When it was almost full, she took her mouth away and let the air out. She gave Chester the balloon and told him to hold onto it until he came back home. She held the piece of string to her heart and then tied it around her wrist, double knotting it and shaping it into a large bow that looked like rabbit ears.

Chester stood on the passenger side of the minivan and waited to be let into the vehicle. He took one last look at Maple Manor before he pulled the balloon from his pocket and blew it up. He got in the van and unrolled his window all the way down. Then he did what none of us expected him to do. He knotted it at the bottom and let it go. It was a windy day, but the balloon barely made it an inch before the agent's van ran it over. Mother and I both jumped when we heard it pop. When the van was gone, Mother ran out and grabbed the broken balloon. She stuffed it in her pocket and ran to her closet. It was the last time she ever saw him.

"Where's your costume?" I asked Chester. I didn't know what else to say. *Where have you been? Why haven't you written or called? Have you heard from your mom? Aren't you surprised how much I've grown?* I wished Emily was there to ask questions that I didn't dare. Not including the day we met him, it was the first time I had seen Chester on his birthday without a costume on. Mother always made his costume when we were kids, even though a teacher usually bought him a plastic one from a store. Mother used cardboard boxes and poster paint, and turned him into a cake or a present. One time she made him go as a baby, with a giant diaper made from towels she used to bleach the floors and walls. She had sewn feet on his pajamas, and made him wear the diaper on the outside so people didn't think he was just a kid without a costume. She said God didn't give every kid a birthday on a holiday.

Even though Chester had already taken his shoes off before I opened the door, I could tell by the way he walked into Maple Manor that he knew Mother was gone.

"Where are *you* living?" I asked Chester, as I closed the door behind him.

"As of today, nowhere," Chester said. "I'm eighteen. Finally." He sat down on his backpack in the front hall and let out a big sigh as if he had just returned from a long day at school.

When I offered Chester one of the upstairs beds, he shrugged his shoulders, walked over to the basement door, and picked the lock with his driver's license. I threw down some pillows for him to make a mattress, and Simon rolled down the sleeping bag from the Star Wars bed. Within ten minutes Chester was back upstairs sitting on the circle stool as if no time had passed since the day he left. We talked about weather for a while until Shilo mentioned Mother. She seemed to want Chester to know that a mother used to live in the house.

"He knows Mother," Simon said. "Before you were born, he was practically our brother."

When Simon asked Chester how he'd been, Chester described his eight years away from us as *okay*.

"But what were all those families like?" Simon said.

"Yeah. How many different families did you live with in all that time?" Rosie asked.

"Mother said you are like a sack of potatoes," Shilo said.

"Waiting to be mashed," Melinda said.

"Sweet potatoes," Magdelene said, trying to make him feel a bit better. I couldn't help noticing that Magdelene's voice was almost the same as mine. She was a runt like me, and she also had the crooked pinky.

"I just stayed at one house," Chester said. "For the last seven years or so anyhow. It was different the first year."

We waited for Chester to talk about the first year, but he didn't say a thing. He looked all around and waited for us to ask more questions.

"What was your family like?"

"Okay."

"He's saying that again," Shilo said. "It's his favourite word."

"There's not much to say. They were regular folks. Jen and John. Two kids. A cat and a dog."

"What kind of kids?" Rosie asked.

"They were okay. They had already moved out of the house when I got there. They left a swing set, which was nice. Kind of felt like home."

"We have a swing," Shilo said.

"He knows!" Simon said, annoyed.

The phone rang and Rosie ran to get it.

"Did you use it?" I asked Chester. "The swing."

"Every day."

Rosie put the phone on the table and said it was for me. As I walked to the kitchen I heard her telling Chester who was calling.

"It's Desiree. She needs directions for a French braid. She's going to a boy-girl party."

I picked up the phone and Chester told me to tell Desiree he said hi. I pretended not to hear him.

"It's not something you can do on yourself, Desiree. Besides, I can't explain it over the phone."

"But I'm going as a French maid. I already have the rest of my costume on."

"So twist your hair up in a bun."

"But can't you just explain it to Dad and maybe he can try. He knows how to do hair better than a lot of girls I know."

Dad came on the phone and I told him to do a regular braid at the top and then add sections from the sides as he worked his way down. He gave the phone back to Desiree while he made an attempt.

"Who was that laughing in the background?" Desiree asked. "Ouch! I heard a man. Ouch, Dad!"

"Trick-or-treaters," I said.

"That wasn't kids," Desiree said. "I heard a guy. I recognized his laugh. It sounded just like—Kyle Fitzpatrick."

*

Within a week of Chester moving in to Maple Manor, Desiree had dropped out of school and decided she was meant to live in *a small town*. She was dressed in Samantha's clothes, and her lipstick was so fresh I knew she had put some on in the car.

"So...where is he?" she asked, after she dropped her bags at the front door.

"You mean Captain Sunshine?"

"I mean Chester."

"He's downstairs studying," Shilo told her proudly.

"Studying for what?"

I explained to Desiree that Chester needed one more credit to get his high school diploma and that he was doing it by mail.

"How do you go to school by mail?" Desiree asked.

"You study at home. They send you the work so you don't have to go to class."

Desiree said that's what she was going to do too. She said Mother always said she wasn't born to sit in a classroom. When I reminded her she still needed eight credits to finish school she said no, she was the same age as Chester.

"Chester took summer school courses so he could get into college a year early," I said.

Desiree shrugged and said she didn't need a diploma to be a hairdresser.

"Samantha and I are going to open a saloon," she said, tucking her shirt deep into her underwear when she heard footsteps coming up the stairs. I didn't correct her or wait for them to say hello before I unveiled the new plan. The idea had come to me on a walk to the creek the day after Desiree called to say she was coming to live with us. She had always wanted to be a Creek Kid, she told me over the phone. If Mother or Dad had given her the choice she would have picked Maple Manor, she said.

"I was just telling Desiree, it was perfect timing that she decided to move back to Maple Manor. The Creek Kids will need some help with laundry and cooking and stuff with us gone. Since you'll be the oldest in the house, you'll be in charge for once in your life," I said.

"What do you mean *us gone*?" Desiree said. She folded her arms in front of her and looked as though she was about to shout to Mother that something wasn't fair.

"Chester and I are starting college next semester. In Kitchener," I said.

Father Marvin sounded different on the phone than he did at the front of the church. He sounded like he looked in his bare feet the day I knocked on his door to tell him the church wasn't locked. I pictured him in a terrycloth robe with little curly hairs poking out the top. In my mind, he twisted the hairs while we talked.

"I hear you and your friend are looking for an apartment to rent. Your dad put a notice in the church bulletin. You need room and board near the college, isn't that correct?"

"Uh, yeah. I'm going to school in January," I said, winding my finger up so tight in the phone cord I couldn't get it out. "We are. He's more like a brother. He's hoping to get in, but if he doesn't then he'll work for a while. Maybe Canadian Tire or something. I'm taking linguistics."

"Well, you're in luck. My sister has a basement apartment she rents out near Conestoga College. It's vacant right now. I've already put in a good word for you two. You're going to love it." The way he said love reminded me of how he used to look at Desiree every Sunday when we came up the stairs to the church. *Hi love,* he always said to her after he said hello to me. I don't think he even knew her name. I wrote down the address and thanked Father Marvin for his help.

"I should mention something about my sis. She prefers to rent to couples."

"Oh."

"What I mean is... it wouldn't hurt to say he's your boyfriend. Sissy might give you a better deal if you do."

*

Chester and I linked arms and walked up the front steps to the landlady's house. He fake kissed me on the cheek as Father Marvin's sister opened the door. She smelled like stale candy canes. I made a face and Chester knew what it was for.

"Welcome, lovebirds."

Father Marvin's sister took Chester's hands and pulled him towards her. The middle button on her pantsuit was undone and a tip of underwire was poking out of a big beige bra. When she shook my hand she left four red nail polish half moons in my palm.

"Her lipstick matches her socks and her headband," Chester whispered to me when she disappeared into the kitchen to fix us some snacks. We didn't even know her name yet.

It was Mabeline, but we could call her Mabel if we chose to stay. "Or shall I say, if I decide to keep you," she said, letting the *p* bounce off her cherry lips. She served us Hershey Kisses and asked us about our relationship.

"We're getting married," Chester said. He flattened the foil wrapper from his chocolate over and over while he talked to the table.

"Don't bother." Mabel said. She turned to me for a second. "Well, no offence honeybun, but—" She put her hand up to block her words as though only Chester could hear. "She'll take all your money when you cheat. Happened to me. Twice." She held up two fingers and then changed it to three.

"I don't cheat," Chester said.

"Let's be straight, shall we son." She peeled one of the chocolates and then stabbed a tiny fork into it and fed it to herself as if she were her own lover. "I rent to couples because of the energy they bring into my house. I don't rent to singles, especially not shrivelled up ones like myself." She smiled as she cupped her left breast and let it fall.

"Okay," he said.

"So long as someone's doin' it, I don't mind who it is. It helps my complexion. You understand, punkin?" She went to pinch his cheeks, but then looked at me and slapped her own hand away. Chester said he understood, but I didn't think he did.

"Well, then the place is yours. I'll just need one signature." She handed the lease to Chester and put her bun in his face so he could pull the pen out of her hair.

"One thing," I tried to say. My voice didn't come out clear, so I said it again. Chester scribbled circles on the lease to get the ink moving. "We'd like to see the suite." Mabel looked at Chester and said that of course we wanted to take a *look-see*. She said she knew we would fall in love with it, though. She could tell just by looking at us.

We followed her down the stairs from the kitchen, and she held on to the banister, pausing to straighten her back and check her posture the whole way down.

"The walls match your lipstick," Chester said. Mabel must have taken it as a compliment because she blew him a kiss.

I walked towards the window and reached up to touch the black velvet curtains. "They're real," Mabel said, but I didn't know if she meant the curtains or the windows.

Chester sat down on the loveseat in the centre of the room. He took off his flip-flops and dug his toes into a giant rug hooked zebra.

"Does that thing work?" he asked, pointing at the fireplace.

"Of course it does, baby doll." She got on all fours and flicked the switch on the underside. Three logs lit up with a fake orange glow. "Give it half a sec. It'll feel like your Mama's apple pie in here in no time."

"Is heat included in the rent?" I asked.

"And the movie channel."

"We'll take it," Chester said laughing, but I asked to see the bedrooms. Mabel took us into one with a bed that took up most of the floor space.

"Is this a queen?" Chester asked.

"It's a triple x, pet."

Mabeline turned to me and whispered, "I don't like calling a bed a king. It's the woman who does all the work after all, wouldn't you say?" The closet doors were mirrors, and she looked at me in them and waited for my answer. Chester jumped into the middle of the bed and patted the spot beside him. I walked away looking for the second bedroom. Chester walked out too, but went a different way.

"Come and check out this tub!" Chester yelled to me from the bathroom. The door was a shower curtain, but there was no actual shower in the room. Mabeline fiddled with the dried up rose petals that were strewn around the ledges.

"You'll get used to which settings you like best in no time," she said, twiddling her index finger at both of us and turning the faucets on. "I warn you, the water comes out pretty hot."

"Where's the shower?" I asked.

"What for?" Mabeline said. She pulled the shower curtain closed and one of the rings fell out and onto the floor. I stared at the loose panel while she spoke. "So, that's it. We share the kitchen," she said as if it were a perk. I wondered if she shared the tub with her tenants, too. We followed her back up the stairs and had a better look around. While Chester looked out the window into the backyard, I stood at the card table and traced the circle stains with my finger. I imagined Chester, Mabel, and I squished together slurping up our cornflakes.

"Thanks for your time," I said, pushing the lawn chair in.

"I'll take four fifty on the months you're short," she said, addressing the numbers to me.

TARA BENWELL

Chester asked her to give us a few minutes to discuss things, and she sent us back down to the suite to do what we needed to do. She tucked a plastic bag of cinnamon hearts into Chester's back pocket before she closed the door behind us.

"There's nothing to talk about," I said to Chester before he could beg. We were sitting on the zebra rug sucking on hearts. I was playing with the mane while he pulled hair out of the tail.

"You don't like it. I knew it." Chester stuck his tongue out at me and walked into the bedroom to check in the closet mirror if it had turned red yet.

"There's only one bedroom, not to mention no shower."

"I like it. Kill me."

"Then you take it."

"Would you be mad if I did?"

When I told him I would be furious, he promised to sleep on the couch and still pay half.

"We'd have to share a kitchen with her!"

"There's a toaster and a microwave down here. All we need is a mini fridge."

"And a sink!"

Chester looked towards the bathroom. "You never cook anything but croissants anyway. How many dishes do you really use?"

"Check out this literature," I said, tossing him one of the books from the shelf. "*Naughty by Nature. Chains, Cuffs, and Lover's Bluffs. Three's For Me.* Seriously, Chester."

"You only live once, Carl. You said it yourself. Besides, there's a trampoline in the backyard."

"So?"

"Maybe it's a sign."

"A sign of what?" We hadn't talked about the circus at all, and I hoped Chester wouldn't want to start talking about it again if we moved in together.

"Like maybe you're ready to graduate from your swing."

I put the books back on the shelf and took a second look at the bathroom.

"I'll try it for one month, Captain Sunshine," I said, when he finally looked up at me again, "I'm not signing a lease."

Chester picked up one of his flip-flops and handed me the other one. I knew they were microphones even before he started singing.

Mabeline slid the lease under the door.

CHAPTER 21—BIRTHDAY SUIT

In Ontario, your nineteenth birthday is supposed to be the day your parents take you out for your first official beer. I figured that was what Dad was going to do when he called the day before my big day to say he was going to pick me up before lunch. I didn't tell him that Mabel had already put a two-four at the top of the stairs for me, or that Chester and I had been getting her to buy us six-packs every Friday night for months. The hall closet was overflowing with empties because we didn't know if minors were allowed to take them back.

Dad was working at *The Mitchell Advocate* again. He had moved out of the apartment and back into the house with Desiree and the Creek Kids shortly after Chester and I moved out. The twins had taken jobs at Canadian Tire and rented a one-bedroom apartment in King's Tower on the seventh floor. Neil had planned on moving in with them too, but Miles convinced him to spend the summer doing deliveries.

"Have I ever forgotten your birthday?" Dad asked, when I sounded surprised to receive his call. *Just last year*, I almost said but I knew that wouldn't be fair. Mother had only been gone for a month when I turned 18, and we had been busy getting things ready for the move back to the house. Still, I remember thinking it was odd that Dad hadn't even reminded the others to wish me a Happy Birthday. That whole day I had wondered if it was some important anniversary of the circus disaster, but I was too afraid to look in the shoebox to check.

"I'll pick you up before lunch. I have kind of a birthday surprise," Dad said on the phone. He sounded excited and nervous, as any dad would probably be to take his daughter to the bar for the first time.

Dad pulled up at noon and honked for me to come out to the car. Chester was running a bath, and I yelled to him that I'd be back around dinnertime.

"Maybe we can order a pizza or something," I shouted.

Usually when we were in the car together Dad would ask rapid questions trying to fill the silence. When he couldn't think of any more he'd talk about all of the people in Mitchell who were dying. "It's like some kind of epidemic," Dad would say, and I'd tell him it's called old age. This time neither of us said anything. I was still upset he had asked me not to bring Chester along. I knew it would be easier to fake my first taste of alcohol with Chester there, but Dad said his surprise was something we had to do alone.

When he started driving back towards Mitchell I wondered where he planned on taking me. *Please not the Chinese restaurant*, I thought. The only time Dad had ever taken us out to a restaurant in Mitchell was the day we buried Mother. It was a buffet style restaurant, and we had sat around a giant circular table trying to eat rice with sticks instead of forks. Dad hardly spoke the whole time we were there. He stood near the plates and kept bringing us new dishes to try, and the lady who owned the place kept telling him to *sit, sit* and *eat, eat*, but he refused. Dad wouldn't let any of us eat a fortune cookie, and when Shilo told the lady we were celebrating our Mother's death, she wouldn't let him pay for the bill. Even though more than a year had passed, I was sure the lady would remember us, so I was thankful when Dad kept driving instead of stopping for Chinese beer. I was beginning to think he was going to hand me my first beer at the house, when he turned the car down the dirt road and drove right up to Whirl Creek. It was the first time we had ever pulled that close to the water's edge in a car.

Before we got out, Dad grabbed a bag out of the glove compartment. I felt the coldness as the bag brushed my lap, and I assumed it was going to be a bottle of wine or a cooler. I wondered if Dad thought to bring glasses or a corkscrew, but when he walked to my side of the car and handed the bag to me I realized it was just a bag of crusts from the freezer to feed the birds. It felt strange knowing Mother was the last person to touch the bread. She always collected enough to fill a whole bag before she took it down to the water on a family walk. None of us bothered to collect and freeze the crusts after Mother died. We ate our sandwiches in full, sometimes even open faced with peanut butter and jam together. Sometimes butter, too.

Dad and I sat on the grass and waited for each other to speak. We took turns tossing the bread bits into the water and watching the bird fights. I wondered if it was the last bag, or if there were more hidden behind tubs of ice cream or boxes of waffles. Dad pulled a folded envelope out of his back pocket and handed it to me as soon as I threw in the last piece. He looked away as my eyes sorted through the first few pages. It wasn't a birthday card or a money gift.

"Mother had a will?" I said.

"Yep."

"But why?"

"What do you mean why? She had more money than most people do, Caroline."

"How? She never worked."

"It doesn't matter how. What matters is what she wants done with it."

I skimmed through the typed pages as Dad played with his hair.

"What is all this?" I asked.

Dad reached over my arm and flipped to the last page for me. "Your mother had a dream, Caroline. She was one of the lucky ones. Not everyone has a dream."

"How long did she have this dream?" I asked.

"It's something she wanted to do even before you were born, but I kind of talked her out of it. I should have just let her do it back then. She wanted to open a store. A store slash service, right at the house. She would have called it *The Birthday Barn*."

I flipped through the pages and felt Mother's voice coming to life as I read. There were detailed notes about how to reconstruct the chicken coop, and what colours to paint the balloons on the walls, where to put the *Birthday Barn* sign, how much to charge for cupcakes, how to make mass confetti, where to find matching paper plates and cups with themes. *You will need at least one helium tank and three pairs of scissors on hand for curling ribbons. Use local dealers. Buy in bulk.* There was nothing that said why she wanted it so bad.

"There's enough money to do it," Dad said. He got up and walked over to the creek to throw the crumbs to the ducks. I couldn't help but think of how similar he looked the day we scattered the ashes. He hadn't even bothered to put on his best clothes. He had just worn blue jeans.

"So buy a new house," I said to his ponytail. "You said you were going to sell Maple Manor and buy a house in the city. I thought that was *the plan*."

Dad turned around to face me.

"But it might actually work. Every day is someone's birthday, right?"

Dad walked towards the trash bin to deposit the empty crust bag. Garbage was overflowing onto the grass.

"Wait, Dad."

"What?"

"Can I keep that?"

"The empty bag? Why?"

He walked back and stood at my feet, stretching the bag out and holding one end with each hand. A few crumbs landed in my lap.

"It might be the last bag," I said.

Dad sat back down beside me and stuffed the bag between my knees so the wind wouldn't take it. The ducks finished eating and set sail along the creek, following the same line we had walked after Dad threw Mother's ashes the day of the burial. The bread bag flew out from under me, and when I tried to catch it, Dad grabbed my hand between both of his and wouldn't let go.

"It was her birthday that day, you know. I know you know about that day, Caroline."

"What day?"

"Today."

"Today? My birthday?"

"Your Mother's birthday. And the day of the circus fire. July sixth. I know you have the shoebox. Your Mother always kept those old articles in there. She tortured herself with them once a year. Maybe more often. Locked herself in that stupid closet."

I tried to get up to grab the bag before it hit the water, but my feet wouldn't move. All I could see in front of me was the headline. *Brother and Sister Lose Everything.* How could it be her birthday? July sixth was my birthday. The unluckiest day of the year. The day after 07 07 when Kyle Fitzpatrick was born. Kyle and Lucy Montgomery's Chester. Today.

"She was two years old. Two exactly. It was lucky she was that young. She didn't remember much. She can't picture the fire like I can. She couldn't, I mean. All she remembered was a bad smell. I can still remember everything. I was seven, you know."

I said I didn't know. I mean I knew, but not how old. I didn't do the math. There was no use pretending I hadn't read the newspaper clippings. I could tell he knew I had.

"Both of my parents were trapped. They were pinned beneath all of those chairs. They didn't have a chance, Caroline. There were so many chairs. I couldn't have saved them. But my little sister—" His voice broke up.

"Dad. It's okay," I said. I hoped he would skip the part about who he and Mother really were since he knew I already knew their secret.

"My sister. I saw her blonde hair underneath a burning chair, and I just yanked it. The hair kept falling out as I pulled, but I finally got a big chunk. My sleeves were on fire, but she was all I had left." Dad lifted his sleeves and showed me the marks on his arms. "I didn't care if her hair burned. I was smart enough to know it would grow back."

"You saved her life," I said. All those years I thought the marks on his arms were from cutting down trees to make thinking chairs. Even after reading about the fire, I never considered the fact that he had escaped death or saved a child's life. All I thought about was the brother sister part. All I thought about was what it meant for me.

"It wasn't until after I piggybacked her out of the smoke that I realized my mistake," Dad said.

"What mistake? You saved Mother. Us kids wouldn't be here if—"

"I saved the wrong little girl, Caroline! I piggybacked a complete stranger to safety instead of my own sister. Little Nel. Natalie. She was probably already gone, but still…"

I took my hands away from Dad to remove a strand of hair that had blown into my mouth. I pretended I already knew what Dad was telling me.

"I knew it, Caroline. As soon as I looked into her eyes I knew it. Even though your mother was covered in ash, her eyes stood out in the smoke. Those lost blue eyes. They stared right through me and begged me to stay close by. Nelly's eyes were brown. Those two girls weren't even wearing the same coloured dress that day at the circus. It was just the hair that was the same. It was the same blonde, like Shilo's. Nel was more like you, though. She was small. Petite, my mother used to say to Natalie because she wanted to be a big girl. Even her name was too big for her—that's why we called her Nel. It's probably where you got it from. Your smallness. That and your pinky finger," Dad said, grabbing my hand again.

"Hers looked just like this, only kid-sized," Dad said, trying to straighten out my little finger. "Shilo's getting it too if you look closely. My mom had it. Your Grandma. I remember how Grandma's pinky stuck out from her teacup all the time. And her big feet that only fit in men's shoes. It's funny what you remember about people."

Dad told me how he had lied to the police right after he rescued mother from the fire. He told the police he and his *sister* had watched their parents die under the chairs.

"No one questioned me about who she was that day," Dad said. "They just assumed. They called me a hero." Dad snorted. Then gulped.

"You pretended Mother was Natalie? Your real sister?" I stared at my little finger. *How many promises had I made with it?*

"Well, your mother's name was on her loot bag and she was still holding it. It said *Happy Birthday Sherry.* I wanted her to be my sister. I guess I told the police what I wanted to believe myself. That I had saved my sister."

"But didn't anyone look for Mother? Didn't her family try to find her?"

"Your mother's whole family was at the circus for her birthday party. Mom, Dad, baby brother, grandparents. Even the kitten she got as a gift that morning. There were no relatives left to claim Sherry. I couldn't help what I did. There was no one to claim me, either. I didn't have grandparents, or uncles, or cousins like your mother did.

Dad knew my question before I even asked. *Did he ever tell Mother? Did he tell her before she died? Did she live her whole life thinking he was her real brother?* He answered without my asking.

"A woman spotted your mother down at the orphanage about a month after the circus fire. She was the family's next-door neighbor. She looked straight at your mother and said, *That little blonde girl.* I can still hear her goddamn voice. *That little blonde girl's last name isn't Quartz. And she don't have a big brother. She had a baby brother and he burned in his mother's arms. That kid is Sherry Roodie.* Your mother ran up to her and called the woman by name. *Mrs. Smith.* She asked Mrs. Smith to put her hair in ponies like she always did for special occasions. Cecile Smith adopted your Mother that day. Changed her name too. Called her Joan for years. I guess she thought it would help your mother forget her real family."

For a moment I forgot that I was listening to a real story about my own parents. My own parents. My own grandparents. My own aunt and uncle. "And did she? Forget them?"

"Nope. I remember when we were in the orphanage she told me her mother loved cherries and that's why she named her Sherry. The people at the orphanage couldn't get her to eat anything, and I told them to try giving her cherries. Eventually she moved on to other berries like strawberries."

"That's why she liked that Neil Diamond song so much. *Cherry, Cherry.* She used to love it. I mean a long time ago used to," I said. I pictured Mother washing the dishes and singing that song. She had sat me on the kitchen counter with a towel so I could dry the cutlery. It was my first memory of Mother.

"Music sort of helped her remember things. She changed her name back to Sherry when we moved to Canada."

When Dad said the word Canada I tried to stop the next part from coming. I wasn't ready to hear more about Neil and why he didn't belong to us.

"But what about you? You stayed in the orphanage all alone?"

"After Cecile Smith adopted your mother the people who ran the orphanage began to introduce me to all of the visitors as the *liar with his pants on fire*. A couple finally adopted me, but only because their own son got hit by a truck."

"You mean Miles," I said. I don't know how I knew it, but I just did. Maybe I knew all those years but was too afraid to ask.

"He wasn't the same after the accident, but Miles wasn't dead. It was no reason to adopt another boy. One child can't replace another."

Dad explained how he had spent years looking through phonebooks and calling up all of the Smiths in Connecticut trying to find that little Sherry again. He couldn't find her because of the whole name change thing. He finally found her when she was fourteen.

"It was pure luck when I did," Dad said, "though your Mother always called it a gift from God. I recognized her right away even with that dumb fake name. Joan. Miles and I were horsing around at a park one day and there she was eating candy floss with some friends. She invited us to her house for a party. That's when the thing happened between Miles and your mother's stepsister. They disappeared into the basement at some point; I was just so busy flirting with your mother."

"What thing happened?" I asked, but Dad didn't have to say any more.

"The girl was only thirteen. It wasn't normal back then. Girls like that had to get rid of their problem, or find a way to disappear."

Dad said Cecile blamed him for bringing Miles to the party and that after the baby was born she convinced Mother and Dad to take it and go someplace far where nobody knew their names. If they'd keep their mouths closed, she'd send money every year. "We figured why the hell not.?" Dad said. They went to Canada and they called the baby Neil. "Your Mother said she picked the name Neil because she loved Neil Diamond, but I think it was more her way of honouring little Nell."

"What about your parents? Miles' parents, I mean." I wondered if it was them who sent gifts to the house from Connecticut, but by the way Dad shrugged and looked up into the sky I had to assume it was Cecile who had sent the gift packages.

Just when I thought Dad couldn't possibly have any more secrets to share, he stood up and said he had something *sort of important* to tell me.

"There's a reason your birthday seems like such a coincidence. You know, sharing the same date with your mother. Not only that, but the same date as the lousy circus fire," Dad said.

I was sure he was going to start using Mother's voice. He'd start talking about God's plan, and how nothing in life happened except for good reason. I waited for a minute, but Dad's voice didn't soften like I expected. He sounded sorry and angry and afraid all at once.

"You weren't born two months early, Caroline. You were born right on time. On your very own birthday. You were actually a September baby."

"September baby," I laughed. "Very funny, Dad."

I thought about the Family Feud episode that cracked us up all those times. It got us so bad we had to cross our legs and shake ourselves around to hold in our pee. *During what month does a woman start to look pregnant?* Dad was never the type of person to come in and ask *What's so funny?* He probably had never even seen the classic episode.

"What about that guy and the creek you told me about before the move? We were right here when you told me, Dad. Remember? My baptism." *The nude guy.*

"That all happened, Caroline. Only you weren't there."

"What do you mean I wasn't there?"

"Well, I guess you were there, but you were still tucked up tight inside your mother. She wanted you to come out early so bad. She wanted to make that day better. July sixth."

"But I didn't come out?"

"She blamed herself, you know. For being born that day. Her family might have gone to the circus a different day if it hadn't been her birthday, right? There was supposed to be a show on July fifth, but it got cancelled because the trains were late."

"But circuses are never cancelled. It's bad luck," I said. "Simon says."

Dad nodded and sighed, and told me it was cancelled anyway. The circus jinxed itself.

"Before you were born, Mother had this thing. This *feeling*, she called it. She thought it came from God. She had this idea that she could reverse all of the pain somehow—not just hers and mine, but all the other people who had lost loved ones that day in the circus fire."

"How?" I asked.

"She thought if she had a baby on that day she could somehow make it all better. Like some miracle or something. At first, she thought God was telling her that you were going to come early."

"On July sixth?"

"She said she had dreams with angels in it. They gave her the date. When you showed no signs of coming in those first few days of July she got desperate. She came up with this dumb idea. She faked your birth, Caroline. At least she tried to."

"How do you fake a birth?" I asked. The air was getting hotter and I wanted to jump up and put my hair in the cold creek and slow down my brain.

"She paid some guy a lot of money to pull it over on me. She told me he was an angel. I might not have noticed her belly because she hardly gained any weight with you. You were so tiny. She barely even looked pregnant, especially after how big she got with the twins. I don't know how she was planning on keeping a fake baby away from me until September, though. Even a tiny baby like you. Maybe she would have hid in the closet with her fake bundle for two months or something."

"You mean I was just a doll?"

"Your Mother told Marie to go home and insisted that I go and check on Miles. She said she wanted to be alone with her baby. Marie had already stormed off, and I was about to leave when you—the real you— jabbed a toe or something into Mother's ribs and the doll rolled out of Mother's arms towards the creek. Your mother jumped up to grab the doll. It was all so obvious. There wasn't any mess. The guy left with his picnic basket faster than he appeared."

"What did you do?"

"I had no choice but to go along with her story. It was God's plan, right? She made me pinky swear not to let Neil or the twins get a good look at you until September. She convinced me and some doctor she paid off to put July sixth on the birth certificate. A birthday is just a date to you and me, but it was different to your mother. You understand what she lost, right? She was a baby the day of the circus, but she held on to that guilt her whole life."

Dad waited for me to say something, but I just stared at the ducks and the creek and felt like Alice in Wonderland.

"You were always a September baby to me, Sweet Caroline. I delivered you."

"You?"

"There was nobody else."

"What about Marie?"

"Marie thought you were already born, remember?"

"Oh, yeah."

"It was a pretty special day," Dad said. "I wouldn't want to do it again, but I'm still glad we did it."

I stared at the creek while Dad went on about the song they had named me after. The song about the good times and how they never felt so good.

"It was a September song. I'll never forget it when it came out. There was a rumour Neil Diamond wrote it for President Kennedy's daughter."

I knew then that Mother had lied to me right up to the morning before she died. The last thing she had told me on my final visit at the hospital was that she had finally found someone else who shared my birthday. "His name is George W. Bush," Mother had said, between her gulps of hospital air. "They say he's going to be the next US President, follow in his father's footsteps. Anyway, I got Simon to double check it, so it's official. George W. Bush, born July sixth. Maybe he'll go down in history or something, huh Caroline? Maybe he'll save the world. Wouldn't that be nice?" I had walked out of Mother's hospital room thinking I should go home and pray for that unlucky man, George W. Bush. Born on the unluckiest day of the year.

Mother could have just said it was her birthday too. She never planned on telling me everything. She hadn't told me anything.

"Your Mother didn't see any harm in celebrating your birthday in July every year instead of her own. She always said if the queen could celebrate a few months early then so could our babydoll."

CHAPTER 22—SEPTEMBER BABY

As Dad pulled up to Mabel's after our talk at the creek he asked if I still had the shoebox with the circus articles. "I assume Mother sent you to collect it from the house. It was her last wish, right?" He didn't give me any time to answer. "Mother wanted to be the one to tell you. She wanted you to know everything, even though we promised we'd never tell a soul about our lives on the other side of the border."

When I admitted to having the box, Dad said I could have the articles back later if I wanted. He needed them so he could tell the others. "They deserve to know the truth too, right?"

"If you say so," I said, but I wasn't sure they did.

Dad said it was Mother who had always wanted to keep everything a secret, not him. Part of me wanted to tell him that Mother had nothing to do with me taking the box from Maple Manor that week before the prom. I almost told him the truth. That the reason I had lied about going shoe shopping that day was to put back the letter from the agency. One of dozens of letters that said Mother couldn't have Chester. *Mother died not knowing what I knew. What I thought I knew.* I couldn't say it. Instead, I nodded my head and ran into Mabel's to get Dad the shoebox.

While Dad sat out front in the car, I ran inside and searched the floor of the bedroom closet. I kept the box behind my sweater coat, just as Mother did. I still hadn't looked inside, but I had shaken it. Before finding the torn up letters from the agency I had pictured the shredded newspapers as a giant pile of ashes, like the kind you'd carry out of a funeral in a velvet bingo bag. As I pulled the box out of the closet, I pictured the articles just as Chester and I had seen them the very first time—fully intact with headlines to give you nightmares for years.

The water was running hard and it sounded like Chester was having another bath. He was blaring Neil Diamond, and I was sure he hadn't heard me come in. I ran back out to the car and handed Dad the shoebox through the car window. I wondered if he'd give one story to each kid and tell them all to go out to their thinking chairs and read about the circus fire and the lies our dad told. *Would he tell them the truth about Neil? What about me and my unbirthday? Where would Shilo look at her article— from my stump or my swing?* Hers would be the one with the full page picture, taken on July 6th before the fire ripped through the tent.

"I'm back," I yelled to Chester when I went into the basement the second time. I hadn't decided what I would tell him if he asked about Dad's birthday surprise. The music was even louder than it had been when I first went in to grab the shoebox for Dad. It wasn't just some top 40 song that Chester was listening to. It was my song. When it came to the chorus part, Chester's singing got louder and he knew all the words.

Sweet Caroline. The woman I was named for. I wondered if that part was even true. I bent down to untie my shoes and realized Chester hadn't heard me come in. The bathroom curtain was open, and Chester was standing in the tub, pulling his rugby shirt over his head. I looked away for a second and then looked back. He was naked except for a baseball cap, which he put back on after taking his shirt off. His body was tanned around the edges and white in the middle. I turned away and expected to hear him splashing down into the tub. When I was sure he hadn't seen me, I looked back. I watched him singing and wiggling his hips to the familiar tune. His microphone was a long pink shower hose. The packaging for the new hose was on the bathroom floor.

Chester lathered himself up and then rinsed off, like a soap commercial. The bubbles slid down his legs, and the music stopped. Then it started again. It was the same song. My song. It was on repeat. This time when he was done singing the chorus part, Chester snapped a towel off the rack and began polishing the new shower hose. When it was dry he shoved it back in the box and let his body drip-dry into the tub.

I ran back outside and jumped up on Mabel's trampoline. Visions of Chester flipped around inside my head as I jumped and counted to seven minutes. When the time was up I had to sit on the edge to catch my breath and stop the dizziness. I finally understood what people meant by butterflies.

I went back downstairs, turned off the stereo and announced that I was home, this time using a much louder voice. Chester came out of the bedroom with a pair of corduroy shorts on. He crossed his arms over his bare chest, like a girl caught in her bra. He turned his back to me and did up his fly.

"You're back? What happened?"

"Nothing."

"What about your dad's surprise? Was it beer?"

"Blue cake."

"Oh yeah? Let's see your tongue."

I stuck it out quickly, hoping he wouldn't notice it was pink as usual. I kicked my shoes on the rug and said I needed the bedroom so I could change into my jeans.

"You're already wearing jeans," Chester said.

"I spilled cake on them," I lied, rubbing my hands on my front pockets. "Hey. What's all this?" I asked, standing in the bedroom doorway. Chester's clothes were spread out all over the bed. There were tops and bottoms lined up like headless people.

"Um, I was looking for stuff to give to *The Second Chance*. The closet's getting full with us sharing. You should maybe go through yours, too. There's still such a thing as *The Second Chance*, isn't there?" He grabbed the closest shirt to him and tried to pull it over his head. The buttons were done up, and when he got stuck in it I didn't offer to help.

"I haven't started dinner yet. I wasn't expecting you until after six. I was going to decorate," he said from inside his shirt.

Chester told me to stay in the bedroom so he could wrap my present. He brought me a beer for company and told me not to come out until he said the magic words. While I drank the beer I stared at the clothes people on the bed. The shirts Chester had spread out weren't old ratty ones. They were good ones without any holes or stains. His favourites. I lay down on them and smelled him. I heard him fiddling with paper and scissors on the other side of the door. I closed my eyes and imagined him unbuttoning his shirt as he wrapped my gift. I wondered if Dad was going to show the Creek Kids the articles from the shoebox as soon as he got back to Maple Manor. I wondered where Neil was. I wondered if Chester's mom dreamt of her son as a grown-up.

"Come out, come out wherever you are," Chester said, opening the door for me. He passed me my gift and cleared a spot on the couch for me to sit down. I peeled away at the tape with my fingernails and pretended not to notice that the paper was damp.

"Just rip it open. It's newspaper for god's sake," Chester said.

"What's this? A shower hose?"

"You said you wanted one."

"I did? When?"

"In your sleep. A few nights ago. In your dream." Chester closed his eyes and made a talking motion with his hand.

"Dream. How do you know?"

"You were talking in your sleep. Like you always do."

"About what?"

"Duh. The shower. That's how I knew you wanted one. Come on, go try it. It just hooks onto the faucet. At least that's what it says on the box." Chester said. He was a bad liar, and he knew it himself.

"I had a bath this morning," I said.

"Just see if it works."

I agreed to take a shower so Chester could prepare the English muffin pizzas. He took out the instruction booklet and pretended to follow the steps to install the shower hose for the first time.

"Happy Birthday," he said, when he was done setting it up. Then he closed the curtain door behind him and left me with my unbirthday gift.

I undressed, turned on the water, and pulled out the lever for the shower. My legs shook as I climbed into the tub. I sat down and stuck my heel in the drain hole, letting the hot water sprinkle over me as I soaked in the shower bath. I tried to get Chester's suntan out of my mind, but it just got more and more visible until it felt like he was sitting in the tub with me. We were under the waterfall and no one could see us touching each other. He sang Happy Birthday to me while he scrubbed my feet clean. He told me he liked being in his birthday suit with me. He didn't care that it wasn't my real birthday. *My parents were childhood sweethearts*, I told him. *Not brother and sister.* We slipped under the water.

Chester rattled the curtain door and asked how the gift was working out. My fingers and toes were so wrinkly I knew I must have fallen asleep. I pulled my heel out of the drain in a panic, wondering if I had dreamed and not noticed myself talking. *Had Chester turned the music back on? Had he heard me dreaming through the curtain?* I stood under the shower hose and rinsed off with water so cold it ached. The only towel left was the bath mat and it was still wet from Chester's shower. I wrapped myself up with it, and darted for the bedroom. Chester knocked while I was still mostly nude. When he spoke, it sounded like his lips were pressed right up against the bedroom door.

"Well? How was it?"

"Nice. Thanks for the present." *But it's not my birthday*, I wanted to say. I wanted to say it, and then I wanted him to wrap himself around me and tell me none of that mattered now.

I pulled my jeans on over my wet legs and got my arms tangled in my bra. "Is dinner ready?" I asked.

"Almost."

When I came out from the bedroom, Chester was lying on the loveseat blowing up balloons. There was an unopened beer waiting for me beside his. I sat down on the zebra rug and stretched out a red balloon before cracking open the beer.

"Can I tell you something?" he asked. He took his mouth away from a pink balloon with birthday candles all over it. "Promise you won't laugh."

"What?"

"You smell like Mother today."

"My mother?"

"Yeah. Probably because of it being today and all. I always think of her on, well, on birthdays. Maybe it's just 'cause she gave birth to you."

"It's someone's birthday every day," I said.

I finished blowing up the red balloon and taped it to the ceiling. As I reached for another one, I realized Chester's hand was already in the balloon bag. I pulled mine out quickly and stared as he chose a yellow one.

"Do you remember that day? When she gave me that yellow balloon? The day the agent came for me," Chester said. "The last day I saw her."

"Of course I remember. I still don't know why you did it. You broke her heart, you know, when you threw that balloon out the window of the van. I'll never forget the sound."

"She gave me a yellow balloon," Chester said.

"So?"

"So, yellow is for friendship." He put his balloon back in the bag and picked another red one.

"And?"

"I didn't want a friend, Caroline. I wanted a family. Besides, I didn't think that jerk would run over it. I was hoping an angel would catch it and give it back to me when I got to heaven. I didn't think balloons would be allowed where I was going." Chester stood up and went to check on the pizzas.

I punched the balloon I had finished blowing up towards him. The knot came loose and the balloon buzzed around the room.

"You knew your mother tried to adopt me, right?" He came back to the couch and fished around for another balloon.

"Duh."

"Then when she realized she couldn't, she tried to have another boy of her own."

"She never realized she couldn't," I said. "She never gave up."

"She needed a boy." Chester said. He sat back down and held a yellow balloon close to his mouth.

"She had four boys already."

"And five girls."

"So she loved having babies." I stood up and kicked the balloons at my feet out of my way.

Chester said she didn't need to have ten. She should have stopped at Magdelene. Four boys, four girls. He held up four fingers on each hand and put them in front of my nose.

I wanted to say he shouldn't count Neil, but I couldn't bear to say the words "Some people like big families. Sue them."

"You don't get it, do you, Caroline?"

"I don't get what, my family?"

"It all started with the pigs, you know." Chester handed me a pink balloon to blow up.

"What all started?"

"We usually talked when your dad was upstairs in the shower," he told me, as if I didn't know. "We had this secret language." He didn't say what it was, but I figured he meant pig Latin. "One time I asked her why she kept the pig book on her bedside table," Chester said.

"What'd she say?"

"She said that it felt right when she had it nearby."

"It's not that weird. Everyone has a favourite book," I said.

"Did you know that Maple Manor was a pig farm when they first moved in?" Chester asked.

"So?"

"Don't you think it's weird that your dad killed all those piglets?"

I didn't know what Chester meant by piglets. Chester blew up another balloon before he told me what he knew about the pigs. He said that Mother and Dad had inherited two free pigs with the house, and the day that they moved in the mother pig gave birth to seven piglets. "Eight, but one died. It was a runt, just like Wilbur from *Charlotte's Web*. They came one after another and your mother watched it all. They just kept coming and coming. She said it was a sign."

"What kind of sign?" I asked.

"That's all she said. Just a sign. But then your dad sold all those pigs one day when she was pregnant with the twins and that was the end of the pig family. I don't think she ever forgave him. She felt responsible for them for some reason." Chester wouldn't look at me, and I knew he was telling the truth by the way he kept rubbing the balloon in his hair.

"My dad's not like that. He wouldn't kill baby pigs."

"He waited until they were grown up so they weren't babies anymore. Then he and Miles took them to the city and sold them so they could buy some beds."

Chester said I wasn't born yet, so how was I to know if it wasn't true. He said that as far as he knew even Neil didn't know the truth. "Neil was a baby when they moved to Canada."

"I know," I said. It seemed like he knew everything I knew.

Only one balloon was left in the bag, and Chester seemed to be waiting for me to reach in and blow it up. It was yellow, just like the one he was holding in his hands. Just like the one Mother had given him the last time she saw him.

I finished the last swig of beer in my bottle and grabbed the balloon. I tried to inflate it, but it was one of those tiny balloons that are impossible to blow up no matter how hard you stretch them. Chester grabbed it from my hands and put it to his mouth without wiping off the opening. He blew it up in one try, then he tied it up, and offered it to me. It was half the size of the others. It reminded me of me.

"I have to tell you something about Mother and Dad," I said to Chester. "I just found out today." I drank as much beer as my mouth could hold and then swallowed and took another big sip.

"Found out what?" he asked.

"The truth. About the circus. The newspaper clippings. It's not what we thought when we were kids."

"You mean the brother sister thing?"

"Yes, the brother sister thing. It's not what we thought—"

Chester stopped me before I could even start to explain. He said he already knew everything.

"What do you mean, everything?" I said.

Chester asked me if I remembered the day he stole one of the articles out of the box. *Do you think your Mother would notice if I took just one article? There's a whole pile of them. Do you think she counted them?*

"It was published a year or so after the circus, and it explained the whole mix up—your Dad's lie, how the neighbour found your mother at the orphanage. It was a front page spread, Caroline. I don't know how we missed it."

"You shouldn't have taken it," I said. I didn't know how we missed it the first time, either.

"Maybe your mother was holding on to it the first time we looked. Or maybe your dad. She always kept something inside her shirt."

Chester disappeared for a minute and I heard the sliding doors of the bedroom closet open and close. When he came back he had the article he had stolen from the box. It had been folded so many times some of the words were hard to read. The headline was still legible: LOCAL CIRCUS HERO CAUGHT WITH PANTS ON FIRE.

"Your Mother knew this article was missing from the box," Chester said, folding it back up. He tucked it in my back pocket, and I wished his hand would stay in my jeans.

"How do you know she knew?"

"She asked me if I had it. She figured it was either you or me."

"What do you mean she asked you? When?"

"In one of her first letters. She started off by saying she had a Neil Diamond name for me, *Captain Sunshine*. Then she asked me if I had the missing article from the shoebox."

"What do you mean her first letters?" I asked.

"She told me you chose to stay at Maple Manor," Chester said. "I had no idea you were living with your dad." One of the balloons popped near his foot and we both jumped. "Sorry, birthday girl."

"It's not my birthday," I said. I didn't want him to know that I had found out about the doll that was born on my birthday, but I could tell by the way he said *birthday girl* that he already knew.

"Your birthday is in September. Your Dad told you today, didn't he? I can tell by looking at you. That was his surprise. I tried to tell you. As soon as your mother found out what I knew about the circus she started telling me everything. I wrote to you all the time. I never once heard back from you."

If she knew he knew, then she knew I knew too. Chester kept talking. He spoke faster this time, juggling a few balloons with his hands and his head.

"I think I was supposed to be his replacement, you know. She never said it like that, but I sensed it. She said I had his eyes. "

"Whose eyes? Dad's?"

"Her baby brother, the one who died at the circus. She showed me a picture of him once, but I don't know. All babies look the same if you ask me, especially in black and white."

I grabbed Chester's yellow balloon and walked back outside.

*

"Psst, Caroline?"

"Dad? What are you doing back here?"

He was on his hands and knees peeking under the trampoline where I was laying down. I had expected Chester to be the one to come looking for me. I noticed something cradled in Dad's elbow.

"What are you doing under there?" Dad asked. "I was just about to knock, but I spotted your feet."

"Just thinking," I said.

"One of the articles is missing," Dad said. He reached an arm out for me to take it, but I didn't budge. "I just spread them out on the seats to make sure they're in the right order and realized, well, maybe you forgot to put it back. It's the, uh, last one." Dad laughed nervously. "Without it—people might think…well you know. You read it, right?"

"I'm sorry they called you names. That must have been hard." I slid out a little from the trampoline, but decided not to come all the way out.

"I'd like to put that missing story with the others, so your brothers and sisters can read for themselves. You know Simon. He likes to have things in writing."

"Right." I took the missing article out of my back pocket and reached out to give it to Dad. I had already read it while I was under the trampoline. It smelled like Chester. Dad tucked the article into his pocket and then took a bundle of envelopes out of the shoebox and threw them on the trampoline. They were wrapped in the green

TARA BENWELL

ribbon Mother always used to tie birthday balloons to the mailbox. One end of the ribbon was frayed at the bottom and I recognized it instantly as the one Mother had tied around her wrist the day Chester was taken away. She had worn it for weeks after he left, even though the rabbit ears kept getting caught on everything.

"I found these in the shoebox. They belong to you." *Hadn't I seen them there,* he asked. *Hadn't I looked inside the box recently?*

"They're for me?" *Of course I hadn't looked inside the box. I already knew what the articles said. Besides, I was worried it would just be a box full of shreds.* I slid the rest of the way out and hopped up to take a seat beside the envelopes on the trampoline.

"They're letters from Chester. They're addressed to you, but I'm guessing you haven't seen them before."

"No."

"You'd think your mother would have at least written back to him with our apartment address. She knew what a good friend Chester was to you guys. To you, especially. It might have helped you back then when you were the new girl. I guess your mother tried to forget about Chester. If you want you can keep the shoebox," Dad said, taking a long breath of air as if it were his last. He put the box on the trampoline beside the letters. He was about to say something else, but instead he turned it into a wave. I knew what he wanted to say, though. *If Mother couldn't have Chester, then neither could you.* I picked up the first letter.

> *Dear Caroline,*
> *I promised your mother I wouldn't tell you what she told me. She wants to tell you herself when you are old enough. You're older than me, so I'm going to tell you everything. I'll write short notes on tissue paper and she'll think they're just paper flowers. Love Chester*

Each letter was no more than a few lines of kid writing. I read through them all, half wanting to bury or burn them or tear them in pieces and half wanting to tuck them in my bra and never change my clothes.

Dear Caroline: Your mother and dad are not brother and sister…
Dear Caroline: Neil is not your real brother …your mom says family
is family… Dear Caroline: My sister died before she came out…Dear
Caroline: Your real birthday is September something…Dear Caroline:
My mom asked your mom to take care of me but your mom's not
allowed… Dear Caroline: Maybe we can be brother and sister one
day…

I stood up on the trampoline and tossed the balloon into the air. I imagined Mother with her wings reaching down through the clouds to collect it. There was no wind to catch it, though, and the balloon fell back to the ground and got caught under the trampoline. The balloon reminded me of Mother's dream for the birthday store, and I pictured Desiree and the others folding up the newspaper articles Dad had passed around for them to read. Maybe they were already getting started on the Birthday Barn. If there was anyone who could live out someone else's dream it was Desiree.

I placed Chester's letters in the shoebox and walked towards the door.

"I have an idea," I told Chester the moment he saw me. I put the shoebox down beside the door and walked into the bedroom. I wondered if he would look down and recognize the box, but he seemed too nervous to move, and it was too light out for the box to glow. When I started to hum, he came over to the bedroom closet to see what I was doing.

"More beer?" Chester asked.

"Help me take this thing down," I said. I pushed up on one of the closet doors and pulled it out of its tracks.

"Why?" Chester asked, but I was already putting the door against the wall.

"It will give us more room in here," I said. It was already easier to breath with just one door off.

"Aren't mirrors supposed to make the room look bigger?" Chester asked. He was looking at me in the closet doors, and I stared back at him and heard my own whisper in my ear. *Ask your question, Caroline.*

"Chester, do you think of me as a ...sister?" I asked.

"Excuse me?" Chester said, but I was sure he had heard me perfectly. He looked away from the mirror and searched for something else to stare at besides us. I waited for him to look back before I spoke again.

"You heard me," I said. I was trying to pull the second door out of its track, but it didn't come out as easily as the first one. Chester walked out to grab his beer and then came back and stared at my arms and legs. The door finally popped out. "Well?" I asked.

"Not really," Chester said. "I mean, not these days."

"But you did at one time?" I said. I rested the second door against the first one and walked over to grab my beer. I sat on the bed on top of Chester's clothes and then stood straight up again.

"I haven't for a while," he told me, and I nodded and said, "Me neither." Then, just when I thought he was going to ask if I was ready for another beer, he grabbed my hand and pointed at us in the mirror. I pulled his hand up to my mouth and kissed my own knuckle by accident. Chester let go of me and put his bottle on the ground, then he grabbed my beer and put it down next to his.

"I wasn't done," I said, but Chester walked away without asking if I meant my drink, or the hold, or the kiss. I heard the click of the stereo and then he was back beside me grabbing my waist and turning me around to face him. As my song began again, he reached out for my hands and we made a London Bridge. It was low at my side, but anyone could have fit through it just the same.

We looked at each other and I imagined all of the people in our lives taking turns ducking under the bridge. I wished we could catch each one and ask the questions we deserved to know. *Who told you? What stopped you? Where were you? When will you? Why didn't you? How could you? Is there anything else I should know?*

Chester held his arms high and let each person pass through without a care. "Your hands are warm," he said to me as the chorus began.

His were too.

TARA BENWELL

Acknowledgments

I once read about a waitress who refused to buy a new pair of work shoes until she published her first book. Having delivered my fair share of hamburgers, I appreciated her determination, and vowed in February 2008 not to buy another pair of socks until my own novel hit the shelves. Before I go sock shopping, I would like to thank the following people.

Thank you to Roberta Georgiadas and Jane Crosbie for encouraging me to write stories as a child, even though I held my pencil wrong and failed the spelling bees. Thank you to Samantha North, wherever you are. Your phone call many years ago gave me the courage to take this dream beyond the first submission. Thank you to Kris Rothstein at the Carolyn Swayze Agency for never giving up on Caroline. Thank you to my editor, Alethea Spiridon, and to her husband for sticking up for writers, even though his wife was right. Thank you to Paul Battle, Josef Essberger, and Ben Buckwold for providing me with creative work with such a short commute. No words can express my gratitude for the four amazing women who supported me throughout the last ten years. Andrea, Janette, Tammy, and Karen, you are the sisters I never had. To Jackson and Joey, thank you for understanding (at least once in a while) that writing *is* playing for Mama. And finally to Dean. Thank you for letting me dip into your sock drawer on those odd occasions when I actually left the house. You have put up with the coldest feet in the world.

www.ingramcontent.com/pod-product-compliance
Lightning Source LLC
Chambersburg PA
CBHW020747250626
47155CB00003B/960